The Headless Lady

The Complete Great Merlini

from

Gregg Press Mystery Fiction Series

Otto Penzler, EDITOR

The Headless Lady

By Clayton Rawson

With a New Introduction by
Otto Penzler

GREGG PRESS
Boston
1979

Republished in 1979 by Gregg Press, A Division of G. K. Hall & Co., 70 Lincoln St., Boston, Massachusetts 02111

First Printing, June 1979

Library of Congress Cataloging in Publication Data
Rawson, Clayton, 1906-
The headless lady.

(The Gregg Press mystery fiction series)
Reprint of the 1962 ed. published by Collier Books, New York.
I. Title. II. Series.
PZ3.F1982He 1979 [PS3535.A848] 813'.5'4 79-11659
ISBN 0-8398-2544-7

Introduction

"A MYSTERY STORY IS REALLY A MAGIC TRICK ON PAPER," WAS ONE of Clayton Rawson's favorite lines. He often performed magic tricks for the Mystery Writers of America and other groups while lecturing on "Misdirection and Suspense in Magic and the Mystery Story." During his discussions of the theory of magic and mystery, he illustrated various points with sleight of hand and illusions that delighted and perplexed his audience.

His talks, although informal and friendly, had been carefully conceived in advance, and he regularly worked from thoroughly detailed lecture notes. Those papers have never been published, but Hugh Rawson, the son of the popular author and editor of *Ellery Queen's Mystery Magazine* and an editor in his own right, has pulled them out of a hat and made them available for this edition of *The Headless Lady*. Some excerpts, some words of expertise from the master of the combined art of prestidigitection, follow:

"The mystery writer and the magician are both entertainers with the same end in view. They both deal in the same commodity—the production of mystery. And they both do it in very much the same way, using the same basic principles.

"The main ingredient—the *raison d'etre*—of any mystery is the creation of suspense. And suspense consists essentially of uncertainty as to what will happen next. Both the writer and the magician must always stay at least one, and preferably two, jumps ahead of the reader or the audience. He must know what the reader or viewer thinks will happen next and then give him something unexpected. This is the principle of surprise. If your storyline is run-of-the-mill and the reader correctly figures out what is coming on the next page, there is no suspense—and, if this goes on very long, probably no reader, either.

"Suspense must always begin as soon as possible because there is no suspense in waiting for suspense to begin.

"The first step toward achieving suspense is to attract your reader's attention with something that intrigues him. Then, as soon as possible, surprise him so that he is uncertain as to where you—and he—are going.

"The writer can't always do this all at once. He may have to set the stage a bit first, but he should begin to work toward that goal as quickly as possible. The first three things he must do are: (1) introduce some interesting characters; (2) set up an intriguing situation; and (3) have that situation develop in unexpected ways.

"The characters must be people worth putting into a story. They must not be garden variety, standard brand types who act in obvious and predictable ways. This is the trademark of the cardboard character. If they act and talk like real people they will, automatically, be interesting.

"Actions must be convincingly motivated. They must have what seems *to them* good and sufficient reasons for what they do. They must not perform actions simply because the plot demands it. They must seem to be acting of their own volition for their own—not the author's—reasons. The author must think himself inside the character: 'If I were this kind of person in this situation, what would I do?'

"If suspense consists of being uncertain about what will happen next, the reader must become interested enough in the characters so that he wants to know what will happen to them next. He should become more than merely interested, but also emotionally involved—especially with the identification, or viewpoint, character, who must have some quality or qualities with which the reader can sympathize.

"One of the great difficulties of the crime story, unlike other forms of the mystery genre, is that all the characters so often are unlikable; they are crooks or psychopaths headed for disastrous ends. If there is no one in the cast whom the reader likes, he is not likely to wonder what will happen next. He will not care enough for anyone to care what will happen.

"Of course, he usually knows what will happen anyway. The "hero" who is a villain generates little uncertainty or suspense because the reader knows from the beginning that this bad guy will have a violent end.

"It seems likely that the best medium for the crime story is the short story. It is easier to induce the reader to become interested in a criminal protagonist for the length of a short tale than for a full novel, and the reader does not feel so let down after a dozen pages as he does after two hundred.

"Many of these short stories fall into the 'biter-bit' category. The criminal makes one little mistake that undoes him at the end—just the reverse of the detective story, in which the detective unearths one little but important clue that solves the case. The major difference is that in the 'biter-bit' story the criminal tries to do something and fails, while in the detective story the detective tries to do something and succeeds. It is more satisfying. There are, naturally, exceptions, as in the Karmesin stories of Gerald Kersh and the Arsene Lupin tales of Maurice Leblanc, but these criminals are romantic and sympathetic, and their crimes are something less than murder.

"Take, for example, the case of Jack the Giant Killer. The story has interest and suspense because Jack—the hero—fights against ever-increasing odds and eventually wins. The mystery and suspense do not arise from the question: 'Does he win or not?' but from the question: 'How can he possibly win under the circumstances?' If the reader is playing ball on Jack's team because he likes Jack and hopes intensely that Jack will somehow win, he is not going to be very happy to see Jack lose and the giant win. This may be realism, but it isn't fun.

"The magician tries to conceal his clues completely; the writer can't. He must explain all at the end. This is why writers have to write new stories, but magicians continue to repeat the same tricks.

"And what is magic? Most people think of it as sense deception. They believe the hand is quicker than the eye. It is not—but it is cleverer.

"Nor is magic, as many people believe, only a matter of gimmicks (a word derived from magic): mirrors, trapdoors, false bottoms. Its real secret lies deeper than a mere deception of the senses. The magician uses a much more important basic weapon—the psychological deception of the mind. 'Don't believe everything you see' is excellent advice. But there is a better rule: Don't believe everything you think!

"The psychological principles of deception are what the writer must use in fooling his reader. The mystery writer, the magician, and the murderer try to induce the reader, the audience, or the police to make false assumptions and false deductions which end in false conclusions.

"The mystery writer has performed a trick—on paper."

And what tricks Clayton Rawson performed, both on a stage and on paper. He was both a member of the Society of American Magicians and the Mystery Writers of America, and it was only natural for him to create a fictional character who was equally successful as a magician and as a detective. The Great Merlini was the first and most famous of his magician detectives, appearing in four novels: *Death from a Top Hat* (1938), *The Footprints on the Ceiling* (1939), *The Headless Lady* (1940) and *No Coffin for the*

Corpse (1942), and twelve short stories, collected for the first time in *The Great Merlini* (1979).

Rawson also created another magician detective, Don Diavolo, about whom he wrote four novelettes under the pseudonym Stuart Towne. The four adventures appeared originally in *Red Star Mystery* magazine in 1940 and were later published in two volumes, each of which contained two novelettes: *Death out of Thin Air* (1941), with "Death from the Past" (originally titled "Ghost of the Undead") and "Death from the Unseen" (originally titled "Death out of Thin Air"), and *Death from Nowhere* (ca. 1942), with "The Claws of Satan" and "The Enchanted Dagger", called simply Act I and Act II in the book.

The magician detective is a rare breed indeed. It takes a special combination of talents to bring it off, and Clayton Rawson did it better than anyone else. The Great Merlini exemplifies this singular type of character, and *The Headless Lady* is one of his greatest cases. It is a book to be enjoyed by all who enjoy the worlds of mystery and magic, of detection and illusion, of crime and conjuring.

Otto Penzler
New York City

With thanks to

JUSTUS EDWARDS
and
BEVERLY KELLEY

who duked me in

The Headless Lady

With wily brain upon the spot
A private plot we'll plan,
The most ingenious private plot
Since private plots began.
That's understood. So far we've got
And, striking while the iron's hot,
We'll now determine like a shot
The details of this private plot.
—UTOPIA, LIMITED

Performing Cast

STARS

MAJOR RUTHERFORD B. HANNUM—Owner of The Mighty Hannum Combined Shows.
PAULINE HANNUM—His daughter. Wire-walker and high perch performer.
JOY PATTISON—The Major's niece. Wire-walker and aerialist.
J. MACALLISTER WILEY—Legal adjuster.
KEITH ATTERBURY—Press agent.
IRMA KING—Elephant trainer and equestrienne.
TEX MAYO—Featured Wild West performer and ex-movie star.
MATT GARNER—Tramp clown.
THE HEADLESS LADY—Featured side-show attraction.
JOHN WILKES BOOTH—A mummy.

TOWNERS

THE GREAT MERLINI—Professional magician and amateur detective.
BURT FAWKES—His assistant and factotum.
ROSS HARTE—Free-lance writer and the narrator.
STUART TOWNE—A detective-story writer.
DR. LEONIDAS TRIPP and DR. ISHAM BYRD—Physicians.

SUPPORTING CAST

SWEDE JOHNSON—Sword-swallower.
GUS and STELLA MILBAUER—Mentalists.
FARMER JACK—Three-card-monte grifter.
EVERETT (CALAMITY) LOVEJOY—Front-door superintendent.
DEEP-SEA ED—Bull boss.
STEVE KUZMIC—Acrobat.

9

HOODOO, THE HEADHUNTER—Abraham Lincoln Jones of the Bronx.

THE FUZZ

CHIEF INSPECTOR HOMER GAVIGAN—of the New York City Homicide Bureau.
CAPTAIN LEONARD SCHAFER—of the New York State Police.
CHIEF OF POLICE SAM HOOPER—of Norwalk, New York.
SHERIFF WEATHERBY—of Waterboro, New York.
DETECTIVE LESTER BURNS; TROOPERS: PALMER AND STEVENS; OFFICERS: ROBBINS AND CROSSEN; DETECTIVE BRADY.

WALK-AROUNDS

BEVERLY KELLEY and JUSTUS EDWARDS, press agents on advance; LEE DANIELS, side-show manager; LILA DEVEREAUX, bird trainer; WALTER JENNIER, equestrian director; ETHEL JENNIER and LOUISE ATTERBURY, aerialists; BOB O'HARA, reserved-seat superintendent; IRVING DESFOR, photographer; ELSIE, MODOC, and RUBBER, elephants.

Contents

Chapter 1

Two-Headed Girl

"Ladeez and Gentulmen: In just about sixty minutes or one hour tickets to the big show will go on sale in the red ticket wagon directly across the show grounds. In the meantime, the management presents for your edification, mystification and amusement. . ."

DURING THE night Manhattan Island had apparently slipped its moorings, drifted southward with incredible speed, and come to rest somewhere off the coast of Equatorial Africa. The great city lay submerged like a lost Atlantis beneath the heavy waves of hot moist atmosphere that all day had moved slowly in from the steaming ocean. The blazing tropical sun was nearer. Even the tall solidity of the buildings seemed limp and jellylike as their outlines wavered in the damp haze. The nervous and excited rumble of the traffic had slowed to a fitful murmur of protest. Policemen growled; truck drivers cursed languidly; pedestrians mopped hot faces. New York was enduring the first heat wave of summer.

I called up a final spark of energy and pushed at the door of The Magic Shop, that curious commercial establishment in which the Great Merlini carries on his darkly nefarious business of supplying miracles for sale.

"If you were really a magician," I announced, "you'd do something about the weather. You'd make a pass or contrive a spell and—"

I stopped. My only audience was the shop's mascot and living trademark, the white rabbit that stretched lazily on the counter, a look of vast boredom in his round pink eye. Even his ears drooped disconsolately; and he paid no attention at all to my complaint.

Neatly lettered on the wall above the cash register was Merlini's business slogan: *Nothing is Impossible.* The annoying confidence of that statement had aroused my skepticism before. I decided now to give it the acid test. I closed my eyes and intoned loudly.

"Hocus-pocus. Abracadabra. Fe-fi-fo-fum. I want a long cool drink, an ice-cold shower, an electric fan, a lot of air conditioning, a—" My eyes jerked open.

This really was fast work! I looked around apprehensively, still hearing the sound of ice clinking in a glass and the rushing siphon-swish of soda. But the wishful thinking together with my fevered temperature had apparently combined to produce an auditory hallucination—an empty, hollow illusion of a piece with the rest of Merlini's deceptive stock in trade. There was no drink, and the cool sound had only accentuated my discomfort.

Then Merlini's voice came from beyond the doorway that connected the outer salesroom with the workshop and office in the rear.

"Come and get it!"

For the first time that day I moved with some degree of haste. There *was* a Santa Claus after all; the age of sorcery was not yet dead. In the back room, Burt Fawkes, Merlini's shop assistant and general factotum, reclined at full length on a long, low box that had the sinister shape of a coffin. Beside him on the floor stood a container of ice cubes from the corner drugstore, a soda siphon, and a none-too-full bottle of Scotch. In one hand Burt held his own half-finished drink; in the other, a nice fresh one that he held extended listlessly in my direction. His remarkable lack of animation was so complete that I was about to diagnose a seriously advanced state of cataleptic trance when he spoke.

Merlini is the one who usually quotes from his favorite Gilbert and Sullivan, but on this occasion Burt beat him to it. Lazily he sang:

> *"Why, who is this approaching,*
> *Upon our joy encroaching?*
> *Some rascal come a-poaching*
> *Who's heard that wine we're broaching?"*

Then he added, "Hurry, Ross. It's slipping."

I rescued the glass from his limp, wavering grasp and

turned to find two more bodies laid out on the surface of the long workbench. Merlini's lank frame, in an undignified half-lying, half-sitting sprawl against the wall, had, like Burt's, apparently settled there for the duration of the summer. He was in his shirt sleeves, tieless, his collar open. The keen, forcefully cut lines of his face were utterly relaxed; the interested curiosity that is ever present in the sharp glance of his black eyes was concealed behind closed lids. The buoyant vitality that bubbled in his personality seemed to be almost completely turned off—but not quite. It appeared in the voice he used—though the voice was not his. It was, instead, the youthful alto of a brash, irrepressible child; and it came not from Merlini, but from the grinning, red-haired ventriloquial dummy that lay beside him trying vainly to match the superior example of immobility that Merlini had set.

The dummy's hinged lower jaw moved slowly. "Simple as that," he said. "Just name it and there you are. We stock only the best grade of witchcraft, every item fully guaranteed or your money back."

On a raised dais near by was a great thronelike chair whose curving design and brightly gilded, grimacing dragons bespoke an oriental and ancient origin. Carefully I tested the seat for trap doors, and, finding none, sat down.

I gave some attention to my drink and then inquired, "What about that shower, the fan, and the air conditioning?"

"Be reasonable and settle for the drink," the dummy retorted lazily. "The Djinn-of-all-work hereabouts has had a hard day. We were just about to let him knock off and go home."

"That's a new excuse," I said. "What kept the Djinn so busy, and why do your boss and Burt look as if the referee had just counted ten? I thought that all the Great Mysterioso had to do was wave his hand—simple as that—and the Djinn did all the work? Big husky fellow like that didn't need help, did he?"

"Those cases and cartons over there"—the dummy's head inclined toward a stack of boxes in one corner—"had to be packed. It took a great many mystic passes."

I eyed them, noticed a suitcase or two in the lot, and sat up suspiciously. I ignored the dummy and addressed Merlini.

"You're not leaving town *again?*"

Merlini tilted his glass and drank long and deep, a procedure that did not prevent the dummy from answering, "Give me just one good reason for *not* leaving a place that has weather like this."

I banged my glass down on the chair arm. "I'll do exactly that! Where do you think you're going?"

"Albany. New York State Convention. Society of American Magicians. Driving up tonight through the cool countryside. Won't you come along?"

I had my hands full; I saw that. "Merlini," I said heatedly, "stop fiddling with that dummy and be reasonable." I held up the roll of galley proofs I'd brought along. "This is the second set of galleys on your 'Footprints' case.[1] You were so involved in constructing a new levitation you couldn't check the final typescript. You chased out to Chicago to attend a National Convention of Witches, Warlocks, and Banshees or something when the first proofs came through. And now, if you think—"

Merlini spoke for himself this time. "But it's business, Ross. I've planned a mouth-watering display of the very latest conjuring—"

"What do you think *this* is?" I waved the proofs feebly. "You signed a contract. Our publishers, to put it very mildly, are beginning to fret. They'll begin making passes themselves shortly—but not at the empty air."

"I thought they published books, not a weekly magazine. No one reads in weather like this anyway. It's too hot—"

"They answered that one," I replied. "Said *we* seemed to have the erroneous impression that they published bicentennially. I know what's eating them. They'd sort of like to get back those advance royalties we've already spent. Ever think of that?"

The sound of a buzzer indicated that a customer had entered the shop outside.

The dummy said, "Take it, will you, Burt? We're in conference."

Burt finished off his drink, pulled himself up onto his feet,

[1] *The Footprints on the Ceiling*—G. P. Putnam's Sons, 1939

and went out, moving at about half the speed of a sleepy snail who hasn't made up his mind.

"And," I continued dyspeptically, "when I try to tell them how busy you are, they always counter with, 'Well, he's a magician, isn't he? Have him wave his wand or something.' I'm sick and tired of that crack. I don't know an answer for it, if any. Why haven't you done something about a science of practical and applied magic? I'd take a course myself if I could say 'Hey Presto' and have something useful happen. Rabbits from top hats, ladies sawed in half, ducks that vanish! Why? Who cares? Phooie!"

"Not so fast," Merlini rebutted. "You got the drink, didn't you? Have another. Some liver pills, too. But, seriously, I will make a deal with you. Drive up with me tonight. Burt has to stay on the job here, and I'd love company. After the convention is out of the way, we'll vanish into the Adirondacks beside a mountain stream for a day or two—I know just the spot. We'll cool off, and I'll give some attention to those proofs. Honest Injun, cross my heart."

"Well," I said, "I would like to see a tree again for a change. But no soldiering, understand. If you cross me up—"

Burt returned from the shop, walking a shade faster. We couldn't know it then, but this slight change of tempo was the cue that dimmed the house lights and sent the curtain rolling up on Act I.

"Customer outside," he announced. "Wants to see a headless lady. Looks like a sale. I think you'd better see her."

"Headless lady?" I asked, suspecting a gag. "Now what? Has the firm added a body-snatching department?"

"Yes," Merlini said. "We're changing the name to Ghoul & Co. Who is it, Burt?"

The latter shook his head. "Don't know. Girl who won't take no for an answer. In a hurry, too."

He was right about that. The door from the shop swung inward abruptly, and she came toward us moving with a graceful but determined stride and a display of energy which in that temperature was almost foolhardy. She was as interesting and—as we were about to discover—as tantalizing a young woman as had ever set foot on the premises. She was in her middle twenties, tall, dark-haired, undeniably good-

looking—and as nervous as a cat. Nervous in the same way
—outwardly poised, self-assured, sleek—but jumpy. Beneath
the dark outdoor tan of her complexion there was a hard,
taut quality that was also present in the deep-throated mascu-
line voice.

She gave me a glance whose briefness was no compliment,
decided I wasn't it, and turned to face Merlini as that gentleman, finally coming into action, swung down from the workbench.

"Mr. Merlini?" Her tone was polite but businesslike.

"Yes." He nodded, taking her in.

"I need a headless lady," she said. "I have to have it at
once. This gentleman says—"

"That at once is too soon," Merlini finished. "I know. That
particular item has been selling faster than twenty-dollar
bills wrapped around cakes of soap at two for a quarter. It's
a good pitch. Everyone wants a headless lady."

"Except me," I corrected quietly but firmly.

The girl went on, "He says you have one here. A demonstrator."

Merlini nodded. "Yes. But I can't display it for you at the
moment. The Merlini Super-Improved Model with the visible,
circulating blood feature and the respiratory light attachment,
built to last a lifetime, takes down quickly, easily, and packs
for carrying in two suitcases. Those." He pointed toward two
squat squarish cases that were with the others in the corner.
"It's there now. I'm taking it to a magicians' convention in
Albany tonight."

"I don't need a demonstration," the girl said. "I know what
it's like. The price is three hundred dollars, isn't it?"

"Yes. Discount of two per cent for cash."

"We'll skip that," she said, flipping open her purse. She
took out a folded packet of perhaps a dozen bills, dealt off
three, and handed them to Burt. They were hundred-dollar
bills. Burt's response was automatic and prompt. He procured
a receipt pad in about the same length of time it takes Merlini
to produce a coin from thin air.

"Name?" he asked, pencil poised.

She scowled at him. "Is that necessary?"

Burt nodded. "Yes."

She looked at him thoughtfully for a moment longer, then said suddenly. "Christine—Mildred Christine."

"Address?"

"Wait," she said. "You don't understand. I'm taking it with me."

Burt looked at his boss. Merlini absently took a playing card from the workbench and balanced it impossibly on one edge on the back of his hand. "I'm sorry, Miss"—he paused noticeably—"Christine. I can't let you have this one. The factory is a week behind on orders. I couldn't possibly make delivery before—well, I might get them to rush an assembly by Monday. Today's Thursday. Will that—"

"No." Miss Christine was quite certain. "I'm leaving town tonight. I have to have it *now*."

"I'm sorry." Merlini was equally definite. "Perhaps an Asrah Levitation, a 'Burning a Woman Alive,' or a nice fast trunk-escape at one-half off, or—"

The girl took a step or two toward Merlini, restlessly. "Look," she said. "You'd sell the demonstrator at a price, wouldn't you?"

Merlini considered that for a moment, frowning. His dark eyes met hers intently. "I might," he said finally. "It would be more, of course." He drawled his words, slowly, as if puzzling over something.

"I realize that," she said.

Merlini still hesitated, his frown deeper. Then he said quickly and flatly, "It would be three hundred more."

Burt gave a surprised start that was almost a jump, but Mildred didn't as much as blink. The corners of her mouth even curled upward slightly. She promptly repeated her production trick with the purse, and three more hundred-dollar bills passed across to Burt.

"My car is down the street," she said. "I'll be back in half an hour. Will you have the cases taken down for me, please?" She turned on her heel, and started for the door.

"Just a minute," Merlini said hastily. "This has gone far enough."

She stopped in the doorway. "What do you mean?" Her eyes snapped. "You named your price. You got it. You can't—"

"I know." Merlini took a cigarette from his pocket and hunted thoughtfully for a match. "I wanted to see just how badly you did want it. You surprised me. But I'm not a shakedown artist. You may have it at the regular list price —on one condition."

"Yes?" She scowled.

Merlini lit his cigarette, leaned back against his workbench, and observed calmly, as if he were thinking aloud, "You don't need the apparatus so quickly because it means a job. You've got too many of those century notes. Possession and exhibition of the illusion four days sooner than I can supply one from regular stock will hardly net you the extra three hundred you're willing to pay. If you'll explain this curious haste and tell me why the monogram on your purse is an H rather than a C—you can have it."

Merlini's business is mystery and the mystification of others, yet the one thing he can't abide is to have someone drop anything even faintly baffling into his own lap. Everything Mildred did and said bristled like a hedgehog with question marks—big curly ones. Merlini was puzzled, and he didn't like it. He apparently didn't like it three hundred dollars worth.

Mildred wasn't exactly overjoyed. "You mean that?" she asked, frowning.

Merlini nodded.

She unsnapped her purse again. "I'll make it *seven* hundred."

Merlini shook his head decisively. "No."

The girl looked at Burt. "Is he always like this?"

Burt glanced at the money he held. "You can expect anything, Miss. He's stubborn, too."

"So am I." She took the bills. "But if I *should* change my mind . . . How much longer will you be here?"

Merlini consulted his watch. "Not long. But you can reach me at my home until about eight o'clock."

"Thanks." She put the bills in her purse, turned and strode through the door into the shop. We heard her footsteps cross the floor beyond, heard the buzzer as the outer door began to open, and then heard it gently close again. She came back at once. Merlini smiled—but only temporarily.

Miss Christine was agitated. "Is there a rear exit here?" she asked. "I'd rather not—"

Then she saw the open window and the fire escape beyond. She took half a dozen steps, put one hand on the window sill, and went through the opening with the fluid grace of an acrobat. Before any of us had recovered enough to speak, she had gone. It was rather like one of Merlini's tricks.

Merlini raised an eyebrow at me and then moved quickly to his desk in the corner, picked an envelope from a pigeonhole, sealed it, and scaled it at Burt. "Take this out and drop it in the mail chute. Keep both eyes open. And report back as to the nature of the menace that seems to be lurking in our corridor."

Burt asked, "Why pick on me?" But he went.

The back issues of *Billboard Magazine,* the showman's bible, were stacked high on the filing cabinets by the desk. Merlini took down the top half-dozen copies, separated one, and flipped through it rapidly as if he knew what he wanted.

I crossed to the window, leaned out, and looked down. Mildred Christine was just vanishing through another window four flights below.

"Can't I do something?" I asked. "Tail the gal, perhaps?"

Merlini was preoccupied. "What?" he said.

I repeated my question.

He gazed thoughtfully at his magazine for a moment, and said, "No. That won't be necessary." He removed the page that had caught his interest, folded it carefully, and placed it in his billfold. "I think I know—yes, Burt?"

"Corridor peaceful and deserted," the latter reported, "except for the guy that ducked into the men's washroom down the hall just as I went out. The door didn't quite close behind him, so I figured maybe I was being watched. I proceeded to go powder my nose, but he took cover just as I got there. So I didn't get a look at much except his feet. Number nines or thereabouts. I don't suppose that's a lot of help?"

"It's a beginning," Merlini said. "We'll go on from there, and we'll give him something to think about. We'll close up shop—nearly time anyhow. Burt will go first, wait in the lobby downstairs, and sit tight. Ross and I will stall a few minutes, then lock up and follow after. That will give him a vanishing lady to worry about. Burt will see what he does about it. Tail him when he comes down."

Burt put on his tie and went out. Merlini and I locked up and followed a few minutes later. I glanced along the corridor out of the corner of one eye. The washroom door was suspiciously ajar. Merlini didn't appear to notice, but he gave me a wink and said, for the benefit of any listening ears, "That vanishing cabinet will have to be worked over. It's impractical as it stands. We put the girl in; she disappears and then doesn't come back. Won't do at all. Can't use a new girl every time. It'll have to work both ways. . . ."

He kept that up until the elevator door had closed behind us.

We took a taxi, made a stop at my apartment on East Forty-first Street while I packed a toothbrush, and then went on to Merlini's at 13½ Washington Square North. The schedule we planned consisted of a cold shower apiece, a change of clothes, cocktail, dinner.

Merlini was in the shower, and I was working with the cocktail shaker when the phone rang. I took it.

The phone said, "Burt speaking. Ask the boss what I do now. I'm at the drugstore, Eighth and Fifth, just around the corner. The subject tailed you and I tailed him. All we lacked coming down Fifth Avenue in our three taxis was a parade permit, confetti, a band, and Grover Whalen. He's in the park across from you."

"Who, Grover?"

"No, you dope. The mystery man."

"Hold everything." I put the phone down, stepped to the window without going too near, and peered out between the curtains. The running splash of the shower had stopped, and Merlini asked, "Yes, Ross?"

Across the street, not directly opposite, but somewhat to the left, a man sat on a park bench. He held a newspaper spread before him that concealed all the upper part of his body except the dark felt hat that projected above its top edge. I suspected that his eyes were not on the print, but rather were aimed in my direction, surveying the house through the narrow space between the paper's top and the lower edge of the hat's brim.

I told Merlini what Burt had reported and what I saw. "Perhaps he thinks we cut the girl up in little pieces," Merlini said, "and brought her—"

I interrupted, jumping for the phone. "He's shoving off. Want Burt to carry on?"

Merlini hurried from the bathroom, toweling himself and leaving wet tracks across the carpet. He looked out the window. "Yes," he said, "have him do that."

"Step on it, Burt. He's coming your way."

"Aye, aye, sir," Burt said. The receiver clicked.

A half-hour later, as we were about to leave in search of a restaurant, our special investigator phoned again. "Operative Q-X9 reporting," he said. "The subject proceeded to 19 West Thirty-first Street. Business building. Small. The lobby directory lists the following: "The Sylph Brassière Co.; Gerald L. Kaufman, Architect; A. Shapiro, Dresses; and The Acme Detective Agency, Martin O'Halloran, Prop. Tell Merlini I think so, too."

I relayed that and added, "Burt thinks our man is a brassière salesman. Now what?"

"Tell him to eat and then wait for us at the shop. As soon as we've dined, we'll pick up the car, load the luggage, and head for Albany."

That wasn't at all what I expected. Merlini saw it on my face. "Go on, tell him," he repeated.

I did.

Burt didn't get it either. "Doesn't sound right to me," he commented. "Merlini not feeling well?"

"Too well. He's master-minding again, pretending he's way ahead of us. Wants us to think he's solved the curious case of the Vanishing Lady and the Disappointed Shadow. But don't believe all the rumors you hear. We'll be seeing you."

Merlini grinned. "Your tactics are crude. I'll tell you one thing, though. I'll tell you who the real Millie Christine was. Knowing that, you may be able to figure out who Miss H is. I did."

"Well?" I said suspiciously, afraid with good reason that

any information he gave away free at this point was going to be cryptic.

"The real Millie Christine," he said, "was one person who would have had a really practical use for a Headless Lady Illusion. She was a freak in Barnum's Museum—*a two--headed girl*. Come on. I'm starved." [2]

It wasn't until dinner was over and we had started uptown in Merlini's car that I was able successfully to get him back on the subject.

"Why don't you send Burt to the convention with your bag of tricks?" I said. "We'll stay here and snoop."

"I thought you wanted those proofs checked?"

"Hell with 'em," I said. "I want to know—"

"So do I," he grinned. "Convention first. Check proofs on Monday. And Tuesday we snoop. In Waterboro, New York."

"Waterboro, New York. Oh, I see."

Merlini grinned again. "You do *not*," he contradicted.

We parked the car and went on up to the shop and the remaining surprise that lay in wait for us that night. Burt supplied it the moment we entered.

"Thriving little business we have here," he said. "It flourishes even while we sleep. Like an automat."

"What," Merlini asked, "does that mean?"

Burt led us to the inner room and pointed a finger at the window on the fire escape. Merlini, I remembered, had closed and locked it before we left. But it was open now, and there

---

[2] Millie-Christine (1851-1912) were really two negro girls, Siamese twins of the ordinary Chang and Eng type, whose manager always spoke of them and often advertised them as one girl with two heads. They were given musical instruction, one girl singing alto, the other soprano; and their vocal duets and performances upon musical instruments were, from all accounts, quite creditable. They also appeared in side shows with Adam Forepaugh's, Coup's, Batcheller & Doris', Barnum's, and other circuses, as well as making a European tour.

The closest nature has ever come to a freak having two heads on one body, which lived and was on exhibition, was the Locano prodigy, Johann and Jacob Tocci, born in 1881, in Turin, Italy. They had one body, one pair of legs; but above the sixth rib the body became double with two heads and two pairs of arms.

was a jagged hole in the pane above the window catch.

Merlini sent a swift glance around the room. "Miss Christine," he said then, "is undoubtedly one of the most determined young ladies I've ever encountered."

Three hundred-dollar bills lay beneath a paper weight on the desk. The cases that contained the Headless Lady apparatus were gone.

Chapter 2

Side Show

". . . this great combined outside show and international congress of weird people, the most amazing, Gargantuan, awe-inspiring, cataclysmic collection of strange oddities, living freaks, and curious wonders ever assembled under one canvas! The show starts right away! No waits. No delays. No extra charge on the inside. Step right up to the ticket boxes on either side! Fifteen cents to all . . . "

CONVENTIONS ARE uninhibited, haywire affairs. I imagine that even the annual conclaves of the Society of Ancient Historians, the United Association of Embalmers, and, possibly, the left wing section of the D.A.R. have their moments. But a convention of magicians, coin kings, card manipulators, illusionists, mind readers, hypnotists, and ventriloquists *is* an experience. The Mad Hatter's well-known tea party was, by comparison, as humdrum, staid, and decorous as a seminar in quantum mathematics.

The nimble-fingered delegates practiced their deceptive skill in the corridors, the elevators, and at the table. I think I saw every accepted scientific axiom of physics and logic shattered beyond all mending. The effect was rather like living in a room paneled with the curved distorting mirrors from an amusement park's Fun House. After two days and nights of concentrated trickery I essayed a little vanishing act of my own. At 3 A.M. on Sunday morning I sneaked quietly off to the room Merlini and I shared, locked the door with the only key, and crawled into bed.

I woke less than an hour later to find the door wide open, the room full of smoke, shop talk, and magicians. Several of them sat on the edge of my bed playing a curious kind of game with a deck of cards, never dealing but passing the complete deck from hand to hand, each man as he reached for it, saying, "That reminds me—have you seen this one," or, "Here's another way of doing that."

I sat up, swearing sleepily, only to have the cards spread in an expert fan beneath my nose with the command, "Here, take one, any card at all."

Automatically I obeyed, looked at the card, and then shuffled it back into the deck as directed. The magician, a fat little man with a bland grin, took the cards, held the deck between forefinger and thumb, and gave it a smart rap with the edge of his right hand. The cards fell in a shower to the floor, all except one, which remained in his fingers. "And your card," he said confidently, making ready to turn it face up, "was—?"

There is, I knew, one thing that makes a magician feel like going into retirement. I supplied it.

"I couldn't say," I replied. "You didn't ask me to remember it."

"Oh, it's *him!*" someone else said in a tone that made me feel as if I had six legs and lived in a drain. "Here, take this and be quiet." He handed me a highball. I couldn't smell any bitter-almond odor, so I drank it.

There were more tricks on Sunday, and a banquet. I met a blonde who is sawed in two twice a day for a living, discovered that she didn't require more than the usual amount of care in handling, and had a pretty good time. Monday morning we caught up on sleep, and in the afternoon Merlini packed what miracles remained unsold and we took them to the Express office.

Monday night we had a session with the proofs. Merlini's job was to check them for facts, but I had the devil's own time trying to keep him from adding a lot of fiction. On nearly every other galley he'd say, "Of course, I know it didn't happen just that way, but don't you think it would have more punch if—" I managed to stop some of his "improvements"; but at that there were enough facts to be trued up so that I spent most of Tuesday madly rewriting. I finished just in time to make the post office before it closed, and sent the proofs off by registered mail. Then, finally, after giving the car a feed of gas and oil, we pulled out and headed west on Route 20—smack into trouble.

Waterboro, according to the road map, is a wide spot in the road (Pop.: 5,000 to 10,000) some seventy-five miles out of Albany in the middle of nowhere, and noted as far as I knew for exactly nothing at all. I'd never heard of the place until Merlini had pulled it out of his hat on Thursday night, and I'd long since given up trying to figure out how the mysterious Miss H——, her unholy desire for a headless lady, and her use of the name of a two-headed freak had suggested it.

I said as much, and insisted, with some annoyance, on an answer.

"Circus," Merlini replied. "The Mighty Hannum Combined Shows is playing Waterboro today. And I'll drink all the pink lemonade on the lot if we don't find that headless illusion of mine working in their side show."

"A particle of dried mud that I didn't notice on Miss Christine's left shoe, I suppose," I said. "An unusual type of red clay that you immediately recognized as coming from nowhere else but the northeast corner of the circus lot in Waterboro, New York."

"You *don't* know my methods, Watson," he paraphrased.

"No. Hardly that. The show plays one-day stands. Last Thursday when Miss H, as I prefer to call her, made her brief appearance, the show was playing Newark, New Jersey."

"Take it from there," I said. "I'm listening."

"The Headless Lady is this season's wow exhibit in the open-air amusement world. Miss H's healthy tan, her too-contrasty make-up, and her athletic manner taken together, suggested outdoor show business. Circus, carnival, or exposition. There were half a dozen playing within a two-hundred-mile radius of New York City. Then, when Burt asked her name, she gave a phony. She's too quick-witted to give out something like Mary Smith or Jane Johnson, but she found herself hesitating, and she popped out with the first other name that entered her head, Mildred Christine. Simple matter of association. We were discussing a headless lady, and she thinks of a two-headed girl. My deduction that she knew her circus history was elementary. I consulted *Billboard* for circus routes. There were three shows in the neighborhood. One, I knew, had the illusion; one was a dog-and-pony show that couldn't afford it; and the other, the one nearest New York at that, was the Hannum show. It looked possible."

"Then you added in the H monogram on her purse, I suppose?"

"Exactly. At the beginning of the season, *Billboard* prints lists of the personnel of the various shows as they leave winter quarters. Major Rutherford Hannum, an old-time circus man who dates from the wagon-show days, owns the show, and one of its featured performers is his daughter, Pauline. I haven't seen the Major for years, and I failed to recognize Pauline because the last time I saw her she was in pigtails and short dresses. She's changed."

"She performs, you say?" I asked.

"Wire-walker," Merlini replied. "And good, so I hear. She also doubles this season in the swinging ladders, perch, and double traps."

"Perch and double traps?"

"Perch act. The girl who does the hand and headstands atop a pole balanced on the head of the understander. You've seen the Walkmirs with the Big Show. Double traps means double trapeze. You'll have to learn the language."

"So," I said, "she didn't really need that fire escape at all. She could have gone into a human-fly act down the side of the building. But why does their side show need a headless lady so badly and so quickly that she commits an illegal entry to get one?"

"That," he said, "is what I'm going to find out."

"Three-ring outfit?"

"Yes. It works out of Peru, Indiana, and ordinarily sticks to the Middle West, which is why I haven't caught it lately. It's one of the larger truck shows, though if you're polite when you're on the lot, you'll refer to it as a motorized show. And don't call the tents, tents; they are tops except for the one you eat in. That's the cook-house. A mitt camp is the fortune-teller's booth; zebras are convicts; barkers are never called that, but talkers, openers, or grinders; show elephants are all female, but are referred to as bulls; a rubber man is not a freak—he sells balloons; the picture gallery is the tattooed man; a mush is an umbrella and a skinned mush, consequently, a cane. A grab joint is a hot-dog stand; a grease joint is a lunch wagon or stand; a juice joint, the lemonade—"

"That," I said, breaking in on the foreign language broadcast, "is a good idea." I pulled off the road before a white house with a neatly dignified sign that read, "Ye Old-Fashioned Cookie Jar—Chicken and Waffles, Our Specialty."

"This grease joint do?" I asked.

We reached Waterboro at eight o'clock and, as I braked before the town's one traffic light, I hailed a boy on the corner. "Which way to the show grounds?" I asked.

Merlini's voice beside me answered. "Turn right, here."

"Oh. You know the town, then?" I asked, turning.

"No. Never set eyes on it before. Now turn left."

"Clairvoyance?"

"Something like that," he said. "Just give the car its head. I've had it so long that it turns in at circus lots automatically. Force of habit."

I could believe that. Merlini, as I should have explained before now, was born to calliopes, elephants, spangles, and sawdust. His mother was turning somersaults on a resin-back as late as five months before he was born and within a couple of weeks after. At one time or other when you were in kneepants or short dresses you probably saw the Riding Merlinis, an equestrian act that circus people still talk about. Merlini, himself, began his career of mystification as a side-show sorcerer, and he still has a very warm spot in his heart for the whitetops. I'm fairly certain that he'd have found himself at Waterboro that night even though the headless lady incident had never happened.[1]

[1] Lovers of coincidence will be interested to note that Philip Astley, often referred to as the "Father of the Circus," was also a magician. Many historians trace the origin of the modern circus back to the first exhibitions of horsemanship Astley gave in an open field near the Halfpenny Hatch Inn, Lambeth, London, in 1768. Later, after establishing Astley's Theatre, he also undertook the role of magician, and in 1784 published a book on conjuring, *Natural*

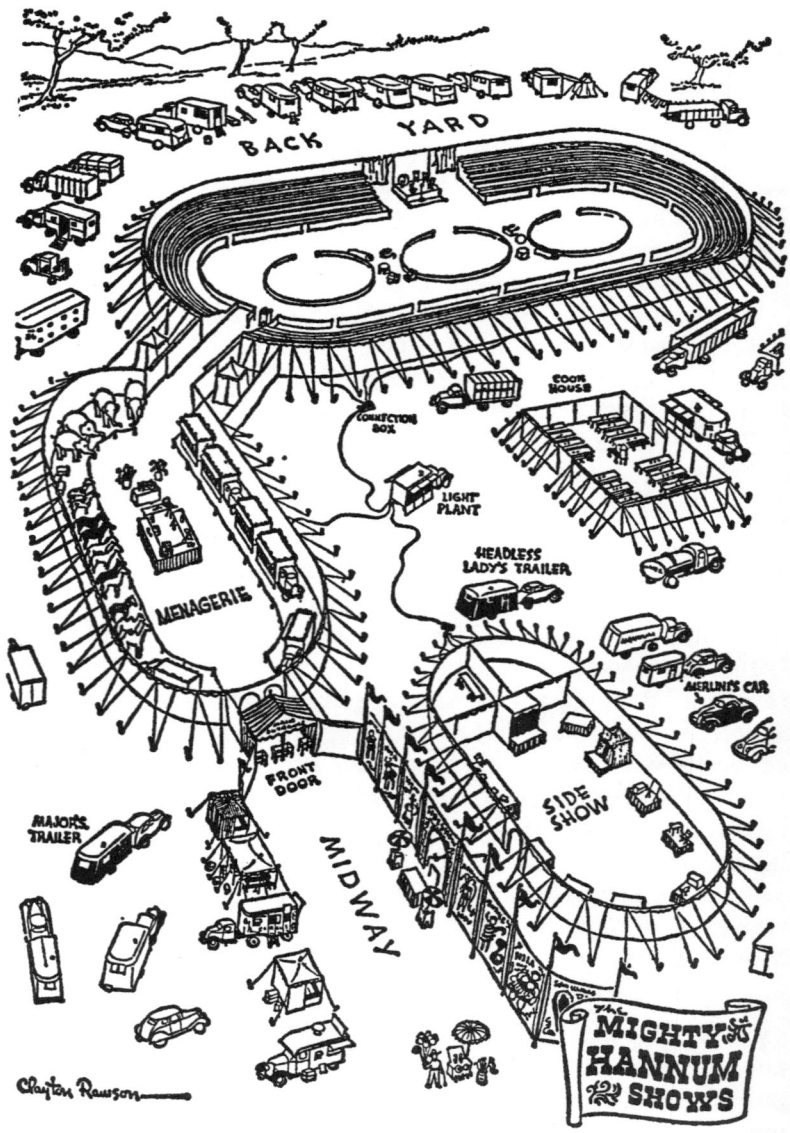

BACK YARD

COOK HOUSE

CONFECTION BOX

LIGHT PLANT

HEADLESS LADY'S TRAILER

MENAGERIE

MERLINI'S CAR

SIDE SHOW

FRONT DOOR

MAJOR'S TRAILER

MIDWAY

Clayton Rawson

THE MIGHTY HANNUM SHOWS

We made one more turn at his direction and came onto a street at the town's edge lined on either side with parked cars. At its further end there were lights and music, the gay, thumping, nostalgic sound of brasses that held all the old gala promise of excitement, color, and pageantry. As we came closer, I glimpsed the bellying, pennon-topped silhouettes of the tents rising above the brightly lighted side-show banners with their hot, garish splashes of color. We were downwind, and all at once I got the first whiff of that inimitable circus odor, the complex blended smell of elephants, cats, horses, hay, sawdust, crackerjack, hot peanuts, and candy floss.

"Is that your secret?" I asked. "Hypersensitive sense of smell?"

"The telephone poles were chalked," he explained, sitting forward expectantly in his seat. "When the show moves, the crew on the first truck out puts arrows on the poles, marking the turns so that the following drivers can dispense with maps or having to ask questions."

We turned right, up over the curb and onto the lot, pulling in and parking near several trailers behind the side-show top. Merlini was out almost before she stopped rolling.

He didn't bother to circumnavigate the tent, but went directly to the side wall. His tall figure, silhouetted against the lighted canvas, stooped as if to lift its lower edge, then stopped. I hurried toward him as he picked something from the grass at his feet.

"Well!" he said in a faintly surprised voice. "A grift show."

He fanned the three purses and then flipped them open one at a time, looking at the identification cards behind the celluloids. As he glanced at the second, his voice showed real surprise.

"That," he said, "is definitely a bloomer. I wonder . . . "

"Now what?" I asked. "Not clues already?"

He stuffed the billfolds into his pocket, bent quickly, lifted the side wall, and said, "Come on."

He held the canvas up as I ducked in behind him. We emerged between two of the dozen or more low platforms

Magic, in which he claimed to have invented the Bullet-Catching Trick as early as 1762.

that were set at even intervals around the interior. A tall square-shouldered man in an ankle-length, gaudy, somewhat soiled red and yellow robe, was arranging, on the table before him, a glittering assortment of long knives and swords. He turned, hearing us, and scowled ill-naturedly. His forehead had a Neanderthalian slant, and his bony underjaw projected belligerently.

"Where the hell duh ya think you're going, Mac?" he growled.

"Nowhere," Merlini said calmly. "We're here. We're with it."

The reception committee was skeptical. "Oh, yeah? Since when?"

"Since now." With his customary deftness, Merlini produced a cigarette from thin air, reached again, and got a paper of matches. "Magician," he explained somewhat unnecessarily. "Where's the mitt camp? I'm looking for Gus and Stella Milbauer."

The sword-swallower's suspicion melted slightly. "Over there," he said, jerking his head to the left. We stepped out from between the platforms and saw a small tented structure of awning-striped canvas down the line. Above its entrance hung a large drawing of Cheiro's chart of the hand. Merlini started toward it.

There were twenty or thirty customers within the sideshow tent, mostly gathered in a group at the far end listening to a five-piece negro band that was playing with more fervor than harmony, and watching a buxom, coffee-colored and undulant wench who shouted a faintly off-color lyric to one of Mr. Handy's Blues. She wore a skin-tight scarlet evening gown, and her hips operated on the principle of the universal joint.

Just beyond the band there was a platform surmounted by a square boxlike enclosure formed of dark red drapes, the front curtains tightly drawn.

Merlini pointed. "Success," he said. "That's it."

The singer stopped just then, and the band music faded. From outside on the midway came the leathery exhorting voice of the opener shouting, ". . . and the weirdest sight of all, my friends, the sci-un-tific mahvel of ouah time—Madem-

*wahselle Christine, the lady without a head! Positively living
and buh-reathing! While the big show is going on you see it
all for the one price—fifteen cents! Step right up . . ."*

Gus, standing by the mitt camp, greeted Merlini with
pleased surprise. He was a skinny little man with a scrawny
neck, thinning gray hair, a black-rimmed pince-nez, a rather
hammy dignity, and a warm smile.

"Stella," he exclaimed, turning. "Look who's here!"

A middle-aged, completely ordinary-looking woman sat on
a camp chair before the tent. She wore a black evening gown,
too much eye shadow, and an abstracted air. She looked at
Merlini with faded blue eyes and nodded politely but with
little enthusiasm.

Gus and Merlini, however, burst into a rapid-fire exchange
of reminiscences. "Haven't seen you since Coney Island in '33
. . . played the Orpheum circuit together . . . remember the
Curtises? . . . They're on the Russell show this season. . . ."

I looked interestedly around the tent at the silent gaping
crowd and at the blasé, matter-of-fact freaks and performers
who were awaiting their turns. Hoodoo, the Headhunter from
the Amazon, an inky-black, fuzz-topped colored man with
war paint on his face, sat on a campstool before his collection
of war clubs and shrunken human heads, cleaning his finger-
nails with a jackknife. One of the grass-skirted cooch dancers
was knitting busily at a small pink sweater.

My attention shifted suddenly back to Merlini and Gus, as
I heard the former ask, "When did the Headless Lady join
up?"

"Friday, I think," Gus replied. "Wasn't it, Stella?"

Stella, the woman who, according to the inscription on the
chart behind her, knows all, sees all, and tells all, answered,
"I guess so."

"Who is she?" Merlini continued off-handedly. "Anyone I
know?"

But Gus didn't get to answer just then. A lean, lantern-
jawed gentleman with a pair of innocent brown eyes and his
hat brim turned up all the way around, stepped from the
crowd and touched Merlini's arm.

"Pardon me, brother, but can you tell me how soon the
big show starts?" His voice was that of the country yokel,

but there was a knowing grin on his face.

"Holy jumping camelopards!" Merlini ejaculated. "Farmer Jack!" They shook hands energetically. "Ross, step over here. I want you to meet the dean of the broad tossers, the best three-card-monte man in the business. If he offers you a little bet on a sure thing, run for the nearest exit! Tell me something, Farmer. Last I heard this was a Sunday School show. When did the grift come back?"

Farmer grinned. "It's coming back on a lot of shows. Last season was a bloomer for one thing, and the grift's a sort of insurance. And then, too, when the fixer walks into Johnny Tin Plate's office and says, 'No grift at all this year, Chief,' for an answer he gets, 'Oh. That's nice. But how the hell do I get mine?' And the fix has to be paid off anyway. So why not frame a store or two?"

"I can't think of a real good answer for that one, Farmer. You're on the pay roll then?"

"Yeah. I think so. But maybe I'm wrong. Orders came through to lay off a few days. But if I don't get the office soon, I'm blowing. Seems like every time I take a vacation the chumps walk right up asking for it."

"Why the layoff? Too much heat in these parts?"

"No. There aren't many beefs the way I dust 'em off. Don't know what it is. Something goin' on around this outfit that I'm not hep to."

"It's the advance crew for one thing," Gus put in disgustedly. "Kelley and Edwards. They've gone nuts. Here, look at this route card."

26th Annual Tour-Season 1940

MIGHTY   HANNUM
COMBINED   SHOWS

Winter Quarters—Peru, Indiana

Mon.	Stroudsburg, Pa.	29
Tue.	Newton, N. J.	33
Wed.	Morristown, N. J.	24
Thu.	Newark, N. J.	19

Fri.	Bridgeport, Conn.	66
Sat.	Peekskill, N. Y.	48
Mon.	Kings Falls, N. Y.	58
Tue.	Waterboro, N. Y.	92
Wed.	Norwalk, N. Y.	80
Thu.	Watertown, N. Y.	77
Fri.	Ogdensburg, N. Y.	59
Sat.	Winchester, Canada	35

Total miles for season 2,820

Gus continued, "Seventy, eighty-mile jumps every day, and a lot of wrong towns. Waterboro's a grass town. Show this size hadn't oughta be here. We won't come close to making the nut. Norwalk tomorrow, and that's worse. I don't get it. We even played Bridgeport less'n two weeks after the Big Show."

"And," Farmer added, "we just got out of mine strike territory in Pennsy, and we're heading smack into a milk strike upstate. But it's not the advance crew, Gus. They don't know no more about it than we do. Couple of them back on the lot Sunday and crabbin' about it. It's orders from the old man."

"Salaries paid up?" Merlini asked.

"Yes," Gus said, "but that's funny, too. We were six weeks behind up until Saturday. Lots of folks were all set to blow. Three or four big top acts did leave. Then we got the whole thing up to date, all at once. Like that."

"The Major land an angel?" Merlini asked incredulously.

"Looks like it," Farmer answered. "High-class sucker, too. I'd like to have his phone number. But say, hasn't anybody told you . . ."

The lecturer's voice cut in above Farmer's. "Over here, ladies and gentlemen—the strangest, most startling scientific exhibition ever shown, Mademoiselle Christine, the Headless Lady."

Merlini gave me a glance. "Christine," he said. "Perhaps we'd better watch this." He started toward the crowd that stood before the speaker.

"Two years ago," the lecturer stated in a brisk clinical tone, "a terrible railway accident occurred near Paris, France. Many of you doubtless read about it. Mademoiselle Christine, who you are about to see, was in that accident. They found her among the dead and dying in the twisted wreckage with the bony structure of her skull horribly crushed. But she still lived! By a fortunate chance, the accident happened close to the private villa and research laboratories of the great surgeon, Dr. Josef Veronoff, world famous, as you all know, for his wonderful experiments in keeping human and animal tissue alive in chemical solutions. He saw at once that Mademoiselle Christine's head injuries could never be repaired by any surgical means. He kept her alive for three days with adrenalin and serum injections, while his technical assistants hastily constructed the marvelous apparatus you are about to see. Then Dr. Veronoff completely amputated the young lady's head! And substituted his astounding machine!"

The lecturer pulled a cord; the curtains drew apart. "Ladies and Gentlemen, may I introduce Mademoiselle Christine, the Lady Without a Head! The eighth wonder of the world of science!"

The display was obviously the lecturer's favorite. He really went to town and put oomph into his buildup. He did it well; the spectators, up to this point, had expected to see something falling as far short of the painting on the banner outside as did some of the other exhibits. But they were fooled. The side-show banner artist had, for once, found it impossible to gild the lily. The Headless Lady was exactly that.

Her body, dressed in brief shorts and brassière, sat on a high hospital stool made of metal tubing. Her figure was Grade A plus in all respects—except that it simply stopped short at the base of her neck. A cup-shaped rubber attachment was fixed between her shoulders, and six slender glass tubes rose upward from it, curved in a half-circle, and terminated in six descending tubes of rubber. Three of these were attached, on the left, to a radiolike apparatus, the front panel of which was covered with rheostat dials and electrical switches. The other three tubes led off to a chemico-electrical apparatus on the right, fitted with pressure gauges of strange design, an electric motor with visibly moving eccentric parts, and a complex hookup of chemical glassware—beakers, retorts, and flasks in which a red fluid bubbled. The same liquid could also be seen circulating through the glass tubes that led into the body at the base of the neck. A green light pulsated at a respiratory rate.

Above the girl's shoulders there was simply nothing but the curved glass tubes and empty space!

"This apparatus," the lecturer went on, "substitutes for all the physical activities of the missing brain. It supplies nervous stimulation to the body, and feeds it with a carefully regulated chemical diet and a steady flow of blood.

"The machine on your right is Dr. Veronoff's elaboration of the diagram you see here." With a perfectly straight face, the lecturer exhibited a framed, glass-covered Sunday Supplement double-spread. The article was headed: *Carrel Keeps Tissues Alive in Serum*; and the diagram he indicated was a schematic drawing of the Lindbergh heart.

The lecturer continued, "Many people, when they see Miss Christine, are skeptical. They have said that her body is merely a cleverly constructed dummy. I'll let you decide that for yourselves." He lifted a limp arm and pressed his thumb for a moment against its flesh. He removed his thumb, and we saw that its pressure had left a white spot on the arm which gradually faded away as the blood returned.

"I will now," he said dramatically, "turn on the nerve exciter." He threw a switch and moved several of the dials on the electrical equipment. A four-inch spark suddenly spit and leaped with a bright flash between two copper electrode terminals.

The body moved for the first time. The fingers of the hands twitched. Slowly the lecturer turned a rheostat, and slowly the sputtering, intermittent crackle of the spark grew faster. The girl's arms moved upward from their position on her thighs; her fingers jerked spasmodically in a clawing, galvanic movement that accelerated with the spark's increasing frequency. This continued for half a minute; then the crackling subsided; the finger jerks slowed; the arms settled again into their former position, and finally came to rest. The spark ceased abruptly.

"Her arms always return to their former position," the

lecturer explained, "because, having been in this condition
now for nearly two years, Mademoiselle Christine's muscles
have become set to a certain extent. If any of you have any
questions to ask I will be happy to try to answer them for
you." He stepped forward and drew the curtain to behind
him.

"Do *you* have any questions?" I asked Merlini.

"Yes," he said, "I do; but I doubt if the lecturer is the
man to ask. I still want to know who the girl is. I've a feeling
in my bones that *this* Millie Christine is not the one we had
the pleasure of meeting. Did you like the illusion?"

"If I didn't know it as an illusion, and if I failed to realize,
as many of this audience seem to, that no bona fide scientific
marvel of this caliber would ever be on tour in a side show, it
would give me the creeps, the fantods, and the willies. Look
at that woman over there. She's a kind, sympathetic soul;
and it's obvious that she is feeling sorry as hell for poor Miss
Christine. It's a bit thick, isn't it?"

"I know," Merlini said. "He played it straight from start
to finish. The illusion is so perfect that it would still be a
socko draw if it were announced as an illusion instead of as
the real thing. But the lecturer is a circus man and a showman. The townspeople, to him, are chumps, linguistically
and literally. It hasn't occurred to him that he's doing his bit
toward making science our modern superstition. If it did, he'd
say, 'What the hell! My job is to pack 'em in.' He has, of
course, a notable precedent in Phineas Taylor Barnum. I
think, however, that I will tell the Major that the Carrel-
Lindbergh patter is not only a little too far over the edge,
but quite unnecessary as well."

Gus, who stood beside us, said, "Then I was right. You
haven't heard. Farmer started to tell you a few minutes ago
that you won't be seeing Major Hannum this trip—or any
other."

Merlini turned on his heel, sharply. "Why not?" His words
were definitely apprehensive.

Gus said, "They shipped his body back to Indiana this
afternoon. He was killed last night. He—"

The lecturer led the crowd in our direction. He spoke to
Gus. "Let's go. You're next."

"Right," Gus said, and to us, "Sorry. See you later."
"The woman who sees all, knows all and tells all," Merlini
commented thoughtfully. "I do wish that wasn't just another
snare and delusion."

Chapter 3

Gun Talk

*"If he's old enough to enjoy the show, lady—he's old enough
to need a ticket."*

MERLINI WATCHED Gus mount the low platform before the
mitt camp and stand waiting beside his wife as the lecturer
rattled off his introductory talk.

"Ross," he said after a moment, "the Mighty Hannum
Shows have attractions that aren't mentioned in the advertising."

"Yes," I agreed. "The way things are shaping up, I wouldn't
be a bit surprised but what I'll have to report to your wife
that you've run off and joined a circus for the duration of
the summer."

"That's quite possible," he said seriously. "The side show
could use a magician. And you can sign on as a punk around
the elephants.[1] Come on. Let's go ask questions."

We turned toward the entrance and went out just as Gus
tied a blindfold over his wife's eyes and launched into the
second-sight act that sold Madame Stella as a seer and preceded the later request for "the small sum of twenty-five cents
more that entitles each and every one of you to a personal
horoscope, a private reading, and a full and complete answer
to any question concerning the Future, Love, Travel, Business
—"

Before the side-show top and the line of violently colored,
somewhat Dali-esque banners that pictured a "positively un-
equaled display of Believe-It-or-Not freaks and oddities from
the four corners of the earth" stood a raised platform, flanked

---

[1] Boy who waters the elephants. Anything young is a punk.

on either side by an umbrella-covered ticket box. A talker walked back and forth on the platform, mopping his brow with a damp handkerchief and trying with little success to get a reaction from the scattered groups of townsfolk who stood stolidly watching him.

"Lot-lice," Merlini said. "Folks who stand around with their hands in their pockets and don't buy."

On the opposite side of the midway, reading from left to right, were a frozen custard stand, a grab joint, the ticket wagon, a grease joint, and a juice joint. In the center of the midway on the left a pitchman was selling balloons, whips, and replicas of Charlie McCarthy. We turned right, toward the canopied marquee above which, in ornately serifed letters, were the words, "*Main Entrance,* THE MIGHTY HANNUM COMBINED SHOWS."

"This," Merlini said, determined to see that I was properly educated, "is the front door. And the performer's section of the lot behind the big top is called the back yard."

As we came up to the entrance, we were accosted by a short and extremely wide man who had been constructed, through some error, according to architectural specifications intended for a hippopotamus. He held out a large hairy paw and said, "Tickets, please. You'll have to hurry. The big show is now going on."

"Is Mac Wiley around?" Merlini asked.

The hippopotamus gave us a sour and speculative once-over.

"No," Merlini said, apparently reading the man's mind, "no attachments, no damage suits, no shakedowns. I just want—"

One of the two men sitting inside the enclosure on folding camp chairs suddenly hopped to his feet and stepped briskly forward, hand out. "Well, you old son of a gun! Come in! Come in! Been wondering why you hadn't showed up before now." He took Merlini's hand in both of his own and pumped at it enthusiastically.

He was a lean, wiry individual with graying, brittle hair and bushy black eyebrows that jutted out with a Mephisto-phelean twist above a knowing and extraordinarily penetrating pair of small bright eyes. The hard muscles of his face were covered with a tough and weatherbeaten hide that had seldom been indoors, the leathery tan of which was spotted with an overlapping accumulation of darker freckles. A limp felt hat was pushed far back on his head.

"You couldn't keep me away, Mac," said Merlini. "How are you? Meet a good friend of mine, Ross Harte. This is J. MacAllister Wiley, legal adjuster extraordinary, technically known as the fixer, or the patch."

"Glad to know you. Any friend of Merlini's . . ." Mac nodded at the other man, who had risen from his chair, a hatless young man with a rumpled thatch of sandy hair and an intelligent, worried face that I noticed grew suddenly intent at that first mention of Merlini's name.

"Don't think you know Atterbury, here, do you?" Mac said. "Keith Atterbury, press agent on the lot. Young squirt. Since your time. But he writes a nice notice. Sit down, Merlini, and tell me about yourself. It's been years."

Atterbury acknowledged the introductions somewhat perfunctorily and pulled up two more chairs. He lit a fresh cigarette from the end of the butt he held and watched Merlini with a nervous and calculating air.

"Last time I saw you—" Mac pattered rapidly. "Wait. I know. Night of the blowdown on the Hagen show." His thin-lipped mouth spread in a wide grin, and he addressed me. "The Great Merlini was working the kid-show and the blow hit us before the boys could finish double-staking. The top came down while Merlini was floating a lady in midair. One of the customers that I had to argue out of a damage suit —he got conked by a falling quarter pole—said afterward, 'Why in hell didn't that damned magician use some levitation on the tent?' Ho! Ho!"

Merlini grinned. "I couldn't let the lady down, Mac. That *was* a night, wasn't it?"

"It was. The bulls stampeded into the next county, and when the attachments and damage suits began to come in, the show folded then and there. Don't know what either of us was doing on it. It was a traveling crash-pile anyhow."

"Remember the mountaineer boy who showed up in Hillsvale, Kentucky, wanting a job?" asked Merlini.

Wiley grinned all over. "Will I ever forget him," he said,

chuckling. "Tell them about it."

Merlini addressed Atterbury and myself. "Old man Hagen had bought a lion from the Robbins show at the start of the season, sight unseen. They guaranteed him to be as gentle as a lamb. That was an exaggeration; he was as mild as a full-grown typhoon. The cat would hardly let an animal man on the lot get near enough to the cage to feed him. When the hillbilly arrived asking for a job, Hagen, whose practical jokes were famous, said, 'Why, yes. Guess I could use a young fellow like you. Tell you what. You go over and clean out that lion's cage. If you do a good job, I'll put you on.' The kid went off and then—nothing happened at all. Finally Hagen began to worry. He was afraid that perhaps the kid *had* tried to enter the cage. So he investigated. He found the boy actually in the cage, and calmly doing a good workmanlike job of cleaning it out. *But the door was wide open and the lion was gone!*"

"Luckily we cornered the cat," Wiley added, "before it chewed anybody, though we had to shoot it to get it. Hagen didn't as much as think of another practical joke for nearly a month. Reminds me of the time . . ."

For the next five minutes Merlini and Wiley, ignoring Atterbury and myself, exchanged a rapid barrage and counterbarrage of reminiscences. It was interesting, but largely historical; and there were several times when, in spite of the glossary of circus terms Merlini had already shoved at me, I got completely lost. Finally, their cavalcade of memory returned to the current date, and Merlini asked, "Good show this year, Mac?"

"I dunno. Ask Keith. He's the P.A. I haven't seen anything but small pieces of a circus performance in fifteen years." He glanced at me, saw the incredulous look on my face, and added, grinning, "Nothing odd about that. I knew a clown once who *never* saw a complete show until after he retired at seventy-three."

A neatly dressed stoutish man came in from the midway and approached us with a smile. "I just picked up a couple of dandies, Keith," he said. "Seam-squirrels and circus-bees. Nice."

Mac grinned. "I'd say they were *lousy* myself. When you

hunt for them it's called 'reading your shirt.' " Mac turned to us. "This is Mr. Stuart Towne, a First-of-May visiting author. He's spending a week or two with the show. Says he's going to do a circus murder mystery, but he spends most of his time collecting words. The man with the high pockets, Towne, is the Great Merlini in person, and this is his friend, Ross Harte."

Towne acknowledged the introductions and then turned back to Mac. "The words will come in handy," he said, "but I've been picking up murder material too. That single-edged grub-hoe the working men use would be a nice original weapon. Never saw it used in fiction."

"I've seen it used in real life though," Mac said. He rattled off an account of a circus murder by a drunken prop-man while I noticed that Towne, like many another author, didn't look the part. He was middle-aged, blue of chin, and altogether too ordinary-looking. You wouldn't have given him a second glance in a crowd, though once you had talked to him you did just that. Behind the commonplace, rather trite face, you soon detected the busy clockwork of a clever and active brain. His character at first seemed as colorless as his face; but as I came to know him, I found that it had an annoying chameleonlike way of appearing to change, as soon as you were on the point of defining it, into something quite different. He chewed gum incessantly.

When Mac had finished, Merlini, whose interest in murder since he went in for a sideline of crime has been boundless, said, "The grub-hoe's a weapon, Mr. Towne. And here's a method. You can use it nicely on a clown. Clown white, a preparation of pre-Elizabethan origin, is a mixture of zinc oxide, lard, and tincture of benzoin, dusted over with talcum. The great Humpty-Dumpty pantomimist, George L. Fox, and others are said to have died because they mistakenly used bismuth in place of benzoin. Use any poison that can be absorbed through the skin, and there you are. No charge." [2]

"Thanks," Towne said. "There's another thing *you* could give me, if it's etiquette to ask. I saw you vanish an elephant

[2] Merlini's formula dates from his own circus days. Clown white now is usually compounded of zinc oxide, olive oil, and glycerine.

at the old Hippodrome ten years ago, and I've been annoyed
ever since. I might be able to use the method to vanish a
murderer sometime."

"That trick was designed to vanish an elephant," Merlini
smiled evasively. "Vanishing a murderer by that particular
method would be like killing a fly with a sledge hammer. And
besides, you do pretty well on your own. You got off a very
neat vanish of a corpse in *The Empty Coffin*."

"He gave me an autographed copy of that," Mac put in.
"I'm looking forward to reading it this winter. There's a circus saying, Mr. Towne, that circus people do their sleeping
in the winter. That goes for reading, too. There never seems
to be time for it on the road."

"By the way, Mac," Merlini put in, "that book title reminds
me. What is this that I hear about the Major?"

Mac sobered a bit. "Auto smashup. Tough break for the
show. Happened last night just outside of Kings Falls; his
car hit a bridge abutment. Pretty bad smash. He was dead
when they found him."

The fat ticket taker behind Mac, engaged in counting a
pile of ticket stubs, muttered something half under his breath.
Mac turned.

"Oh, sorry, Cal. Merlini, this is Everett Lovejoy, better
known as 'Calamity.' Our front-door superintendent. Pay no
attention to him at all. He thinks the show is jinxed—as always. Every cloud has a black border."

"Well," Calamity scowled, "what would you call it? First
it's mine strikes, then the Major, and now . . . you hear that
band in the big top? Suppé's 'Light Cavalry March,' for God
sakes! Where has that boss windjammer been all his life? You
know as well as I do, first time that was played on a circus
lot they had a train wreck and sixteen people killed. Merle
Evans played it once on the Miller Bros. 101 Ranch Outfit.
I was there. We had a blowdown and thirty-eight killed.
He played it just once after that, and a cornet player died
soon's he'd finished. I got a damn good notion to blow right
now."

"Forget it," Mac said heavily. "You're twice as superstitious as a tribe of Ubangis." He frowned. "That *is* a little
thick, though. Our bandmaster's a Johnny-Come-Lately. May-

be he doesn't know. I'll speak to him. Some of the performers
are apt to get a mite nervous."

"Sure, that's just it," added Calamity. "And break their
necks. Accidents always come in threes. We've had the first.
That leaves two to go." He scowled, then said almost inaudi-
bly, "If it was an accident."

Mac caught it, though. "What," he said with a sudden
sharp bite in his voice, "do you mean by that?"

There was a short uneasy silence until Calamity answered,
"Oh, nothin' at all. I just don't understand why the Major
left the lot at that time of night with a blow comin' on,
where the hell he could have been goin', and why he piled
up—a cautious fussbudget like him. With that bum ticker of
his he never drove faster than a trot, and he was so afraid
he'd scratch the cream-colored paint job on that new sixteen-
cylinder Cadillac, he moved it around like he was truckin' a
load of eggs. He musta been goin' sixty-five to—"

Mac threw up his hands. "You can think up the damnedest
things. If somebody sneezes you're afraid of a blowdown.
Business is always lousy. And if we do have all the blues up
and are putting the customers in the straw you worry because
one of the bulls looks like he might run wild or—" [3]

"And what happened this Friday morning this side of
Bridgeport?" Calamity sputtered. "The elephant truck lands
in a ditch, Rubber and Modoc get away and it takes all
morning to round them up. I suppose you don't count—"

"No, I don't. The publicity we got packed the house in
Peekskill that night. Forget it, Cal. You've been jumpy ever
since the fuzz came on the lot tonight."

"The fuzz, Ross," Merlini footnoted, "is the local con-
stabulary. Cal might be right at that, Mac. Sheriff Weatherby
is going to be howling in your ear before long. That's a prediction."

Mac looked startled. "What do you mean? Do you know
him?"

"No, never saw him; but the cannon mob that's working

[3] Blues: Unreserved seats at the arena ends, traditionally painted
blue. In the straw: Overflow customers are seated on straw spread
around the hippodrome track.

tonight pulled a boner. They should know better."

"What do you mean? There aren't any pickpockets on this show."

"No?" Merlini produced the billfolds. "You wouldn't kid me, would you, Mac? Someone weeded these leathers and ditched them behind the kid-show top. And this one belongs to Sheriff Jonas Weatherby. Don't the boys know enough to lay off the law?"

Mac grabbed it. "I'll be damned! It's a local mob. I'd better see about this."

"I think I've spotted them for you. Skinny guy over there this side of the ticket wagon is the wire. Talking to one of his stalls. Probably waiting to work the connection after the blow-off." [4]

"Excuse me," Mac said hastily, "while I go cause a little trouble. Come on, Cal. Keith, you watch the door."

Towne spoke up. "Cannon mob, wire, stall? I don't have those. Dip is the word I know." He took an envelope from his pocket and made a notation.

"Dip is a winchell," Merlini said. "A sucker word. It's so well known to the layman that only the old-timers among the professionals still use it. Gun, from the Jewish *gonnif*, meaning thief, is preferable, or even the more recent variant, cannon. The gun who does the actual picking of the pocket is called a wire, tool, or hook. Guns work in mobs, the wire being assisted by stalls, sometimes called pushers-and-shovers, which is what they do. One of them prats the mark in, and as soon as the wire gets the okus he weeds it to another stall so if he's tumbled he won't get sneezed with it on him."

Merlini grinned. "Is that clear?"

"To another gun, maybe," Atterbury said. "There are some new ones on me there."

"It's thieves' argot rather than circus," Merlini explained, "You'll find that the grifter and circus argots overlap considerably. You hear less of the former on a circus now than in the good old days."

"Prat the mark in?" Towne asked. "Okus, weed? What—"

[4] Blow-off: Finale.

"Okus and its older synonym, poke, mean pocketbook. Poke was once pokus, and both terms obviously derive from a term connected with my own profession, hocus-pocus. Weed, as I used it, means to get rid of the okus by passing it along to a stall; and prat the mark in. . .here, I'll show you."

He took up a position behind Towne. "You're a mark out in front of the bally platform listening to an opening. You stall for me, Ross."

I had seen Merlini demonstrate the gentle art of pocket-picking on other occasions and knew what was required. I stood in front of Towne and edged back against him, shoving impolitely with my fanny and stepping on his toes a bit, to make him give way.

"Here," he started to object. "What the—"

"You see," Merlini explained, stepping out from behind him. "It's the old story again. Misdirection and distraction of attention. The chump's attention is all on the clumsy oaf in front of him. He doesn't feel the duke slip into his kick at all. And usually a second stall is so placed that he shades the duke and prevents any bystanders from seeing the action. Duke is, of course, hand. A kick is a pocket, and specifically a coat pocket. A breech kick is a trouser pocket; a prat kick or a prop is a hip pocket. The fob is the watch pocket, and the insider is self-explanatory."

Towne was investigating his pockets. "Do you mean that—?"

"Sure." Merlini held out a billfold. "From your left breech. I don't know if you realize it, but that's the smart place to carry it. Except for the fob, it's the most difficult one to beat. Of course, if a wire had trouble with it, he'd resort to rip-and-tear methods—cut the pocket open."

Towne hurriedly took back the billfold and began exploring another pocket. His face was annoyed. "Very educational demonstration," he said. "May I have the other—"

Merlini nodded. "Hope I'm not embarrassing you." He held out two objects. "Right kick," he said, passing over a pack of cigarettes. "And left prat." Merlini looked curiously at the ivory-handled revolver in his hand. "Metzger .32-caliber. Do all detective-story writers carry heaters?"

Towne took the gun and replaced it in his pocket. "I've got a collection of firearms," he said quickly. "Picked this up in Bridgeport the other day."

Merlini said, "Now I know why the ballistic dope in your stories is so well done. I liked that trick you used in *The Phantom Bullet* where the victim was killed with a shotgun loaded with water."

Towne nodded. "Yes. There was a real case of that several years—"

Mac returned and interrupted. He was replacing some bills in the sheriff's wallet. "I got his dough back. Guess I'd better rig up a story about someone finding it on the lot and turning it in."

"If you want him to believe that one," Merlini said, "you'd better get it to him quickly, before he misses it. Want me to slip it back in his kick for you?"

"No," Mac said. "If he caught you, he'd think you were taking it out and I don't want any trouble." Mac started into the tent. "Coming?"

Merlini nodded. "Yes, I want to get a look at the performance."

Towne and I followed them, and Calamity took his stand again at the entrance. Atterbury said, "See you later." He went out toward the midway.

As we walked through into the menagerie, Merlini asked, "By the way, Mac, I understand the eagle screamed hereabouts on Saturday in a big way. And business has been spotty. How does that happen, or am I being nosy?"

Mac turned his head and squinted at Merlini sharply. "You heard about that? Um. If you find out, let me in on it. I asked the Major if his rich uncle had died and he said 'Yeah.' Nothing wrong with that except he didn't have one."

"Who owns the show now? Daughter Pauline?"

"Uh huh. And I hope she knows the answer. We might need more dough any day. She has a lot of stubborn notions about how to run this outfit, and some of them ain't too hot. Expecting a purge around here most any time. You showed just in time for all the excitement."

"Yes," Merlini agreed, "I'm beginning to think I did."

Chapter 4

Suspicion

". . . You have ample time before the big show starts to inspect this amazing traveling menagerie with its priceless specimens from every clime, its strange and wonderful array of curious beasts and zoological wonders . . . get your peanuts for the elephants . . . hot buttered popcorn . . . soft drinks . . . souvenirs . . ."

THE ANIMAL cages, parked end to end, lined half the interior of the menagerie, not the gay and gaudy gold-encrusted parade wagons of memory, but great, simply painted, red and white trucks and trailers. They held a pair of lions with cub, two leopards, a brown bear, a hyena, a colony of chattering monkeys, and a trained chimp. The lead and ring stock was lined up on the opposite side; two bored but supercilious camels, a bright-eyed zebra, a sleepy ibex, and the horses—broad-hipped resin-backs, high-school and liberty horses and cow ponies. Near the entrance that led into the big top itself, just beyond the stand that sold Coca-Cola, popcorn, and peanuts, were four elephants, their trunks moving in restless exploration. An attendant was sweeping the broad back of one of them with a broom.

Near the horses stood a lanky figure in an especially resplendent costume of tight white trousers, high-heeled boots, bright blue shirt, and ten-gallon hat, coiling a long lariat. His hard, angular face in the shadow of the hat brim had a very familiar look.

"Tex Mayo," Mac said. "The movie star. Featured in the after-show with Blaze, his educated pony. Fancy roping, riding, shooting, and bull-whip snapping. You must meet the horse."

"What's wrong with Tex?" Merlini asked.

"Prima donna," Mac said. "He was a big shot in Hollywood until the singing cowboy came in; Tex is tone-deaf. Made a lot of dough in his time and spent it all on swim-

49

ming pools. He gets a bigger salary than any other performer on the show, but to him it's still peanuts. The Major
was ready to put the skids under him, too—he's been liquored
up pretty much lately, and it interferes with his marksmanship. But he'll be around awhile longer now, I guess. He's
been making a play for Pauline—and she likes it."

Mac went on into the big top; and Merlini, Towne, and I
stood just within watching the clowns, who were slapping
each other down with oversize gloves in that perennial bit
of circus tomfoolery, the clown prize fight.

Merlini watched it a moment and then asked, "Just what
did happen to the Major, Towne? Mac rather shies from the
subject."

Towne turned to look at him and raised a questioning
eyebrow. "You don't think Calamity's remarks have any
foundation, do you?"

"I don't know," Merlini said. "That's why I asked."

Towne shrugged. "Don't know a lot about it," he said.
"They found him around midnight last night, quarter of a
mile or so from the lot at Kings Falls. He'd piled up against
a concrete bridge abutment at the foot of a hill. Nearly
threw him through the windshield. I missed all the excitement. I heard about it when I got on the lot this morning."

"What do you do, tag along in your own car and stop at
hotels?"

"Yes."

"You don't agree with Calamity, then?"

"I hadn't considered his remarks very seriously. I've heard
him do a lot of grousing since I joined up Saturday. I don't
know what he thinks it is, if it wasn't an accident. Suicide's
not very probable by that method, and it's a damned impractical murder method. You could drug a man or knock
him out, then put him in the machine and pull the throttle
out at the top of the hill; but you couldn't be at all sure
you'd kill him."

While Towne was speaking, the clowns finished and ran
off, and the announcer's voice came from the amplifiers: "*The
Mighty Hannum Shows now take great pleasure in presenting
an outstanding feature of the circus world, those two amazing
dancing queens of the tight wire, Pauline and Paulette, in*

their death-defying, somersaulting feats of grace and impossible skill!"

"Oh," Merlini said. "Miss Hannum is working tonight?"

"Yes," Towne replied. "Looks that way. It takes a lot to stop her. Very determined young lady."

Merlini glanced at me. I knew he was thinking that the phrase had a familiar sound.

Two girls in Spanish costume, flaring trousers, bolero vests, and wide-brimmed, scarlet hats took their bow in the center ring and ascended swiftly to the small platforms, ten feet high, between which stretched the thin steel wire. At this distance they were merely two dancing figures, either of whom might be the girl we were looking for.

Singly at first and then together they ran and postured on the slender, bouncing wire in a sort of two-dimensional dance, a routine that was such an expert and unusually graceful exhibition of balance that even my layman's eye tagged it at once as big-time.

The announcer broke in again for a moment: *"Pauline will now attempt a feat equaled by no other woman on the wire, a backward somersault from feet to feet! Watch her!"*

One figure ran lightly to the center of the wire, balanced slowly, stood perfectly still with arms outstretched, held it, waited, and then repeated the maneuver, taking short, calculating steps as she watched the wire, building up to her climax. She did it finally—a sudden rising lift, a backward swirl of color, and a precarious, shaky landing, the wire vibrating from side to side beneath her feet. It seemed for a second impossible that she could maintain her balance; and then suddenly she stood straight and still, and walked without haste to her platform.

"The announcer exaggerates," Merlini commented. "She's not the only woman to do that, but she is good. Let's get a look at her as she comes off. Under the side wall there and around—" He stopped suddenly, his gaze fastened on the center ring. "Towne," he said, "does *that* happen at every performance?"

"That? What?"

"The other girl. She just completed as nonchalant a forward somersault on the wire as I've ever seen."

"Yes. She's done it each time I've seen the act."

"And the only special announcement was the one Pauline got, like now?"

Towne nodded. "Uh huh. Why?"

"There's a story for you," Merlini answered. "The forward on the wire, any place for that matter, is far more difficult than a backward. Try it sometime. Find out why the wrong girl gets the announcement and you should have a story. Come on, Ross. See you later, Towne."

I followed Merlini as he ducked under the side wall on the left and out into the back yard. Star Avenue, or Kinker's Row, as it is sometimes called, lay before us, an orderly line of autos, trailers, sleeping cars, and prop trucks drawn up paralleling the big top.[1] Halfway along the side wall were two openings, the entrance and exit used by the performers in entering the arena, called the back door. Walking in the space between the cars and the tent, we started toward it.

We had gone only a short distance when Keith Atterbury came from the dark between two trailers and stopped us. There was a seriously worried expression on his face.

"Could I see you a minute? I've got something I'd like to show you."

Merlini nodded. Atterbury moved to the nearest trailer and, standing in the light from its window, opened a large manila envelope. He took out three glossy 8 x 10 photos and gave them to Merlini. I looked over his shoulder. A strip of copy paper pasted along the lower edge of the first photo bore the typed caption: *Circus owner killed in auto crash near Kings Falls, N. Y.* The photographer had done a professionally competent job. The shot, although taken at night with flashlighting, was clear and sharply focused. But it was not the sort of picture you would enter in a salon exhibition or care to look at during a meal.

Major Hannum was a heavy-set man with an almost totally bald head. His body was lying halfway through the shattered windshield of the car, the front end of which, jammed against

[1] A kinker is a performer.

a concrete bridge abutment, resembled a battered accordion. His face was badly lacerated. The second photo was a close shot from another angle and the third a long shot. Merlini looked up and gave Atterbury a sharp glance. "Why," he asked, "are you showing these to me?" Atterbury tapped a cigarette nervously against the back of his hand. He spoke hesitantly, jerkily. "I know Sigrid Verrill and her father. I was on the Webb Show with him last year. He told me about that Skelton Island case you solved. I don't like that photo. You know about such things. I want to know if what I see in it means what I think it does—before I stick my neck out. You—"

Merlini broke in. "Do you have anything more than just this?"

"You do see it then," Atterbury said. "I've been hoping all day that I was wrong. Yes, I've got more."

"I see enough to want to know a lot more," Merlini replied. "Let's have it."

I took the photos from Merlini and gave them a closer look. I didn't get it.

"You heard Calamity," Keith began. "There's more of the same. I went back to Kings Falls this morning, as soon as I heard about the accident. They hadn't moved the car yet. I didn't like what I saw. Then, at the newspaper office, I happened to see the photos."

"What didn't you like?"

"Well, for one thing, the Major put nine or ten thousand miles on his car every season. He's never had as much as a dented fender before. The cops figured he was drunk and speeding. But he had a bad heart, he never drank, and no one ever saw him go faster than forty-five on a straight stretch. We kidded him about buying a sixteen-cylinder speed-wagon and then driving it like a horse and buggy. He was as proud as Punch of that shiny cream and chromium. Afraid he'd scratch it. Then, suddenly, he smashes it all to hell."

"Where was he going?" Merlini asked.

"That's funny, too. Nobody seems to know. He couldn't have been headed for the town ahead. He always moves with the show the next morning, for one thing; and the road he was on was headed south. Waterboro's north of Kings Falls. The road was a side road at that. It doesn't hit anything but tank towns for sixty miles."

"Picture taken at night," said Merlini. "Just when did the accident happen?"

"They found the body at midnight. He'd left the lot in Kings Falls at 10:45, during the concert.[2] I've checked that. The kid stationed at the lot entrance to direct parking saw his car leave, driving like hell. Almost ran the kid down. But the queerest thing is that the Major would even think of leaving the lot at a time like that. Just before the main show blowed, he gave orders to have the menagerie top double-staked for the night. It was getting damn windy, and it looked like blowdown weather. The Major told 'em to run through the concert on the double-quick so we could get the customers out and the other tops sloughed before we had trouble.[3] Then, just as the customers that didn't stay for the after-show were coming out, he says he is going to his trailer for a slicker. That was ten-thirty. He never came back. That's what made me wonder in the first place. He wouldn't leave the lot in the face of a possible blowdown."

"That a first-hand account?" Merlini asked. "You were on the front door when he left?"

Keith nodded. "Yes. I'd been there all evening, and I stuck around with Calamity until the concert was all out and all over about eleven, when I left to go ahead to Waterboro. I usually make my jump after the night show so I'll be on deck in the next town early to contact the papers."

"And you think that this photo—"

"Cinches it. Yes."

"Newspaper photo. Who took it?"

"Photographer on the Kings Falls *Gazette*, Irving Desfor. He had a lucky break. He was the guy who found the body."

"He took his pictures before anyone had touched the car or body?"

"Yes. First thing he did. Even before he reported it."

[2] Concert: The extra show after the main performance—once a musical program, now usually a Wild West exhibition. Also called the after-show.

[3] Slough: Take down. Pronounced to rhyme with bough.

"The paper hasn't printed these shots?"

"They used the long shot. Not so much detail in it. The others are a bit strong for public consumption."

Merlini looked at the photos again. "Judging from the matter-of-fact caption, neither the photographer nor his editor saw in the pictures what you think you do? And the medical examiner—?"

"They'd have spread it all across the front page if they had. The medical examiner hasn't seen the photos, as far as I know. And he didn't see the body until it was in the undertaking parlor in Kings Falls. I checked that."

"Going to show it to him?"

"I don't know. Should I? Have I got enough evidence? The medical examiner's an elderly stuffed shirt, and now that he's given his verdict of accidental death, he won't want to back-track without some damned good reason. Besides, he's nearly a hundred miles behind and in the next county. Tomorrow we'll be eighty miles further away."

"That's awkward," Merlini admitted. "Who else have you shown these to?"

"No one—yet."

Merlini looked surprised. "And you've had the pictures all day? Why not? Shouldn't Mac see them?"

Atterbury shook his head. "It's dynamite. You saw Mac's reaction when Calamity aired a few doubts. Hush, hush. A police investigation on a circus is poison. They might hold up the whole show while they nosed around asking questions. We'd maybe blow the next stand, and the fuzz on the route ahead might make trouble about issuing readers.[4] At a time like this that could fold the show. Mac's job—"

"Dammit!" I exploded impatiently. "What is it in these pix that I don't see? Mind?"

"Something you can't see because it isn't there," Merlini answered. "Something that isn't there but should be. That it, Atterbury?"

"Yes. Blood."

"Blood?" I looked at the prints again.

Merlini said, "Those cuts on the face, Ross. And that

---

[4] Reader: a license to exhibit.

whopping big gash along the neck. His head and shoulders are lying out on the engine hood. That cream-colored paint job should be well smeared with blood. But it isn't. There's just one small dark streak across the top of his head that might be blood. That's not nearly enough."

I got it then. It hit me like a ton of high explosive. The cuts had been made *after* death—some time after. The accident . . .

Merlini was speaking. "Why haven't you shown these to Miss Hannum? After all, he was her father. Even though it may affect the show, if the accident is suspect she has a right to know—and to decide if the police—"

"*That*," Keith said, "is the trouble. You see, just as the Major left the front door last night headed for his trailer, I saw someone come from the back yard and follow after him. They went into the trailer together. The last person to see him alive was Pauline Hannum!"

For a moment no one said anything. Then Keith added, "And, unless we do something about it, there's another murder to come."

Chapter 5

Burglars We

". . . Watch the little lady closely, boys. Now she's here; now she's gone. The trick that fooled Houdini! For ten cents more you can step right up here on the stage, look into the cabinet, and see just how it's done. Don't crowd. . . ."

WITHIN THE tent the music of the band changed from waltz time to the sprightly rhythm of the "Beer Barrel Polka" as a group of liberty horses trotted in.

"There would seem to be something happening in all three rings at once," Merlini said quietly. "But let's take them one at a time. Assuming that it may be murder, you've given Pauline opportunity. Anything else?"

"Motive," said Keith. "The show's hers now. And the Carnival Equipment Company. Or most of it is."

"Carnival Equipment Company?" Merlini asked. "Most of it?"

"That's his estate," Keith explained. "He owns a carnival-game manufacturing company, the circus, and a little real estate back in Indiana. But Pauline only gets two-thirds. The Major promised Joy Pattison a third. She's his niece. And Pauline won't stop till there's another 'accident.' That's what is driving me nuts. I need help. I checked all of Joy's rigging myself before she went on this afternoon. I'm doing the same tonight."

"Joy Pattison?" Merlini asked. "She wouldn't be Pauline's partner, the Paulette of the 'sister' wire-walking act, would she?"

"Yes, she is. Why—"

"What else does she do?"

"Swinging ladders and double traps. And it would be so damned easy to—"

"The 'sisters' don't get along too well together, do they?"

Atterbury looked at him sharply. "What makes you ask that?"

"I caught the act just now. There was a misplaced announcement."

Keith nodded. "You understand. Joy's mother was a Hannum. When she died six years ago—her mother and father were both killed in a circus train wreck—Joy came with her uncle. Pauline was already doing the wire act and needed a partner. The Major coached Joy in the act, and then she made the mistake of getting too good for her own good. She practiced that forward all last winter and added it at the beginning of the season. Pauline had a fit. She wanted the Major to make Joy leave it out. He simply told her to get to work and see if she could top it. But Pauline *was* his daughter, and she kicked up so much fuss that he had to compromise by leaving her the announcement."

"And the audience," Merlini said, "doesn't realize what they are seeing."

"No," said Keith. "Not many of them know that a forward is a damn sight harder than a back flip. But the show people do, and it burns Pauline up. Another reason I've got to work fast on this is that Pauline knows that I side with Joy. And now she's the boss of this outfit, I expect to get the ax any minute."

"I see," Merlini said. "Complications already. Tell me, why does Joy stay on? She could get a job with the Wait Brothers any time she wants it.[1] She's doing a big-time routine."

Keith nodded. "Yes, I know. The Major asked her to stick it out the rest of the season. Said she had what it takes, and that he could make her the best woman wire-walker in the business. He was helping her dope out a single routine. He was pretty proud of her ability and his coaching."

"Major Hannum used to do trapeze in his younger days, didn't he? I seem to remember—"

"Yes. The Flying Hannums. Back around about '14 and '15."

"You haven't told Joy any of this?" Merlini asked then.

"I haven't shown her the photos or hinted anything about the accident yet. But I'm going to now."

"Here come the fireworks, Ross," Merlini said. "An extra-special set-piece with fourteen kinds of colored fire and the very choicest serpentine aerial bombs, all spelling out the blazing word: Murder. I suggest we touch off the pyrotechnics as gently as possible, Keith, so that we don't get a face full. The photos are the only real evidence you've got. The rest is all guesswork. And the scene of the crime—if that's what it is—recedes rapidly. We need more evidence. The Major's trailer. Did that come over with the show?"

"Yes. It's out front now, parked behind the ticket wagon. The Major's driver brought it along as usual when we moved. But it'll be locked, and Pauline will have the keys."

Merlini gave me a wink. "I don't imagine the lock is anything too unusual. Come on."

He didn't wait for Keith to lead the way. He started off at once through the dark—quickly, as if the blackness of a circus lot was as familiar as his own bedroom. We went with him, skirting the menagerie top back toward the front door.

---

[1] The Wait Brothers Show: Ringling Brothers, Barnum & Bailey, so-called by other circus men because of their habit of posting "wait paper"—posters that read "Wait for the Big Show."

"Lot layout anything like this, last night in Kings Falls?" Merlini asked, his voice low and conspiratorial, in keeping with the illegality of our burglarous mission.

"Pretty much," Keith said. "The Major's trailer is parked in the same place."

On our left now, I saw the lighted side-show banners across the midway, rising above the nearer ticket wagon and line of concession stands. The dark square shapes of several parked cars and trailers showed dimly before us.

"Who else parks here?" Merlini asked.

"Mac, Bob O'Hara—he's the reserved-seat ticket superintendent—Brown, the treasurer on the ticket wagon, and Calamity. I park here sometimes. The Major's trailer—" Keith stood still. "There's someone in it! There's a light."

One trailer only showed a light, a faint glow from beyond the window curtains. Then the light moved.

"Flashlight," Merlini said. "On your toes."

There were two windows on this side of the trailer, one aft and one in the door. The window sash of the rear one, hinged at the top, had been propped open. We moved quietly toward it for a look.

As a Fenimore Cooper Indian, I'm a washout. Beneath my foot a discarded crackerjack box crunched loudly. It almost seemed to be connected with a public address system.

Instantly the light within the trailer vanished.

We halted abruptly and stood waiting. I swore under my breath.

For an instant I thought I saw, framed in the black rectangle of the open window, a lighter blur against the dark that might have been a face. It showed for half a second and then was gone.

"Windows. Other side!" Merlini ordered quickly. "Hurry! Watch them."

I jumped, not bothering now about any noise I might make. The trailer's occupant knew we were there. I circled the trailer, keeping in close to its side. There were two windows, both closed.

I heard Merlini rattle the doorknob, and I looked in cautiously. Then Merlini knocked.

There was no answer. After a moment of complete quiet

I heard the faint click and scratch of metal on metal. I knew what that was. Merlini was picking the lock. Whoever was inside was completely surrounded—trapped. I felt the way an inexperienced speaker does just before he steps out with an impromptu speech to face a large and formal audience. I wondered how the person within the trailer felt.

The door's hinges creaked then; and immediately after, the interior of the trailer was filled with light. I saw Merlini's hand on the wall switch, reaching in through the partly open door. My eyes swept the interior.

There was no one there.

The furnishings of the trailer were obviously custom-built. The room was fitted out as an office and living room. A desk of modern design and a tubular chair replaced the sink and kitchen equipment carried by most stock models. The walls were covered with circus memorabilia: posters, and photographs of performers, freaks, and animals. I noticed a miniature model of an ornately carved parade band wagon and, above the door, an elephant tusk. There was a table in the extreme rear flanked by built-in seats that, at night, could be converted into a bed.

Then Merlini's figure filled the doorway, and he stepped in, picklocks still in hand, Keith behind him. I left my post, circled the trailer hastily, and went in after them.

It was then I saw the gun, a Colt automatic, in Keith's hand.

Merlini noticed it also. "Where'd that come from?" he asked.

Atterbury, looking blankly around the room said, "Bought it this morning. I thought—"

"Good," Merlini cut in. "Just point it this way." He stood with one hand on the knob of a wardrobe door at the forward end of the trailer close to the outer door. "No one left by the open window. All the others, I see, are closed and locked on the inside. So—"

With the traditional gesture of the conjurer when he exhibits the magical cabinet that has previously been shown empty, Merlini turned the latch and swung the door wide. Just as with the conjurer's cabinet, this time too, there was a young lady inside, a girl with golden hair and round, frightened blue eyes. She stood there, crouched back against the clothing on the hangers. She had a flashlight in one hand, and in the other, half upraised, a curious but familiar weapon, a heavy, rounded, three-foot length of wood that ended in a steel-pointed combination of prod and hook. I recognized it as an elephant goad. When the girl saw Keith, the bull-hook dropped from her fingers and fell with a solid thud to the floor.

Then she stepped from the wardrobe, and the light shone scarlet on the bolero vest and flaring trousers of her wire-act costume. She blinked in the light, the fear in her alert eyes replaced now by relief and, as she looked at Merlini and myself, by curiosity.

Keith said one word, "Joy!"

He stepped forward and grasped her arm. "What are you doing here?"

Joy's eyes sought the door through which we had come. "The door, Keith. It was locked. How did you—"

Merlini jingled the picklocks on the key ring and dropped them back in his pocket. "Locks are made to be picked, Miss Pattison. Aren't you going to introduce us, Keith?"

Atterbury was still looking at the girl with a completely bewildered expression. Still watching her, he said, "This is Merlini, Joy. You remember, Sigrid told us about him. And his friend, Ross Harte. But why—what were you doing here? Did you climb in at the window?"

Joy's voice had a cool liquid quality that was easy on the ears. "Yes," she said. "I was looking for the Major's will." Her statement was simple, matter of fact.

Merlini went toward the open window. "Wasn't this one locked like the others?" he asked.

"Yes," she replied, "but there's a hole in the pane. I reached in and turned the catch."

Merlini examined the neat semicircular opening from which a section of glass had been removed.

"You used a glass cutter?" he asked.

She shook her head. "No. I found the pane that way. I noticed it this afternoon. So tonight, after the wire act, when Pauline told me the Major hadn't made a will, I—"

"Pauline said that?" Keith asked sharply.

"Yes. And she said that he wouldn't have left me anything in any case."

Keith turned quickly to Merlini. Excitedly he said, "So that's the gaff.[2] I should have thought of it. There won't have to be another murder after all; this is just as good. Pauline simply destroyed the will!"

"No other relatives, then?" Merlini asked. "The Major dies intestate and Pauline gets it all? Like that?"

Keith nodded. Joy was staring at him. "*Murder?*" Her eyes were wide. "Another murder? Keith, what do you—"

"Easy, kid," Keith said, his arm around her. "I didn't mean to blurt it out like that. The Major's auto smash . . ." His voice trailed off; his eyes had fastened on the ten-gallon cowboy hat that lay near the desk on a chair. "Merlini," he said slowly, "the Major always wore a hat. One of those. Sensitive about his baldness. I suspect he wore one to bed. But there was none with the body or in his car. I forgot to tell you that. And this"—he pointed—"is the one the Major was wearing last night."

Joy paid no attention to the hat. She insisted, her voice thin and tight, "What about the accident?"

Keith turned to her and told her what he had told us. I watched Merlini pick up the hat.

"Gaudy," he said, half to himself, "but not too neat."

There were more than the usual number of dents in the hat's crown, and a smudge of dirt on its gray surface. Merlini turned the hat in his hands and looked inside the crown. For a brief second he hesitated, motionless, saw me watching him, and then said, a shade too calmly, "Size seven and three-eights." He placed the hat carefully back upon the chair as he had found it.

Merlini began investigating cupboards and drawers. Suddenly he interrupted Keith's recital. "Miss Pattison, you said you were looking for a will. Did you find one?"

"No. I had just started to look when I heard you outside."

"Sure that was all you were looking for?"

[2] Gaff: Secret device. In carnival games, the unseen gadget which sets the layout so the player cannot win. In conjuring, a "gimmick" which serves the same purpose.

Her eyes narrowed slightly. "Why, yes. Of course. Why—"

"What were you intending to do with that bull-hook?"

"The bull-hook? I—I don't know. I was frightened. I saw the three of you outside, watching the trailer. I couldn't see who you were. Then I heard you at the door. I'd noticed the hook lying on the desk, and I picked it up almost without thinking as I started for the wardrobe."

Merlini took if from the floor. "It's not yours, then? Is it the Major's?"

"No," said Joy, "it's Irma King's. I don't know why it should be—"

Keith said, "I do. Pauline had it when she came in here with the Major last night. I saw her."

"Um," Merlini said meaninglessly. Then to Joy, "Just where did you look for this will besides in the desk there?"

"No place," she answered at once. "I'd just started on that when you . . ."

She stopped, seeing that Merlini had stopped paying attention. He had suddenly dropped on his knees to examine some shiny particles that sparkled in the light on the linoleum floor. He looked up at Keith and Joy.

"Did Major Hannum wear glasses?"

They nodded. Keith said, "Reading glasses. Pair of horn-rimmed ones. Carried them in his breast pocket. Why?"

Without answering, Merlini took one of his business envelopes from his pocket and carefully brushed the dozen or so small bits of broken glass into it. He folded down the flap without sealing it and placed it on the desk top. He took Joy's flashlight from her, went to the window with the cut pane, and snapped the light on. He held it at an oblique angle and peered closely at the window glass, moving his head slowly from side to side.

"Miss Pattison," he asked, "where were you last night between ten-thirty and eleven o'clock?"

Keith started to say, "Now look here, Merlini. What do you mean by—"

"Act your age, Keith," Merlini cut in. "You'll hear that question fired at a lot of people from now on. Well, Miss Pattison?"

She frowned. "That would be during the concert. I was in

my trailer getting ready for bed. We had a long jump this morning, and nearly everyone turned in as soon as they could. Then at one o'clock when we heard about the Major—"

The latch on the trailer door behind us clicked over. We all started with guilty apprehension as the door slammed inward. A girl came through. She wore a white satin cloak over pink tights. Merlini and I immediately recognized an old friend, our determined lady of mystery—Miss Mildred Christine.

Mac Wiley, behind her, stopped halfway through the door, one hand on the jamb, staring at us.

Joy's startled half-whisper said, "Pauline!"

Mildred Christine-Pauline's words shot at us like a rapid staccato burst of machine-gun fire.

"What does this mean? What are you two—"

Only Joy and Keith had registered on her consciousness until then. Now she saw Merlini, and it stopped her cold.

Mac came to life briefly. "What the hell goes on here?" he blurted. "This trailer is supposed to be locked. What—why —" He bogged down.

"I'm afraid I owe you an apology, Miss—Christine," Merlini said gravely. "We're guilty of an illegal entry, a custom that is, unfortunately, all too common."

Pauline glared at him, angry but uncertain. "What are *you* doing here—in this trailer?"

Merlini had the answer to that. And he gave it to her, politely but without warning. I could see the white deadly wake of the torpedo as it went.

"We are investigating your father's murder."

Chapter 6

Fingerprints

THE EXPLOSION had the solid reverberating thud of a direct hit. But before it there was one instant, a long-drawn-out instant of deadly quiet. One thing only, the tinny festivity of the distant side-show band, came to make a disturbing ripple in the tense, tight silence that held us.

Pauline seemed to sway under the impact of Merlini's words as if they were hard, driving physical blows. Her lithe body was taut and rigid, her fists clenched as if she were trying frantically to grasp at something that would keep her from hysteria. The dark eyes were round staring circles, and the full red lips opened as if to speak.

But it was Mac's voice that thundered and smashed the silence.

"What the blazing everlasting hell are you talking about?"

"Murder," Keith said. "If the Sheriff is still on the lot, you'd better get him."

Mac didn't move.

Keith added, "If you don't, I will."

In answer to that, Mac made one swift movement. His hand was on the doorknob, and he turned it with a decisive jerk. The bolt clicked over.

"No, I don't think so. Merlini, will you explain—"

"Mac! I'll handle this." Pauline's voice had no hysteria in it now, only sharp, crisp authority. Her words were slow and precise, eyes narrowed and careful. She took a step toward Atterbury. "All right, Keith," she said. "Spill it. And fast."

Keith glanced sidewise at Merlini, and then said, watching Pauline, "Mac, when the Major left the front door last night, where did he say he was going?"

"You were there. Weren't you?" Mac replied gruffly.

"Yes. He said he was going over to his trailer to get a slicker. But did he, at any time, say anything to you about leaving the lot?"

"No," Mac scowled. "And so what? He didn't tell me every—"

"All right, Pauline," Keith said. "Let's have it. Where was he going? What's the story you've rigged up? I warn you it'll have to be good, very good."

"Atterbury"—Pauline's voice had an Arctic cold in it— "you're fired! Starting now. Get your money from the wagon and get off the lot."

"No, wait, Miss Hannum," Mac interposed hastily. "That won't do. I'm not going to have him running to the cops with whatever he thinks he's got before I know what it is. Nobody sets foot outside this trailer until this is straightened out!"

Keith started toward the door. "I'm afraid this is something our legal adjuster isn't going to be able to adjust as smoothly as usual. Get out of my way, Mac!"

Mac stood directly before the door. He was a much older man than Keith and half a head shorter, but it was obvious that he was perfectly confident of holding his own. He stood lightly poised on his feet like a boxer.

"You heard her," Keith said. "I don't work here any more. I'm leaving."

"Not yet you aren't."

Merlini's voice cut across the tension in the room in the nick of time. "Miss Hannum," he said, "I have no authority to ask questions or to expect any answers. But unless someone can and does explain the very peculiar behavior of the Major just before he died last night, then Keith is right; the police *will* have to be notified."

"Merlini!" Mac shouted. "For God's sake! You don't believe Calamity's beefing is—"

"Mac," Pauline ordered sharply, "I said I'd handle this." She faced Merlini. "What peculiar behavior?"

"Where was the Major going when he left the lot last night?"

"I don't see that that is any of your business."

"It isn't. But unless someone can supply a decent answer, it's police business. If you would prefer to tell them, that's your privilege. That is, if you know?"

"If I don't know, does that prove anything?"

"No. It only makes his death look even queerer."

"I don't understand you. As it happens, I do know where he was going."

Merlini blinked. "You know why he left the lot in the face of a possible blowdown? And why he was in such a great hurry on a road that goes nowhere in particular?"

"Yes."

"When did you last see him alive?"

Pauline's answers were all hesitant, but when she did speak the words came swiftly with a sudden jerk.

"At dinner," she said.

Out of the tail of my eye I saw Keith start and open his mouth to protest. Merlini cut in quickly.

"Is that when he told you about his plans for the evening?"

"Yes."

"And they were?"

"I've already told you that it doesn't concern you."

"Yes, I heard you. I'm glad that you know the answers, because the police are going to want them."

She studied him a moment. "You've got some other reason for saying that. What is it?"

"Show Mac the photos, Keith. Perhaps you'd better not look, Miss Hannum. They were taken at the scene of the accident and are not very—"

She snatched them from Keith's hand as he drew them from the envelope. She looked with wide eyes, Mac crowding behind her.

Merlini spoke rapidly: "The photos were snapped by the man who found the body, before anyone had touched it. The face and neck are severely lacerated. There is no blood except for a very insignificant amount across the top of the head. The deduction is—that the cuts were made a considerable time *after* death."

Both Pauline and Mac looked up and stared at him.

Before either of them could speak, Merlini added, "Mac, is that the hat the Major was wearing last night?" He pointed.

Mac was thoroughly alarmed now. He turned his head nervously, biting at his thin lips. But he was still cagey.

"Maybe," he said. "What about it?"

"Keith says he was wearing it and that there was no hat found on the scene of the accident, although the Major, because of his baldness, invariably wore one. We found that hat here in this trailer; and inside, on the inner surface of the hat's crown, there is a smear of dried blood."

Mac picked up the hat and turned it over. "Blood?" he said skeptically. "Dark brown stain. It might be anything, and it could have been there for days. You've got to do better than that. Dammit to hell anyway, Merlini, what's got into you? The medical examiner—"

Merlini cut him off. "Miss Hannum, were the Major's glasses found with the body?"

The photo had taken some of the starch out of Pauline; and the bloodstain, if that was what it was, seemed to have impressed her. Though I knew well enough that Mac was quite right and that Merlini, before the stain was worth a nickel as evidence, would have to have it tested.

Pauline looked at Merlini without answering, as if she were thinking of something else and had not heard.

Mac answered instead, angrily, and put his foot smack into it. "Yes," he roared, "they were—what was left of them. They were in the breast pocket of his coat, smashed all to hell by the accident.

"And yet," Merlini said quietly, his voice contrasting with Mac's roar, "I found several small fragments of glass on the floor of the trailer here. The curvature of the pieces obviously suggests spectacle lenses." He tipped the envelope and let them slide on to the desk top, where they glinted in the light. "If they should fit the pieces of glass that were in his pocket . . ."

Mac was hard to convince. "And suppose he did break them here; he might have dropped them—any time, a week ago, maybe."

"It won't wash, Mac," Keith contradicted. "He put them on to look at some press clips of mine last night—less than half an hour before he left the front door. You should remember it; you were there. And don't lie about it. Calamity was there, too."

"Okay, maybe he dropped them while he was here just before he left the lot."

Merlini asked, "Why would he gather up the frames and broken glass and put them in his breast pocket? No point in carrying them with him when they were smashed."

"How should I know?" Mac growled. "He did funnier things. You listen to me, Merlini. If there are any murders on this show I'll be the first one to call the cops. But it's going to take a damn sight more than this to make me think that—"

Pauline put in, "The medical examiner said it was accidental death."

Merlini nodded. "Yes, but there seem to be a lot of things he wasn't told about. There's the burglar, for instance."

Merlini was at his old tricks again—taking unexpected rabbits out of top hats without warning. He got his effect. Pauline's face went white; she sat down. Mac gave a distinct start.

"Burglar?" Mac asked.

"Yes. Miss Hannum, were your father's keys found on his body—and who has them?"

"Yes. I do." Pauline spoke mechanically, like a sleep-walker.

"Have you—has anyone—entered this trailer since the accident? As far as you know?"

"I did—this morning. I got a suit of his clothes—for the undertaker."

There was a rattle at the door then, and Mac turned to pull it open. A voice outside said, "Seen Miss Pattison, Mr. Wiley? They sent me to look for her. She's due on."

Pauline was suddenly businesslike again. "Joy, get out there at once. Henry, tell Walter to spot the traps after the concert announcement. She has to change yet."

"Yessir," the voice said.

Joy got up and walked toward the door. With her hand on the knob she turned and looked at Pauline.

"Did you take anything else?" she asked coolly.

I could hear Pauline suck in her breath. "So that's it!" She got to her feet. "Get out!" she said. Her words stung.

Joy looked at her for a moment longer, an odd expression on her face; then, without saying anything at all, she turned quietly and went through the door, closing it after her.

Pauline turned to Merlini. "I've had enough of this! Are you going to the police with this story?"

Before he could answer, Keith said, "*I* am."

"You don't think we should, Miss Hannum?" Merlini asked.

"No. You don't have a thing except some wild accusations by Keith—and Joy. The photograph means nothing—the medical examiner has made his report. I know why Dad left the lot last night. And there's no reason why he should have told Keith or Mac. The stain in the hat could be anything, and it may have been there a long time. He could have broken his glasses before he left. Joy has no proof at all that my father ever made a will. I don't think he did. I looked for it and I found none."

"Then it *was* you who searched this trailer?"

"I looked through his papers in the desk, yes."

"You didn't look in these linen cupboards and these other drawers?" Merlini indicated several near the wardrobe.

"No, of course not. I wouldn't expect to find—"

Something in his expression stopped her. She reached up and opened a cupboard above her head. It was filled with sheets, pillowcases, and towels. They were mussed and disordered.

"Every drawer and cupboard in the place looks like that," Merlini said. "You see, you forget the burglar I mentioned."

"But I don't—" Pauline began.

"Other than a possible will that may or may not exist, what else did the Major have in this trailer that was of value, that someone broke in to hunt for?"

Pauline shook her head. "I don't—" Then sudden suspicion caught her. "How do I know that you didn't do this before Mac and I got here?"

Merlini hesitated over that one. Then he looked at me. "Ross," he said wryly, "make a note of this. The next time you catch me agreeing to undertake an unofficial murder investigation I want you to kick me hard. You have no way at all of knowing that I didn't search the trailer, Miss Hannum. I did search it, but I didn't disarrange the contents of these drawers and cupboards. I found them that way. And I didn't use a glass cutter to make a hole in that window." He pointed toward it. "That also was here when Keith, Ross, and myself arrived. I only picked the lock on the door."

The surprised looks Mac and Pauline threw toward the window seemed genuine enough. But they both regarded Merlini suspiciously, as if they thought he was talking fast, trying to pull himself out of a hole.

As a clincher, Merlini reached into his magical hat and drew forth still another bunny. He passed Joy's flashlight to Mac. "You might take a close look at that windowpane just above the cut-out section. Tell me what you see."

Mac scowled, took the flashlight, and did as directed. I stood behind him and looked too. I saw on the glass three oval impressions that had a familiar shape.

"Fingerprints," Mac said. "So what?"

"Don't you notice anything odd about them?" Merlini asked.

I looked more closely. Then I saw it. These prints were strangely, queerly different from any others I had ever seen. "They have no ridge markings," I said. "No whorls or loops. They're perfectly flat. What sort of a what-is-it—?"

"That," Merlini said, "is the question. Well, Mac?"

"Well, what?" he replied. "You're still making mountains out of mole hills. And *we* can arrest you for breaking and entering if you're going to be stubborn, you know."

"But you won't. Miss Hannum wouldn't let you. There happens to be another case of illegal entry that cancels mine out."

The expression on Pauline's face was ample indication that that shot had rung the bell and won the nickel cigar. But Merlini didn't stop to collect. He went after a bigger prize.

"I've a theory or two about the burglar with the curious fingerprints. One goes like this: Once upon a time, last evening probably, someone removed that piece of windowpane with a glass cutter, released the inside catch, and crawled in. He— or perhaps she—searched this room, hunting for something of an undetermined nature. Whether he found it or not we don't know. But I suspect that he was interrupted in his illegal pursuits when the Major returned to get his slicker."

Merlini was watching Pauline, Mac, and Keith closely. He got just as much attention from them.

"The burglar," he continued, "couldn't escape the way he had come, since that window is on the same side as the door. He hadn't time to crawl out one of the others; the door was already opening. So, when the Major stepped inside, a blow from the dark hit him on the head. He fell. His hat rolled off. The glasses in his breast pocket smashed. The Major's weak heart stopped. We don't know if the marauder knew about the heart, but it makes no difference. Even if he only intended to knock the Major out, legally it's still murder, since he was engaged in burglary when it happened.

"Finding the Major was dead, the killer set quickly to work to cover up. He lifted the body, and some of the smaller glass particles from the broken spectacles trickled from the

Major's pocket. The body was carried out and placed in the trunk compartment of the Major's own car. It was dark and stormy, and with reasonable care, the killer stood little chance of being seen. Hurriedly, so that no one would see that it wasn't the Major who was driving, he drove the car off the lot. On a side road, where it wouldn't be discovered until he had time to return on foot, he faked the accident. I imagine that he put the Major's body behind the wheel, pulled the throttle wide open, and started it down the hill. The body, slumped over the wheel, would hold it fairly steady for some distance. The car hit the bridge. And that theory, you see, explains the cut windowpane, the bits of spectacle glass, the lack of blood on the body, the stain in the hat, and the apparently peculiar behavior of the Major. The Major didn't act normally in leaving the lot because he was dead."

Pauline laughed, a high, nervous laugh, but one that also had relief in it.

"So that's it! All right. Take your story to the cops. Send them to me. But they won't thank you for troubling them. There won't be any investigation, Mac. It won't be necessary. Merlini's theory is so much moonshine!"

"Oh?" Merlini said softly. "Why?" There was a faint undertone in his voice that sent a chill up my spine. I had an impression of a trap, beneath camouflage, its jaws open and waiting.

"Because," Pauline answered coldly, "I came in here with my father. There was no one else here!"

The snap of the trap's sharp jaws as they closed was distinctly audible. But, for a moment, Pauline appeared not to have heard them. Only the sudden and lasting silence that fell over the rest of us made her look around uneasily and then suddenly realize . . .

"It's hard to believe that," Merlini said. "Just a moment ago you told us that you saw your father last at dinner. How do we know which—"

"Damn you!" she said, her eyes throwing sparks. "I know that. I lied. I didn't see that it was any of your business, but if you are going to accuse . . ."

"I didn't make any accusation. But you seem to be trying the shoe on. You've made two flatly contradictory statements.

One must be false. Both might be. Your motive for saying that you came in with the Major is obviously the stronger."

Now what was he getting at? Keith had said that he saw Pauline with her father. Were there more concealed traps? "But if you did come, as you say, with the Major," Merlini went on calmly, "my theory *is* pretty well shattered. I'll have to discard it in favor of the other—the one that concerns the bull-hook which you carried in your hand when you came in."

Pauline's face looked haggard—ten years older. "Then you knew all the time. Someone saw us. . . ."

Merlini nodded. "Yes. I'm sorry. I only wanted to find out what had happened. You wouldn't answer questions. I had to trick you. You've admitted too much now. You'd better tell us just what happened."

"You—you won't believe me." Pauline's fear was evident. "Nothing happened. We talked together for less than five minutes. I left. I forgot the bull-hook when I went. That's all."

"The hook is Irma King's. Why did you have it?"

"She had left it behind in my trailer this afternoon. I was returning it when I remembered something I wanted to see Dad about."

"What was that?"

"I can't tell you." Her chin came out stubbornly at this.

Merlini left it at that. "Where did you go then, after leaving him?"

"To my trailer. I went to bed."

"Did you meet or speak to anyone on the way?"

"I— No, I—" She stopped, her jaw clenched. The muscles at either side of her forehead stood out in rigid lines. With an effort she stood straight. "I've heard enough," she said grimly. "There's just one thing to be done. But first I want to know one more thing. Is this everything? What else do you have?"

Before Merlini could answer someone rapped sharply on the outer door again. "Miss Hannum," a voice called. "Perch act on next."

"Tell him I'm coming, Mac," she said, and then waited for Merlini's reply.

"There's one more thing," he said. "A question. Who is the Headless Lady?"

Pauline's eyes held a defeated look. But she made no answer. She turned to Mac. "Get the Sheriff. Take him to my trailer. And wait there until I finish this next act."

Mac didn't like the way the wind was blowing at all. "But ... but ..." he started to object.

"Do as I say, Mac! Get going now. Tell the Sheriff his name will be in every paper in the country tomorrow morning. I'm afraid Dad *was* murdered after all. But *I'm* not taking the rap. This show moves in the morning, and there'll be no investigation. It won't be necessary by then."

Mac's face was dark with conflicting emotions. He shrugged helplessly, ducked his head, and went out through the door.

Pauline gazed after him thoughtfully for a moment; then without looking at us she gathered her cape around her and followed after him.

Keith, puzzled, frowned and asked of no one in particular, "Now what does all that mean?"

"It's those fireworks I mentioned," Merlini replied. "Put your fingers in your ears. The fuse is sputtering merrily and rapidly. We have started something now. But I'd like it lots better if I knew just what sort of shooting stars were going to burst."

Merlini flipped a fifty-cent piece meditatively in his hand, made it vanish and reappear once or twice in an absent-minded way; and then went to the wardrobe where Joy had hidden and started to examine its floor.

I watched him for a moment with a vague uneasiness, a subtle, uncomfortable feeling that I couldn't quite define. I rather thought, from his actions, that Merlini was similarly disturbed. He got to his feet after a moment, frowned at a smallish piece of dried mud he had scraped from the wardrobe floor, and then wandered to the rear of the trailer, where he stopped to look again at the odd prints on the window-pane.

Suddenly, in my mind, a skyrocket rose and flared brightly. I knew what was wrong.

"Merlini," I said at once, "I don't like this. And I know

why. It's too familiar. I've read it all before. The chief suspect, cornered, announces like a damned fool that she knows
all and is going to tell—*later*. And, while the Great Detective
and all the forces of law and order sit quietly around twid-
dling their thumbs—the murderer promptly goes to work
again! Bang! Chapter ending! And *this* suspect . . ."

Merlini's half-dollar fell from his fingers to the floor and
rolled across the linoleum. "—is going to climb up on top of
a tall pole and stand on her head! Ross—" His voice stopped
with startling abruptness.

Through the open door, as he spoke, I could hear the big-
top band playing a smoothly flowing waltz; but now, strangely,
the tempo stumbled, the whole structure of the music seemed
to break apart, coming to a ragged, slurring halt as if the
instruments had ceased, not all together, but one by one.

The interval was short, and when the music came again
it was a frantic, uneven march in double-quick time.

Merlini moved as quickly as I have ever seen him do. As
he flew through the doorway, he said:

"Ross, you've called it!"

Chapter 7

Center Ring

"*. . . The zenith in deft and daring high perch accomplish-
ments. The lovely Miss Pauline Hannum high above the
center ring, revolving at breakneck speed atop the dizzy pin-
nacle of a thirty-foot pole . . .*"

THE MUZZLE velocities of Hugo and Mario Zacchini, fired
from their mammoth cannon, were never any greater than
the speed with which we left that trailer. Merlini took three
lightning strides, ducked low, and shot through the doorway.
I projected myself after him, springing outward from the door-
sill to hit the ground, running. I heard Atterbury move behind
me.

I plunged after Merlini's flying figure, regardless now of
guy ropes, stakes, or deep ruts the animal trucks had left

in the springy turf underfoot. We ran the length of the menagerie top and turned right toward the back yard and the big top—the big top that for one bewildering moment seemed to have vanished completely. Then, against the stars, I saw its black silhouette loom out. Where the lighted expanse of canvas top and side walls should have been was only darkness—the dark and a low, deep crowd noise, a vast uneasy rumble of sound that was ominous and afraid. The music of the band beat at it frantically, trying to stave off panic.

I swerved abruptly and avoided disaster by inches.

The few lighted windows of the trailers along the left gave just enough light so that I made out the ponderous, lumbering shapes of the elephants a bare second before it was too late.

A woman's voice in the darkness, hard and unyielding, swore at them. "Elsie! Back, dammit, back! Steady, Modoc! Steady, Rubber! Hold it, girl!"

Just ahead now, by the performer's entrance, there was a hurried, confused movement of flashlights and a shouted tangle of commands. One deep voice rose above the others, hard with authority. "The cars! Get those headlights on, somebody! Hurry it!"

Someone else had already had the thought and acted on it. The roar of a starting motor came from near the end of the line of trailers and cars; and then, in a moment, two bright headlights swung around and rushed down at us. Dark figures scattered before the light, and a frightened horse reared wildly. The shapeless figure of a clown, his white face tense, jumped for the bridle, got it, and hung, pulling down hard as the frightened animal bucked. The car turned, aiming its lights at the arena entrance. Another clown, a red-nosed, baggy-trousered tramp, stood there and swung a beckoning arm.

"Get that car inside!" He vanished within the tent, and three other white-suited, grotesquely painted figures ran after him, their large clumsy shoes flopping; but they ran for once with a direct, sure-footed purpose.

I followed the car as it moved in and saw the long beam of its lights cut across the arena, throwing the dark shadows of the center poles and the intricate rigging onto the white faces of the banked crowd beyond.

The clowns tumbled into the center ring, and several prop men lifted and bore aside the long, limber white pole that had lain there, one end projecting out beyond the ring curb. There, between the two rings where several overturned pieces of apparatus waited, two men knelt above something on the ground. One was a muscular gymnast in blue tights; the other, the lanky, hatless figure of Tex Mayo. Now, as the car lights came, the latter made a swift lifting movement and stood upright.

He turned quickly and came toward the light, half running, the limp figure of Pauline in his arms. Her head hung far back, mouth open, and the dark blood that welled from along her cheek ran down across her forehead, a dripping smear of red on the white face. The excited murmuring of the crowd was stilled suddenly as if someone had pulled a switch; then, as Tex moved past and was lost in the darkness behind the lights, it broke out again, a high, nervous gabble of sound.

Out in the ring the clowns swung quickly into a fast rough-and-tumble slapstick routine, trying to catch and hold the attention of the audience. Their somersaulting figures in the low light from the car threw weirdly distorted, monstrous shadows on the big top overhead.

Then a figure ran past me, leaped to the bandstand, and grabbed the mike. The bandmaster saw him, jerked his arms high, and brought the music to a crashing halt. Keith's voice, strident and hollow in the amplifiers, filled the tent.

"Everybody keep your seats! Please! The lights will be on again in just a moment. If there is a doctor here, will he come this way, please." The music swelled again.

I turned and followed the cowboy. Outside the headlights of another car now cut the darkness. Several figures converged quickly on Tex, as if to help, but he pushed past. His voice was a harsh rasp, almost a snarl.

"Get that trailer door open!"

The acrobat darted ahead of him, and in a moment a yellow oblong of light opened in the side of one of the trailers. Tex stood outlined in it for a second as he carefully swung his burden through the door.

And just as that happened, the lights within the big top

flickered uncertainly and then came on. The excited hum of the crowd rose instantly, and the tension that had filled the darkness broke and began to fade.

The car within the tent began to back out, and Mac Wiley with another man jumped to the running board.

"Swing it around," Mac ordered the driver. "Stay in it and keep the motor running. We may have to take her into town."

His companion, a beefy red-faced man, added, "My car's out front. Police siren. Give you an escort."

Mac nodded, stepped down, and let the car move on. "I hope to hell there's a doctor—" He stopped, seeing Keith run from the tent, followed by an elderly little man with gold-rimmed spectacles and a professional goatee.

"Where'd they go?" Keith asked.

"Trailer," I told him, pointing. "That one."

They ran for it, disappeared inside, and then, as Mac, the Sheriff, and I moved toward it, the acrobat came out and approached us.

"Is it bad, Steve?" Mac asked him.

The man wiped his forehead with his arm. "Afraid so. She landed smack in that mess of props for the seal's act, that table, those metal steps, and some dead men.[1] I felt the pole start in that direction and tried to swing it sideways, but I couldn't make it. She was just going into her headstand when the lights— Say, what the devil went wrong, anyway? That never happened before!"

"I don't know," Mac scowled. "But somebody's going to catch merry hell." Mac was no longer the smiling, enthusiastic person who had met us at the front door. His voice had a snappish, worried tone; and, as his eyes happened just then to rest on me, his scowl grew even darker. "Come on, Sheriff," he added hastily.

I watched them go toward the trailer, suspecting now that Mac hadn't given the Sheriff Pauline's message, and wondering where Merlini had gone to. I had last seen him inside the tent, on the arena track, watching Tex as he lifted Pauline's body. I half decided to go look for him, but changed my mind, realizing that what I wanted to know now more than

---

[1] Dead men: Anchors that hold a piece of rigging taut.

anything else was the result of the doctor's examination. Was or was not Pauline going to be able to amplify those cryptic statements she had made? I lit a cigarette, puffed impatiently at it a moment, and then moved to join the group that stood near the trailer door talking in low but excited voices. I saw Farmer Jack, one of the cooch dancers from the side show, and then Stuart Towne hurry up and attach themselves to the group, full of questions.

"Hey, you!" someone yelled, and I looked back to see a workingman pointing at me. "Watch it, Bud. The bulls!"

I wheeled quickly and then backed hastily. A ponderous moving wall of gray swept across the spot where I had stood. Three other elephants followed in single file, trunks grasping tails. The elephant boss, a short, bulky little man in an ill-fitting uniform coat, steered the leader with an elephant goad hooked behind his ear; and on the great beast's head a woman sat, swaying easily. Her straight, almost youthful figure was encased in a tight-fitting scarlet and gold military uniform, resplendent with brass buttons and gold braid. She, likewise, held an elephant hook. Her face had a hard, bony look that the heavy mascara and grease paint could not conceal. The procession halted for a moment just outside the tent, waited until a shrill whistle came from within, and, as the music changed and the clowns poured from the exit, moved swiftly in.

Then a red-coated man with a whistle on a cord around his neck and a harassed look on his face popped out and spoke rapidly to Steve. The latter turned and hurried past me to the trailer, pushed through the group, and knocked at the door.

"Tex Mayo," he called when the door had opened, "can you come now? Walter wants to run your announcement in next."

Tex stepped out, his face grim, and walked with Steve across to where his pony had been tethered to a stake near the entrance. Keith came through the door after him, looked around searchingly, and then hurried toward me.

"What's the verdict?" I asked.

"Not so good. Concussion. Weak from loss of blood. Still unconscious. Have you seen Joy?"

"No," I told him. "Do you think—"

But he dashed off, running back along the line of trailers to one at the end.

I went into the big top, where the elephants in the center ring were standing on their heads. I half expected to see Merlini out there between the rings where Pauline had fallen, searching the ground for clues; but he was not there, nor, as far as I could see, anywhere within the tent, unless he had taken a seat in the stands with the crowd.

I watched the elephants take their final bow and lumber out. As the man at the mike made an announcement concerning the Wild West after-show, several cowboys rode madly in, circled the hippodrome track, and came to attention, lined up on the opposite side facing the reserved seats. *"And now,"* the announcer went on, *"the Mighty Hannum Combined Shows take pleasure in presenting that world-famous western screen star, TEX MAYO, in person, with his wonder pony, BLAZE!!"*

Bugles blared, and Tex made a dashing entrance, standing in his stirrups. He circled the arena once, and then waited in the center ring.

"Tex Mayo," the announcer blared, *"with his cowboys and cowgirls will appear in the Mighty Hannum Wild West Rodeo, presented in this arena immediately after the big show is over! The ticket sellers will now pass among you with tickets for this sensational, scintillating cavalcade of daredevil roughriders, world-renowned rodeo champions, trick ropers, sharpshooters, and whip-crackers in a kaleidoscopic panorama of thrills and chills—a fast-riding, sharpshooting re-creation of the Old West. Tickets are fifteen cents to all!"*

I didn't hear the rest of it because I was watching two performers who had come in, passed me, and were walking out on the track toward the end ring on the right—Steve and Joy Pattison, who was now dressed like Steve in blue tights. They left their slop-shoes at the ringside, stepped to the center of the ring, waited as the Wild West aggregation thundered off; and then, hand over hand, climbed a rope toward a double trapeze that hung above. A second pair of performers did the same in the other end ring. An attendant on the ground below pulled at a rope that set the apparatus swinging, just as Keith Atterbury hurried past me and seemed about to run out after them. But he stopped and watched with a white face.

"What's wrong?" I asked.

"I tried to find Joy to ask her to cut this traps act. I looked all over. Where did she come from? Did you see?"

"No. They came in together just a moment ago. But what—"

"That damned swinging ankle-drop. I don't think after what's happened that either Steve or Joy are in any condition—" His voice trailed off as he watched them intently, nervously.

Steve hung from his knees, gripping Joy's ankles. The trapeze swung in a wide arc back and forth. The bass drum in the band boomed; and Joy dropped, on an outward swing, twenty feet through space! And then the coiled rope that streamed after her, attached to one ankle, pulled her up short. She swung back in a much longer arc, her head just clearing the ground.

Keith relaxed, and simultaneously I jumped. Merlini's voice came suddenly from over my shoulder. "A murderer running wild," he said, "and things like that scheduled twice daily. Ross, it gives me cold shivers. Murder on a circus, as I'm beginning to realize, is as easy as breathing and damned hard to prove. A minor alteration in the rigging, a half-cut rope, this matter of the lights—"

"Where," I demanded, "did you disappear to?"

"Oh, I've been around. Discovering things. Come outside where we can talk. There's much too much band music here."

I followed him outside, side-stepping a troupe of clowns that was on its way in. I had several questions all loaded and aimed, but he fired first. And he scored a bull's-eye.

"Quickly!" he said. "How soon after the accident did Joy Pattison put in an appearance?"

I blinked at that one. "Just how," I asked, "do you happen to know that that is the whopping big question that's before the house?"

"Answer me!" he commanded impatiently. "She'll be out here in a minute."

"She didn't show up until just before she went out there

for that traps act. And Keith was buzzing around excitedly
hunting for her, wanting, so he says, to persuade her to skip
it. He still seems to think she's on the spot, though it looks
to me as if he was calling his shots wrong. He predicted
that Pauline would have a try for Joy, and instead of that—"

I stopped. Keith and Joy came from the tent, and Merlini
beckoned to them.

"Miss Pattison," he said, going straight to the point, "I'm
conducting a little private census of my own. Will you please
tell me just where you were when the lights went out?"

Joy's arm was linked in Keith's, and when that question
hit her she jumped. He felt it, and his head jerked quickly
toward her, his eyes startled.

"You *are* a magician, aren't you?" Joy said, striving to
make her voice steady. "What makes you ask *that?*"

Merlini frowned down at her. "I'm asking that of a lot
of people, starting now. I didn't expect results so soon."

Joy hesitated a moment. "I might as well confess," she
said. "I'm afraid I was in another trailer again where I shouldn't
have been. Pauline's."

"Oh, damn!" Keith said. "You were looking for that will!"

"Yes, I was. I still think it's there, too."

"But you still haven't found it?" Merlini asked.

She shook her head. "I didn't have time. I went to my
trailer after I left you and changed. Then I saw Pauline
go on for her perch act, and—well, I thought if I could find
that will, we'd have some evidence she and Mac would have
a hard time explaining away. I knew I had a good seven or
eight minutes, but . . . I'm a lousy burglar, I guess. I got
caught there too. I heard some shouting outside, and then
someone pulled the door open. I just had time to make the
wardrobe closet again before Tex carried Pauline in. Then
everybody came. Keith brought a doctor, and Mac came in,
and I had to stick there until they had gone. I kept the
door open a crack and finally, after Mac left—I had to take
a chance; I was due to go on and would be missed—I stepped
out."

"The doctor saw you?" Keith scowled.

"Yes, but I think I misled him. He was working on Pauline
at the bed. I put one hand on the knob of the outside door,

slammed the wardrobe door and, as he turned, said, 'Oh, excuse me,' and backed out as if I had walked into the wrong trailer."

Keith groaned. "That tears it," he said. "When that doctor—"

"No, Keith," Merlini said, "that doesn't tear it. If the doctor *wasn't* fooled it gives Joy an alibi." He turned to Joy. "There's another thing I want to ask. After you had left the Major's trailer and just before Pauline left, she said some very odd things. She said, for instance, that she had something to tell the Sheriff, something that would make an investigation of her father's death unnecessary and would put the Sheriff's name in every paper in the country. Can you tell me what she meant, particularly by that last statement?"

Thoughtfully Joy shook her head. "No, I can't. It—it sounds as if she'd intended to accuse someone. But why do you say that, if the doctor knows I was in the wardrobe, I have an alibi? An alibi for what— Do you mean that Pauline's fall wasn't an accident, that the lights . . .."

"Merlini," Keith interrupted, "just what was wrong with the lights? I think you know."

"I think I do," said Merlini. "And I've been collecting alibis. Trouble is, I seem to have too many."

I gave Merlini a nudge. "Prepare to repel boarders," I whispered. "Here comes Mac. I hope your light story is good."

J. MacAllister Wiley came toward us with a determined look in his eye.

"Another council of war, I see," he growled. "Miss Pattison, swinging ladders are due on in a minute."

Joy nodded. "Okay, Mac." She gave Keith an uncertain smile and left us.

"And you, Keith," Mac said. "It's an eighty-mile jump to Norwalk. If you're going over tonight, don't you think you'd better start?"

"I hadn't planned on it," Keith said icily. "Don't you remember? I don't work here any more."

"Nonsense," Mac replied diplomatically. "Pauline has a temper; you know that. I expect her to fire everybody regularly, now she's running this outfit—and then get mad again if they take her seriously. Besides, your contract specifies a week's notice. Run along and forget it."

Keith's expression told me that he was on the verge of telling Mac to go soak his head when he caught the warning nod Merlini gave him, and replied instead, "Okay. I'll stay the week and think about it." He turned and followed Joy in toward the arena.

Mac said at once, "Now you listen to me, Merlini. Pauline—"

"Mac," Merlini cut in, "where's the Sheriff?"

"I don't know. I think he's left. And dammit, you're not going to—"

"Then you didn't give him Pauline's message?"

"No. Luckily I didn't. She fell just as I got to him. She can't talk to him now. That'll have to wait. And you're going to mark time, too. Sheriff Weatherby is a straight-laced old busybody, and though that so-called evidence of yours is a lot of eyewash, I know that the smooth line of patter you can dish out with it is likely to make him hit the ceiling. And then the show'll have cops all over it until she is well enough to talk."

"You heard Pauline agree that it was murder, didn't you?"

"Yes. She also said that when she told what she knew there wouldn't need to be any investigation. So we're just going to sit tight until she talks. And that'll be that!"

"There's a chance she'll be able to talk, then?"

"Yes. But it won't be tonight. And if you sic an investigation on this show that I'm going to be able to prove could have been avoided, I'm going to sue you for every penny's worth of business the show loses."

"Take it easy, Mac," Merlini said. "Besides, I've already had words with Sheriff Weatherby."

"You've *WHAT?*" Mac nearly did an unscheduled balloon ascension without a balloon.

"I talked to him," Merlini repeated. "But I didn't mention murder—just yet. I merely started him going and listened while he told me about Pauline's fall. He said that you had just leaned over to speak to him when the lights went out. Is that right?"

"Yes," Mac said scowling prodigiously. "But—but what—why—" He stopped, and his bushy eyebrows rose. "Saaay!

Are you going to stand there and tell me that Pauline's accident . . ."

Merlini nodded. "I was leading up to that. Hasn't it occurred to you that Pauline's 'accident' was awfully pat? Miss Hannum as much as says that she is going to name a murderer —and then, presto—like that, she takes a tumble. Not just an ordinary tumble, mind you, but one that happened because the lights—"

"Oh, no you don't!" Mac sputtered. "Not this time! I checked on those lights. The light plant is parked on the other side between the menagerie and the big top. The main big-top cable runs to a plug box just outside the end of the big top and branches out into feeder lines. Some idiot tripped over the cable and jerked it loose. Back-yard customer, probably. There are a lot of them around tonight."

Merlini shook his head. "I know, Mac. I looked into that myself. Before you did. But those cables don't come unplugged as easily as you'd unhitch a floor-lamp extension cord from a base plug. It would need a real hefty yank. It might trip someone up, but I don't think it would jerk loose."

"I see," Mac said. "So that's it. I suppose you're going to tell me you found footprints over there. The grass is six inches high."

"No," Merlini said, "nothing like that. And no dropped cigarette butts or cuff links or pants buttons. I wish there were. A child could have caused Pauline's fall without leaving a clue. It's too simple. An acrobat balances a tall pole on his forehead, and the victim does a headstand atop that. If they can't see, they can't balance. Pull the light plug, and gravity does the rest. And in the ensuing darkness the culprit goes away from there fast. I tell you, Mac, there's a murderer on this show, and I don't like his looks. He's too expert. He's simple and direct and no foolishness about it."

"The patter's good, Merlini. Yours always is. I still don't believe it. If you're so sure about it, why didn't you blow to the Sheriff? Answer me that?"

Merlini regarded him thoughtfully a moment. "I had a reason, Mac. A reason that only two people know at the moment—myself and the murderer. So if you don't know, I don't think I'll broadcast it yet. He might just possibly forget himself and let it slip that he knows."

Mac gave Merlini a steady look from level brows. "You said '*if* I don't know.' Are you accusing me of murder?"

"I couldn't do that very easily, could I? You've got two nice shiny alibis. You were with Calamity when the Major got his, and you were talking to Sheriff Weatherby when the lights went out."

"That's a relief," Mac said with some sarcasm and without smiling. "And how long can I count on this mysterious reason of yours preventing you from hollering for the police?"

"I'm not sure," Merlini said, "that you can count on it at all. But I'll make a deal with you. I won't holler without tipping you off, provided you put a guard on Pauline's trailer and keep it there until further notice."

"Meaning?"

"It's obvious, isn't it? Just admit for a moment that maybe I'm not talking through my hat, that perhaps someone did have a try at Pauline. He has stopped her talking—for the moment. But not indefinitely. If the doctor says she'll pull through—he might very well have another try. And she's in no condition to defend herself."

"The doctor wants to move her to a hospital in the morning," Mac said doubtfully.

"That would help," Merlini said. "But I'd suggest you have him get her there now, while she's still unconscious. If she's the sort of trooper her father was, she'll object to a program like that—short of a broken neck."

"I know, dammit. That's what I'm afraid of," Mac scowled. "Okay. It's a deal. You don't talk and she gets a guard. Calamity says accidents on circuses come in threes. Do you think *you* could manage to have the next one? Murderers, bah! Good night!"

Disgustedly Mac turned and stalked off, his limp more noticeable than ever because of the angry way he stumped along.

"Merlini," I said, "don't you think the man protests too much?"

Merlini took a pack of cigarettes from his pocket, offered me one, and took one himself. He tapped it slowly against the back of his hand. "Ross," he said thoughtfully, "when we heard that music change and we ran from the Major's trailer tonight, I left first. Who came through that door next? You or Keith?"

"I did."

"And did he follow right behind you?"

"Yes. I think so. Why?"

Merlini frowned at me. "You couldn't swear that he did, then?"

"Well, no. Not exactly. He wasn't far behind me, though. He was in the back yard here just a few seconds after I arrived."

"A few seconds is too much," Merlini said unhappily. "That complicates matters no end. Come on. I want a word with that doctor."

I grabbed at his arm and issued an ultimatum. "Not so fast," I growled. "I want to know about this. Now! And what, for Pete's sake, is this hocus-pocus about *not* informing the law? *I* didn't promise Wiley not to give the sheriff an earful, and if you don't talk, I'll damned well—"

"I don't think so," Merlini said. "You can't. Mac's quite right. The evidence we've got isn't worth a plugged nickel."

I suddenly felt as if I'd just been stepped on by a full-grown elephant. "But the hat," I protested weakly. "The photo, the broken spectacle pieces, the prints on the window-pane, the elephant hook."

"The bull-hook," Merlini said, "is not evidence. We've no proof that it was used as a murder weapon. And those other things—hm, well—as soon as I saw that Pauline had fallen, I investigated the lights. I was there perhaps five minutes; and then, remembering that we had left it unlocked, I went back to the Major's trailer. Hat, glass, prints, and photo—"

Merlini made a swift smooth gesture and the glowing cigarette he held vanished.

"—have disappeared!"

Chapter 8

Eavesdropper

DR. LEONIDAS Tripp nodded in answer to Merlini's query and replied in a dry, precise voice, "Why, yes. I believe I did see a young woman in blue tights. She came into the trailer while I was busy with my patient. She seemed somewhat excited and had apparently made an error. She excused herself and withdrew rather hurriedly." He frowned. "Now that I think of it, it does seem odd that, being a performer, she shouldn't know—"

"By what door did she enter, doctor? Do you remember?"

"Door?" Dr. Tripp asked. He turned and scowled at the trailer. "But the trailer only has one, doesn't it? I don't see—"

"Thank you very much."

Before the doctor could turn again to face us, Merlini had gone, myself after him. Merlini headed for the big-top entrance.

"We're getting action for our money," he said. "Not ten minutes ago I was afraid I had too many alibis. Two of them are already dust and ashes."

"Alibis for the monkey business with the lights and for the stolen evidence?"

"Yes. Mac Wiley is in the clear on both counts; he was hobnobbing with Sheriff Weatherby. Keith, when the lights went out, was with us; but he left the trailer after we did and, from all you can tell me, could have wiped those prints from the windowpane and scooped up hat, photo, and envelope of glass particles on his way out. Joy—"

"Here, here," I objected. "Keith's the white-haired boy who put the match to these fireworks. *He* started this investigation."

"Yes, I know," Merlini said. He magically produced two dimes, bought two bags of peanuts, handed me one, and found seats on the lowest tier before the center ring. "But I seem to remember a case or two—one that we were mixed up in—where the murderer did just that."

"Okay," I admitted. "That's your point. And Joy?"

"Joy Pattison," Merlini said, thoughtfully cracking a peanut, "deposes that she was engaged in her curious hobby of hiding in a wardrobe cupboard. And further states that she tried to make the doctor think that she had entered the trailer from the outside. For all he knows that is what she did do. And consequently it's not impossible that that is just what she did."

"But why?" I asked.

"Why?" he said. "Why what?"

"Well, if she pulled the light plug and swiped the evidence, why should she go stick her nose in at Pauline's trailer, pretend she'd made a mistake, and back out again? Sounds silly to me."

"A magician, in performing a trick, often does the exact opposite of what he says he is doing. She may have done that. She said she entered from the wardrobe and tried to deceive the doctor into believing she had come from outside. But suppose that she *did* enter from outside, and was trying to make him believe that she came from the wardrobe. If she could do that, she'd have an alibi."

I shook my head. "I don't follow. If she wants it established that she was in the wardrobe, why, in God's name, did she tell us she came from outside?"

"Because she hadn't put it over. The doctor turned too quickly, before she could get the wardrobe door open, and she realized she hadn't fooled him."

"No, dammit," I objected heatedly. "You're assuming that her mind works like yours, like a trick calculating machine. And besides, what if she had put it over? What if she did fool the doctor into thinking she had been hiding in the wardrobe? He'd ask Mac or Pauline: who was that lady I seen hiding in the cupboard? How would she explain that?"

"Same explanation she gave us. She was hunting for the will. The charge would be attempted burglary, not attempted murder."

I thought about that for a moment, but I still didn't like it. "Why," I asked, "are you trying so hard to pin this on Joy—and Keith. There are others we might ask for alibis. Lots of them. What about Irma King, for instance? It was her elephant hook. And Tex Mayo?"

"I've seen to that. I talked to Deep-Sea Ed, the elephant boss.[1] I met him when he was on the Big Show a few seasons back. The acts that were scheduled to follow Pauline's perch act were: Tex Mayo's announcement and then the bulls, in that order. Tex, Ed says, was on his horse at the entrance when the lights failed, waiting to go on. And Ed, with Irma King, was lining up the bulls to follow Tex."

"You have been busy," I admitted. "But there are plenty of other people on this lot. Performers, workingmen, ticket-takers, ushers, side-show freaks, pop-sellers, and half a tentful of audience. It would take Inspector Gavigan and half a dozen squads of detectives working all night to check them. And I hate to think how many wouldn't have alibis."

Merlini scowled at the menage horses, who were bowing and prancing through a musical ride. "That, Ross," he said, "is exactly what is giving me gray hairs. You see, at the moment it looks as if *every last one* of those people do have alibis!"

He paused, and I swallowed hard trying to get the dizzy feeling out of my ears. "Say that again," I demanded.

"You heard me. Alibis for *everyone* except Keith and Joy. If you'll relax and think about it for as much as two minutes, you'll see why. That'll give you something to do while I meditate on a course of action. When you get the answer raise your hand, but don't interrupt me. Boy! This way with that pop."

Two minutes was an underestimate. When the chariot races thundered around the hippodrome track and brought the performance to a close, the three-ring circus under my hat was still in full swing. The answer to the alibi riddle, obvious as it turned out to be, still eluded me. As I got up to go I made a suggestion.

[1] His nickname derives from the fact that he once owned a deep-sea show, an exhibition of marine monsters. Ed is a man of various talents and wide experience. He also once specialized in window-sleeps, a stock type of exhibition in which the performer goes into a trance in a local store window and apparently remains there motionless for a week or two without food or water.

"That photo," I said. "We could get another print, couldn't we?"

"Sit down," Merlini answered. "We're staying for the concert. Yes, we can get another; but even if we have Keith wire for it tonight, the mail wouldn't bring it in until late tomorrow at the earliest.

"But the murderer would know we could get one eventually. What is it, a play for time?"

"Looks like it. And that might mean he has something else planned."

The climax of the exhibition of rodeo stunts was supposed to be Tex Mayo's trick and fancy shooting with a .22 target rifle. His marksmanship was fancy enough, but it could have been a bit more accurate. He fired from a variety of positions at glass balls and toy balloons hanging suspended from the underside of a six-foot circular backstop which was hanging in the top of the tent. He seemed sober enough at the moment, and I suspected that his reaction to Pauline's fall was probably causing the misses. If, as Mac had told us, he was in love with her, I didn't blame him for giving a rather ragged performance.

I noticed that Merlini watched the show with one eye on his wrist watch. And, as we finally got up to go with the rest of the audience, he commented, "If Tex worked the concert last night, *he* seems to have an alibi for the Major's death as well."

Then he nodded toward the tent's far end, where the side walls had been dropped and a crowd of workingmen had dismantled and cleared away most of the unreserved seat section. Some of them were now stacking the flats in a truck that had been driven in, and others began at once on the seats the crowd was leaving.

"And the top," he said, "will be down in no time at all. If our friend Inspector Gavigan had a finger in this pie, he'd be purple in the face. I can hear him explode. A murder case where the murder room is taken down every night, neatly rolled up, tucked into trucks, carted eighty miles away, and set up again the next morning!"

"Yes," I agreed glumly. "I've been thinking about that. And I can see rough water ahead. Instead of a nice tight little matter of half a dozen suspects cooped up in an isolated mansion out at the end of nowhere, we've got a hundred or more all in the open and moving rapidly across-country. To-morrow morning the Major's body will be somewhere in Indi-ana, the scene of his auto smash will be 172, and the scene of Pauline's tumble 80 miles, behind us. Clues, if any, scat-tered halfway across the state! Are *we* going to have a picnic!"

"And, instead of Inspector Gavigan and his metropolitan homicide squad to help, there'll be a brand-new set of hick cops every day, unless the state troopers deal themselves in."

"*The Rover Boys Behind the Eight Ball* would do for a title," I said. "And I suppose you've cooked up a plan of action that eliminates all possibility of sleep tonight."

"You never know," he grinned. "The next item on the pro-gram is a chat with the Headless Lady."

"Sounds interesting. Does she talk with her fingers?"

On the side-show bally platform the two cooch dancers stood with the side-show manager and treated the crowd to a few sample wriggles as he announced, "*A final and com-plete show for the price of one thin dime, ten cents!*"

Inside, Merlini asked Gus, "What act was working in here when the big-top lights went out?"

Gus replied promptly, "The Headless Lady."

Merlini sighed. "I might have expected that. Look, Gus, I want to meet her."

"Well, I don't know," Gus said doubtfully. "She ain't what you'd call sociable. I haven't met her myself. She practically never leaves her trailer except to come in here for her act. Then she ducks right up into her booth from under the side wall, and she leaves the same way so the customers won't see her with a head. You could waylay her there afterward, I suppose. She's getting set in her booth now. She goes on after the mummy."

The lecturer, as Gus said this, led the crowd toward a platform on which an upright coffin rested before a red velvet backdrop.

"The assassin of Abraham Lincoln, Ladies and Gentlemen, was not killed in Garrett's barn in Virginia in 1865, as some of your history books have it. He escaped and he lived, under the name of John St. Helen, in Texas and Oklahoma until

1903, when he committed suicide by arsenic. In those days they also used arsenic in the embalming fluid. Arsenic is an excellent preservative—though I don't advise you to mix your drinks with it. (Laughter by the speaker.)

"Thus it happens that we are able to present to you the mummified body of John Wilkes Booth in an excellent state of preservation."

He opened the upper half of the coffin and exposed to view the age-darkened desiccated torso of a man. The skin of the chest and shoulders was leathery and wrinkled; on the face it stretched tightly across the cheekbones. The open eyes stared fishily. The curly hair and drooping mustache of the Booth pictures were still there, though sparser. As far as visual evidence went, there was a resemblance; this might have been Booth, grown thirty-seven years older than his pictures.

The lecturer indicated numerous legal documents that hung on the backdrop on either side of the coffin, and a tall stack of them that lay on a chair. "We have literally thousands of affidavits proving that this is the real, genuine body of John Wilkes Booth. They are signed, as you can see, by college professors, historians, criminologists, and doctors. This X-ray photo shows you the fractured leg Booth sustained when he leaped to the stage of the Ford Theatre from the President's box after his murderous deed. You can see the scar above his right eyebrow, the memento of a blow from the sword of another actor who slashed him while playing the duel scene from *Richard the Third*. This small piece of gold ring, which bears the initial B, was removed a few years ago, after X-rays had shown its presence, from the stomach of the mummy. On some occasion, fearing capture, Booth evidently swallowed the ring to avoid exposure of his identity. You will also notice . . ."

"What's the lowdown on this, Merlini?" I asked. "Wax, I suppose?"

"You suppose wrong," he replied, "though you're warm. It's *papier mâché*. John Harkin, who used to be the tattooed man on the Hagenbeck show, owns and exhibits a mummy of which this is an imitation. He has a ton or two of real affidavits that say his mummy is actually Booth. Though, affidavits or not, it's still pretty much a moot point. Izola Forester, in her book, *This One Mad Act*, says that she is Booth's granddaughter and presents evidence to show that Booth lived for many years after his supposed death in the barn. The War Department, she says, has never admitted that this might be so because, among other things, they had already paid out the rewards for Booth's capture and naturally disliked to admit that they'd bought spurious merchandise. Carl Sandburg, on the other hand, says that Booth died in the barn. So you can take your choice. At any rate, Harkin's mummy is a first rate side-show attraction—enough so that a man in Chicago has been lately turning out *papier mâché* Booths like this one for the trade. You'll probably find a union label on his feet." [2]

"I must admit," I said, "that the exhibits in this particular side show are intriguing as hell. The replica of a mummy of a famous murderer, a Headless Lady with what there is left of her as nice as anything I ever saw in the Scandals, *and* Hoodoo, a headhunter from the Amazon. That's an idea. Perhaps, if we looked at his collection of heads, we might find the Headless Lady's. I'm not so sure about that train accident story."

"Don't be too sure about the headhunter," Merlini said. "He's never been within miles of the Amazon. He hails from Harlem. And his right name, speaking of Booth, really is a strange coincidence. It's Abraham Lincoln Jones, no less! I was introduced to him once at Coney Island."

"Are you pulling my leg?" I asked. But Merlini had turned to follow the lecturer toward the curtains that concealed the Headless Lady.

We listened again to the lecturer's talk; and then, just before he concluded, we ducked under the side wall and stationed ourselves where the Headless Lady would come out.

"If she'll tell me what I want to know," said Merlini, "I'll buy her a hat."

He made that crack inadvertently, and when he realized its implications was so delighted with it that his attention was

[2] According to Miss Forester, five alleged skulls of Booth have been on exhibition at various times, and there are records of some twenty men who have claimed to be Booth.

diverted, and we muffed our chance. We had miscalculated slightly. When the side wall lifted, and the Headless Lady (with head now), emerged, she was further away than we had expected. She moved altogether too quickly toward her trailer, which was parked less than twenty feet away.

Merlini and I started after her. Then Merlini stopped me, holding my arm. The shadowy figure of a man, who had been waiting unnoticed by the trailer door, joined her as she came up, and went into the trailer with her. We waited a moment, but no glow of light came from inside.

"Suspicious," Merlini murmured.

We closed in, quietly circled the trailer, looking for an open window beneath which we could eavesdrop. They were, in spite of the warm, moist night, all tightly closed. And from within all that we could hear was an indistinguishably low murmur of voices.

"Looks as if we were foiled again, Ross," Merlini said disappointedly. "Apparently an assignation, and I doubt if a social call would be welcome at the moment. What do you think?"

"Barging in to catch people *in flagrante delicto* ain't etiquette," I said. "We're not after divorce evidence. And it isn't my forte anyway. I suggest we skip it for the moment. But I could bear to know who the man is."

"So could I. But I'm not going to sit here till dawn to find out. Let's go get some shut-eye."

This suggestion, coming from Merlini, was unusual, but it was one that I wasn't going to vote down. We got the car and drove into town. I needed cigarettes and stopped for them at a drugstore. Merlini went to the drug counter and made a mysterious purchase that I cross-questioned him about with no success.

"Just a hunch I have," he said. "Wait until I've tested it."

Waterboro's only hotel, the Chesterfield, is an ancient and dusty firetrap with a desk clerk who fits the same description. He showed us to a room that was as homelike and comfortably inviting as a barn, and nearly as large. It was furnished with a brass bedstead, a tired rocking chair, and an early Sears Roebuck dresser.

We left a call for seven and prepared to turn in. When I

trekked back from a safari to the bathroom at the far end
of the hall, I found Merlini in vivid green pajamas pulling
on a pair of red rubber gloves.

"So that's what you bought," I said. "I don't care for the
color scheme. The accessories should be in matching shades.
If we can find some ice skates, you'll be all set to pose for a
portrait by Dali."

Without replying to the alleged wisecracks, Merlini drew
his gloved hand down across the side of his cheek and then,
moving to the window, placed his fingertips against the pane.

I began to catch wise. "So," I said. "The whorlless fingerprints. Is that it?"

Merlini squinted at the glass, moving his head about to
get the right light. "Yes," he said finally, "I think it is."

"But fingers leave prints because the pores exude an oily
substance, and rubber gloves—"

"Can do the same, if they've touched the face, for instance. They pick up the oil and redeposit it, an offset fingerprint job, as it were. If the gloves have any cuts or abrasions
they'd show up, but the ones we saw in the Major's trailer
were, like these, quite without distinguishing marks. We only
know that the person who cut the windowpane wore rubber
gloves, a fact which may or may not be of help. We'll file
it, however." Merlini stripped off the gloves and turned out
the light.

As he got into bed, I asked, "Are you nursing a theory
as to what did happen in the Major's trailer? I figured that
the burglar story you outlined was invented to trap Pauline
into admitting she had gone to the trailer with her father.
She could have done him in and moved the body; she has
no alibi and enough motive. But she turns out to be victim
number two. Where do we go from there?"

"Back to the burglar theory," Merlini said. "There's nothing
wrong with it. The prowler could have come in before Pauline and her father. When they interrupted his search for whatever it was he was after, he took cover in the wardrobe in
the Pattison manner and sat tight until Pauline had gone.
(I found a bit of mud from someone's shoe on the wardrobe
floor.) Then the Major opened the door to get the slicker
he came for, and—"

Suddenly Merlini's feet hit the floor, and I heard him racing through the dark across the room. He twisted the key, jerked the door open, and peered out into the dimly lighted hall.

"What is it?" I asked, half out of bed myself and ready for anything.

Merlini closed the door quietly and answered in a lowered voice, "Someone with big ears. There's a fairly wide streak of light creeps in under this door, and for the past minute or two I'd been wondering what made the shadow smack in the center of it. When the shadow walked off I thought I had better take a closer look. I should have started sooner. The hall is quite empty."

He got back into bed. "I think that from now on we would do well to include Mr. Stuart Towne in our calculations."

"Towne?" I asked. "How do you figure that?"

"His name's on the registry book downstairs, for one thing. And I don't understand why he was having me on when he pretended not to know any of that gun talk I gave him."

"Um," I mused. "The underworld backgrounds in his books are damned authentic. That why?"

"Yes, that and . . . you read his first one, *The Man with the Purple Face*, didn't you?"

"Yes."

"Remember the blurb about the author on the back of the jacket?"

"Rental library," I said. "I don't think my copy had its jacket."

"The publishers proudly pointed out," said Merlini, "that his realistic underworld background derived from the fact that the name Towne is a pseudonym, and that the author is an ex-bank-robber who turned writer during a stretch in Sing Sing. He has also authored several technical and very informative magazine articles bearing such titles as 'The Gentle Art of Safe Cracking,' 'Con-Men I Have Known,' 'Hoboes and Their Habits,' and the like."

"Well, well," I said. "Now I lay me down to sleep with a mind washed free of care and worry. Mr. Stuart Towne, the Emily Post of the underworld, does articles on the technique and proper use of rubber gloves and glass cutters. And our mysterious burglar . . ."

Chapter 9

Impossible Arrow

MY SUBCONSCIOUS mind wasn't as easily satisfied. Sleep was a long time coming, and when it arrived at last it brought dreams that were anything but carefree. All night long I fled endlessly, like a caged squirrel, around an enormous circus ring, pursued with grim and evil intent by cowboys, bank robbers, sword swallowers, the mummy of John Wilkes Booth, and a thundering herd of madly charging elephants. My escape was blocked on every side by a great audience which filled the seats and overflowed onto the arena track—a silently intent, sadistic, sinister, and impossibly grinning audience the members of which were all quite headless.

Finally Merlini's voice came, penetrating faintly through the heavy layers of sleep to send the phantoms flying. But as his syllables slowly coalesced to form words and then sense, they only called up a greater menace, a Hydra-headed monster that even Barnum might have shied from.

"The desk clerk," Merlini was saying, "has been murdered!"

I sat up instantly, fully awake. "Wh-wh—what!"

"Well," Merlini laughed, his words having had their intended effect, "either that or the service furnished by the Hotel Chesterfield is lamentably lax. We weren't called at seven. It's nearly nine, and I'm expecting a busy day. Come, stir yourself."

Merlini's powers of divination were not operating with their accustomed accuracy. His prediction of a busy day was far short of the mark. It turned out to be an incredibly hectic day filled with an army of incidents whose advancing shock troops, in the person of Stuart Towne, met us as we left the room a few minutes later. We encountered him in the hall, clad in pajamas and carrying soap and towel. He greeted us pleasantly and with some surprise.

"Hello," he said. "Staying on for more circus?"

"Yes," Merlini answered, "I think so. There were parts of last night's performance that we missed."

If Towne appreciated the *double-entendre* he didn't admit it. "Good," he said. "I'll see you on the lot, then."

He disappeared into the bathroom and Merlini, as the door closed behind him, scowled at it. Then quickly he took a notebook from his pocket, tore out a sheet, held it against the wall, and rapidly drew on it in pencil these characters:

He hurried with it to the bathroom door and knocked.

"Yes?" Towne's voice asked.

"Sorry to bother you now," Merlini said, "but something extremely odd happened last night. It's just occurred to me that you might be able to explain it."

Towne unlocked the door and stepped part way out, shaving brush in hand. "Something odd?" he asked curiously.

"Yes. And in your line. Do you think the Hotel Chesterfield could possibly harbor a nest of international spies?" Merlini's voice was completely serious.

Towne looked vaguely alarmed. He frowned, glanced sharply across at me, and then grinned. "Sure," he said. "In a Hitchcock movie, but this isn't that. Or is it? What do you mean?"

"I suspect that most detective-story writers," Merlini went on, "like their literary ancestor, Poe, have some interest in codes and ciphers. Do you?"

Towne's slow nod was puzzled. "Yes. I've looked into the subject a bit. I know Yardley's book. But—" His eye caught the slip of paper Merlini held out.

"Some person unknown," Merlini explained, serious as an owl, "shoved this note under our door last night. It looks distinctly ominous, and I don't know whether it's a warning, a threat, a pictographic description of the Army's newest bomber, or a joke. In any case, it seems to have been delivered at the wrong door. It's quite incomprehensible. Can you shed any light?"

Towne scowled at the penciled characters, turned the paper

over to examine its blank obverse side, hesitated, apparently still not quite convinced of Merlini's seriousness, and then studied the inscription again.

I waited almost breathlessly. His hesitation was highly suspicious. I knew what three of those symbols meant, and I was very sure that Towne knew, too. I didn't know why Merlini had set this little trap; but it looked as if he was going to make a catch. Towne was so close to putting his foot in it that I almost uttered an involuntary: "Careful!"

Then he spoke—and the trap clicked.

"No," he said doubtfully, "I can't rattle off a translation for you offhand. It must be a joke of some sort, but I'd like to have a try at it. May I have a copy?"

"You can have the original," Merlini said. "You're probably quite right about the joke. I'm incurably romantic. I'll inquire downstairs if there's a boy about the place. Age fifteen. One who's been reading *The Goldbug*. We'll see you later, then. If you do make anything of it, let us know."

Towne nodded, and we left him standing in the doorway, frowning intently at the paper, his puzzled air, I was certain now, completely false.

"His acting," I told Merlini once we were out of earshot down the stairs, "is amateurish. But why does he pretend not to know those last three signs, the common proofreaders' symbols for *delete, insert quotes,* and *period?* And why did you suspect he might react that way? And what are those other characters?"

"Hobo hieroglyphics," Merlini answered. "The first means *Tough on tramps. Bad dog;* the second, *Follow this street;* and the third is an English criminal sign signifying *A buyer of stolen goods lives here.* The dot within the circle, the proofreader's manner of indicating the insertion of a period, is also a hobo mark that means *You can count on a thirty-day jolt for vagrancy in this town!*"

"Um," I said. "The intriguing reactions of Mr. Towne. They become more cryptic by the minute. Last night he pretended to know nothing about pickpocket language. Now he won't admit knowing anything about hobo graphic signs— or, what's even more amazing—proofreader's symbols. Yet, knowing them, he must suspect that the note is a phony and that you were trying to test him. But he denies all knowledge just the same. Why? It's almost as if he were trying to make us regard him with deep suspicion. I don't get it."

Merlini looked pained. "Ross, your before-breakfast logic is something to behold. Pythagoras, Hegel, Kant, Descartes, Spinoza, and some others must be whirling like electric dynamos in their graves.

"I'm reminded of Isadore Cohen, traveling salesman for Cohen, Cohen and Cohen, Cloaks and Suits. He met a bitter business rival on the train. 'Ver are you goink?' he asked. The rival replied politely, 'Buffalo.' Isadore grew angry. 'Buffalo!' he growled disgustedly. 'You tell me Buffalo so that I think you're goink to Schenectady, ven I know it's Buffalo you're goink to all the time. Vy do you lie to me that way, Jacob?"

"Does that little parable," I asked, surprised, "mean that our author, bank-robber friend—"

"Hist," Merlini warned, "the desk clerk."

That gentleman came hastily through the door beyond the desk, his shirt tail inadequately tucked in behind, his fingers fumbling sleepily at a wrinkled tie. Seeing us, he apologized nervously.

"Just coming up to call you. I'm afraid I slept right through my alarm. Four times I got into bed last night, and then something happened. I got up when you arrived. After that another gentleman checked in, and at two this morning when the plumbing in room 33 sprung a leak, Mr. Goudge, the cream-separator salesman in the room below, was nearly drowned, and—"

Merlini cut in on this tale of woe. "You're the day and the night clerk as well?"

The harried man nodded. "Day clerk, night clerk, general manager, bellboy, and some other things. Twenty-four hours a day. Of course most nights we don't get any business after that 10:40 train, but last night with the circus here and all . . ."

"The gentleman who checked in after we did." Merlini was examining the register. "Is he still here?"

"Oh, Lord! And he wanted to be called at six!" The desk clerk scuttled from behind his enclosure and started for the stairs.

"Wait," Merlini stopped him. "According to the register you put him in room 26—down the hall from us. This looks like his key with some money here on the desk."

"Oh." The clerk looked at the objects indicated. "He must have gone."

I took a quick look at the register. The name signed beneath ours in a large hasty scrawl was Keith Atterbury's.

Merlini ignored the look I gave him, calmly tore two dollar bills several times across, neatly folded the pieces, and handed them to the clerk. I turned and followed him out as the clerk started to protest, then stopped, having found that the bills, unfolded, were fully restored.

Merlini, anxious to make up for lost time, wanted to skip breakfast altogether, but I persuaded him to stop at a lunch wagon long enough for orange juice, roll, and coffee. I made an attempt at conversation, but he would have none of it.

"Eat," he said, "and be quick about it."

It wasn't until we were some ten miles out on the road to Norwalk, following the arrow-marked poles, that he spoke again.

"Ross," he commanded, "stop the car. I want out."

He spoke so suddenly and urgently that I obeyed automatically, jamming on the brakes with an abruptness that made the tires screech.

"Hannum poster on a pole we just passed," he said, getting out. "I want it for my collection. I won't be a minute."

I watched him as he ran back and started to detach the brightly colored "one-sheet" from the telephone pole. He carefully lifted two corners free from the tacks that held them; then, unaccountably, seemed to change his mind. For a space of half a dozen seconds he stood as motionless as a wooden Indian. Slowly he replaced the poster as it had been. He turned, and suddenly, all action, sprinted for the car. He jumped in, slammed the door violently, and barked at me:

"That crossroad just ahead, Ross. Turn right, and step on it!"

He sounded as if he meant it. I let the clutch in and trod heavily on the gas.

For once he explained without prompting. "There's an arrow chalked on that pole *beneath* the poster, but the bill-posting crew travels a good ten days ahead of the show, and the arrows are placed the morning the show moves. It isn't possible."

"Perhaps some other show—"

"No. The arrow is a nice fresh one."

"But if it's covered by the poster—"

"It means—and for once I use the phrase quite literally —it means dirty work at the crossroads."

The car took a corner on two wheels. Mentally I did the same, wondering all at once if the fact had any significance that this road, like the one on which the Major had been found, was a little-used side road. The macadam, in contrast to the smooth concrete of the highway we had just left, was bumpy and the unbanked curves were sharp and numerous. I trod still harder on the accelerator, and we flew, bouncing and swerving like a roller coaster running wild.

I had no time to speculate on what we might find—I was too busy steering a course; but I knew the moment we sighted the roadster and its attached trailer that it was what we hunted. It was parked by the roadside in a lonely spot that offered no apparent reason for stopping, a broad empty meadow stretching away on one side and a wooded hillside sloping sharply up from the road's edge on the other.

"Queer place to stop," I said, pulling off the road just ahead of the roadster and applying the brakes, "unless it's a picnic or a breakdown."

Merlini had our door open and was out and gone before we stopped rolling. I saw that the driver's seat was empty, and I heard Merlini knock briskly on the trailer door as I cut the ignition and jumped after him. He waited a moment, knocked again, and then tried the door. It opened, and he stepped in.

He looked around and, as I entered, said, "Nobody home."

The interior was similar to that of the Major's trailer, but simpler and without the custom-built features. The table between the two facing seats at the rear had been folded away and the seats pulled out to form a bed. It had been slept in and was still unmade.

Quickly I jerked open one of the two wardrobe doors on my right.

"Looking for something?" Merlini asked.

I looked in the second cupboard. "Bodies," I said. "Or maybe Joy Pattison. Wouldn't surprise me."

The cupboards contained nothing at all but a dozen or so wire coat hangers.

Doubtfully Merlini said, "It could be a breakdown. Suppose you investigate, Ross. Look at the gas gauge, and see if the engine is in running order."

"That's a job for you, isn't it?" I asked. "I can't pick the ignition lock, and the keys certainly won't be—"

"They are, though," he replied. "I saw them on the dashboard. Look for traces of another car alongside, too. We met no one on foot, and the next town's ten miles on."

I hurried out. Though lacking bodies, the layout was still promisingly odd. Trailer door unlocked, keys in the dashboard, and, as I discovered at once, an almost full tank of gas and an engine that perked as soon as I put my foot on the starter. I picked up a pair of dark sunglasses that lay on the floor of the car and then examined the roadside. If another car had stopped, it hadn't left the roadway; the only marks in the soft shoulder that bordered the road were those made by the roadster, the trailer, and our own car.

I went back and found Merlini squatting on his heels, contemplating the trailer floor just inside the door. I made my report and exhibited the sunglasses. He nodded in a preoccupied way.

"What do you make of that?" he asked. The linoleum-covered floor was somewhat worn except for a 2 x 3-foot rectangle that was perceptibly brighter and newer.

I took a closer look. "That's easy," I deduced. "A missing rug." I pointed to several tack holes around the oblong's edge. "Tacked down to keep it from sliding around en route. Owner leaves car keys but takes rug. Magic carpet maybe. And he flew away on it."

"She, Ross, not he," said Merlini. "I found a blond hairpin

and some hair combings to match in the wastebasket. When I saw that the wardrobe cupboards were as bare as Mother Hubbard's, I got nosy. Sinkful of dirty dishes. Orange juice, coffee, buttered toast are indicated. The alarm clock was set for six. There's a good supply of groceries, a well-stocked refrigerator, plenty of pots, pans, silverware, dishes, bed and table linen. All normal enough. But those drawers beneath the mirror there, where I'd expect to find toilet articles, underwear, and the like, are all quite empty. There's not a thing in the place that could be called a personal article." Merlini paused briefly, took a final puff at his cigarette, and dropped it in an ash receiver that stood on the floor near by. "She did more than just step out to borrow a cup of flour. She packed for an extended stay."

"It's a Buick roadster," I said. "A '35 model. And a Roamer trailer, dark-green paint job. If it hadn't been so blamed dark on the lot last night, we might know who—"

I looked curiously around, wrinkling my nose. I was conscious of a faint disagreeable odor that grew stronger—the smell of burning rubber. Merlini too sniffed, then pulled open a door beneath the sink and extracted a crumpled square of brown wrapping paper from the built-in trash container on the door's back. He spread it quickly on the floor, picked up the ash receiver, and started to empty the contents of its neck onto the paper. The still-lighted cigarette butt he had discarded a moment earlier dropped out, but nothing else, although there was a metallic rattle within the ash tray's base. Merlini turned it right side up again, reached in with two long fingers, and removed the obstruction—a rubber glove.

He reached in again and found another. He upended the ash receiver once more, and this time the contents descended amid a dusty cloud of ash. The receiver was a treasure chest of clues. The metallic object that had rattled proved to be a cheap dime-store glass cutter.

Merlini poked at the remaining debris and collected several torn bits of white paper. One of these he passed across to me.

"Clues by the gross," he said. "No. 1, Extra Fancy, hand-sorted and government inspected. Nothing but the best."

The scrap of paper was the torn corner of an envelope,

and it bore part of a printed return address *"The Magic Sh——* and below that 1479· *Broadw——*. It was Merlini's own business stationery, apparently the envelope in which last night he had placed the fragments of glass that he had found on the floor of the Major's trailer.

"When that was stolen last night," I said slowly, "only two women could have known the importance of the evidence it held. Pauline was *hors de combat,* and Joy—"

From outside, through the open door, came a sound that jolted us both into instant action. I got through the doorway first, just in time to see the stone that had rolled down the hillside come to a stop a dozen feet away.

From above, near the hill's crest, we could hear the retreating sound of someone running through the underbrush.

Chapter 10

Vanishing Lady

I HOTFOOTED it up the hill, but by the time I reached its top all sounds of flight had ceased. In his headlong rush my quarry had doubtless left a trail that looked to any self-respecting woodsman like a four-lane highway. But since my natural habitat is Broadway, I made no attempt to locate and follow it, not wanting to put the local Boy Scouts to the trouble of a search.

Merlini, slightly more confident, nosed around for fifteen or twenty minutes and finally located the tree behind which the hidden watcher had concealed himself. There was one footprint, an impression small enough to have been a woman's, though it had the appearance of having been made by a male shoe.

"Why the Daniel Boone act?" I asked. "Don't you think it's high time we got a little official assistance on this case? We passed a State Trooper's barracks just outside of Waterboro."

Merlini shook his head. "Not just yet," he said. "But soon. We catch that circus first; there are one or two items I want to check on."

He returned to the trailer and got the torn envelope, the

glass cutter, and the rubber gloves.

Then he said, "Think you can turn this car and trailer here? We'll take it with us. First town down the line that has a Western Union, I'm stopping off for a minute. You keep going; I'll catch you."

We had seventy miles to go; and, though I pushed along as fast as possible, the trailer slowed us so that it was nearly two o'clock when we reached Norwalk. Merlini pulled in before a garage.

"Just to make sure no one tampers with the evidence this time, we'll park the trailer here." Then, seeing a hungry look in my eye, he added, "You can eat at the grease joint on the lot."

"I still think we should send the cops an S.O.S.," I said as we started for the show grounds. "Joy and Keith will be three states away by the time you get the mounties after them. Aren't you afraid that, when you do report, the authorities are going to be somewhat annoyed at your procrastination?"

"I expect they will," he said. "But you must remember that we still have no concrete evidence to prove that either the Major's or Pauline's accident was anything else. The fact that last night's evidence was stolen is proof of a sort—but it *was* stolen. Did you say Joy and Keith?"

"Joy was your candidate last night, wasn't she? Since she ditched her car and trailer in a spot like that, she must have been met by a car. Keith's. You said I shouldn't cross him off just because he started the investigation."

"Joy, then," Merlini summed up, "killed the Major, discovered the will she had counted on was either missing or nonexistent, tried to kill Pauline so as to inherit the show, failed, got cold feet this morning and took a powder. That it?"

"You certainly make it sound cold-blooded enough," I said, not liking the theory at all, but unable to offer any other that would fit as many facts. "I'm only trying to be analytical in the best Merlini manner. Joy and Keith are both without alibis for the Major's death, and either of them might have swiped the evidence. Whereas Pauline and Mac, the only other two who knew that any evidence had been found, both have alibis as big as a house—damn!"

"Something wrong?"

"Yes. It's taken me until now to figure out why you said last night that everyone else on the lot has an alibi in the matter of the missing evidence. None of them knew we'd found it."

Merlini nodded. "You've stated it very neatly. Joy and Keith are the only possibilities, with Joy a good length in the lead. If this were fiction, I'd eliminate her immediately as being too suspicious—but it isn't. What I want to know now is what happened to the pieces of glass that were in that envelope? And to the hat and the photo. They aren't in the trailer.

"If they've been destroyed, why not do the same with the envelope, the glass cutter, and the gloves? Those things, found together, show that the person who burgled the Major's trailer and the person who made away with the evidence are one and the same. They also indicate that both the Major's and Pauline's accident were caused by the same murderer. Why were they left there? And why, of all places, were they hidden in the ash receiver?"

"What do you mean 'of all places'? I thought the ash receiver wasn't a half-bad hiding spot. You searched with your customary thoroughness and missed them. We found them only by accident."

"I wonder," he said. "Would you hide rubber gloves in such a place? I don't think I would."

We pulled onto the lot before I had time to give that the thought it deserved. We parked behind the side-show top near several other cars. A gang of half a dozen negroes moved with unhurried deliberation from stake to stake around the tent tightening up the guy ropes. Their lazy rhythm was timed to the old guying-out chant: *"Hit it. Hee—Hoooooo! Heave it. . . . Heavy! Stake it! Break it! Down Stake!"*

The big-top band, mellow and resonant because of the intervening canvas, was working on the concert selections that preceded the spec.[1] As we got out of the car, a spirited black horse galloped toward us from the direction of the back yard. Its rider wore a medieval riding costume of ultramarine

[1] Spec: Opening spectacle.

blue that was just the proper contrast for the golden hair beneath the tall pointed cap.

"There would seem to be a minor error in your calculations, Ross," Merlini said. "This looks like Joy."

"Yes," I admitted, making some rapid mental readjustments. Then excitedly I said, "It's Pauline that's missing! The murderer sidetracked her trailer and *this* time he—"

"Look before you leap, Ross," Merlini advised. "The hair samples I found were blond. Pauline's brunette."

Joy's horse reared before us and halted. "I saw you drive in," she said. "Keith and I have been wondering where you were."

"We were delayed a bit," Merlini replied. "Where's Pauline? Did she go to the hospital?"

"No. She's here. She exploded when the Doctor suggested she do that this morning. She said it would take more than a cut face, a sprained back, and a knock on the head to put her off the lot. Tex drove her over. He wouldn't let anyone else drive. They just got in."

"What time did they leave?"

"Six-thirty, when I did. But Tex drove slowly."

"Are we the last arrivals?" Merlini asked. "Or has anyone else failed to—"

The side wall of the side-show top lifted, and Gus stepped out.

"Was that you just pulled in?" he asked.

"Yes," Merlini answered.

"See anything of a Buick roadster and a green trailer on the way?"

Merlini evaded a direct answer. "Why?" he asked. "Did you mislay one?"

My reputation for prophecy, if I ever had one, was thoroughly discredited; but I knew now before Gus answered what he would say.

"The Headless Lady hasn't shown up yet. She should have been here a couple of hours ago. Lee Daniels, the side-show manager, is fit to be tied."

Merlini's expression was one of polite interest, nothing more. "What time did she leave the Waterboro lot?"

"I dunno." Gus shook his head. "She was still there when

Stella and I pulled out, but—"

"She must have blowed the chalk, Gus," Joy put in. "I stopped for gas just outside of Waterboro, and she passed me. But I didn't see her on the road any place. Better have Lee report it to Mac. If she doesn't show up soon, he can send out a rescue party."

Gus went back into the side-show tent.

"But I don't get it," I said. "The Headless Lady has an alibi."

"Alibi?" Merlini asked. "For what?"

"Why, for last night, for Pauline's fall . . ."

"You mean, she was working?"

"Yes."

"And what doing? Being headless. How many of the people who saw the act can swear who it was? For that matter" —he turned to Joy—"who is the Headless Lady anyway?"

"Who?" Joy asked. "Her name's Mildred Christine. That's all I know. She's only just joined."

"Yes. I've heard that. But I've a feeling she may be important. Can't you tell me anything more than that?"

"That's all anyone seems to know. She's damned upstage for a kid-show attraction. She hasn't eaten in the cookhouse once yet. She cooks all her own meals in her trailer. I don't think she's been in the show business long. I never heard of her before."

"Description? What's she look like from the neck up?"

"Blond. And without the dark sunglasses she always wears, I think she'd be a looker. I'm afraid that's not much of a description, but I've just barely glimpsed her. As I say, she keeps to herself."

"Sunglasses that she always wears?"

Joy nodded. "Rain or shine. I think she sleeps in them. There's the spec music. I'll have to dash."

Joy wheeled her horse and cantered off.

"The more we discover, the more interesting it becomes, Ross," Merlini said.

"You mean, the more we *don't* discover, the more—There's Keith."

"Where've you two been all morning?" he hailed. "Hell's been popping hereabouts."

"Hell?" Merlini asked in a startled voice. "What sort?"

"Shakedown," Keith said. "The local cops were waiting at the city limits this morning. They got difficult about little details like driver's licenses, noisy mufflers, and the like. They picked up nearly every other driver as fast as they came in, and I raced along just in time to get nabbed for speeding. A dozen of us spent about an hour in the jug until Mac arrived and paid off the Chief of Police. The one in this burg is poison, and I can see where Mac is going to put up an awful beef if we threaten to give him this murder dope."

"Mac late getting in this morning?"

"Late?" Keith asked. "No, not particularly. He comes over with the ticket wagon, Calamity driving. Why?"

"What made you so late? I thought you were making the jump last night?"

"I intended to, but when I started to leave, I discovered my jalopy was missing on half its cylinders, so I left the car at a garage overnight. Figured that anyway it was a pretty long jump, and I could make better time by daylight. I didn't get away as soon as I should have because the desk clerk didn't call me and I had to wake myself."

"Did you know that the side show has a very special attraction this afternoon? Something never before seen on land or sea? Might be good for a press release."

"No. What?"

"A Headless *and* Bodiless Lady. Her head's invisible, and now the rest of her is missing. Ross and I found her empty trailer. It would appear that she has lammed. I don't suppose you know who she is either?"

Keith shook his head, frowning. "No. And I don't know who does. I asked Mac about her when she joined, but he said he hadn't the slightest idea. You might try Pauline."

"I hear she's able to talk this morning."

"Yes. What do we do now? Tackle her?"

"I think so. And in the meantime I've a job for you. I want to know if anyone besides the Headless Lady is missing this morning. Someone with a car. Would you find out and then hotfoot it around to Pauline's trailer? We'll be there."

Keith asked, "Someone else missing? What does that mean?"

"Yours not to reason why," Merlini evaded. "Yours but to get me an answer."

Keith clicked his heels and saluted. "Aye aye, sir!" He was trying hard to be nonchalant, but it didn't quite ring true. Beneath it he was worried.

Merlini started off toward the back yard. The spec had just finished, and we stood aside for a few minutes out of the way of the performers as they issued from the big top and scattered to their trailers to make wardrobe changes. The clowns had their props set up against the side wall near the entrance, and were making their changes in the open. One of them was inserting himself into a prop horse, donning the costume in such a way that the horse appeared to be walking on his forefeet, his rump high in the air.

A big grinning negro buck on a campstool was tipped back against the side of Pauline's trailer by the door—fast asleep.

Seeing him, Merlini scowled. "It doesn't look as if we would have any trouble getting in to see Pauline," he said. "Let's go, before Mac sees us and tries stalling. If he's been having cop trouble already this morning . . ."

Merlini never finished that sentence. His hand was on the trailer door, turning the latch, when a loop of rope settled quickly around his shoulders and jerked him backward. Tex Mayo on his horse was at the rope's other end, hauling in.

"Who the hell are you and where do you think you're heading for? There are more damned lot-lice around here today than—"

Merlini loosened the lariat, stepped out, made a reaching movement with his hand, produced a business card from nothing, and handed it up to the cowboy.

Mayo looked at it and tossed it aside. "Magician," he growled. "See the side-show manager out front. But stay out of this back yard." He called to the man who had been bossing the guying-out gang. "Hey, Joe. Chase these back-yard customers behind the ropes and keep them there."

"We weren't looking for a job, Mayo," Merlini said. "We've got one. I thought that, since the guard I asked Mac to post had fallen asleep, I'd take a look and see if Miss Hannum was all right. Someone tried to kill her last night; and, if she isn't

looked after better than that, a second try might very well
be more successful."

Tex stared at him. Merlini, holding a four-foot length of
the lasso's end, tied several knots in it without letting go,
impossible as that may sound, of either end.

And before Tex replied we heard Mac's voice behind us.
"Damn!" it said. "You two still around, are you?"

"Morning, Mac," Merlini answered, rapidly tying more
knots in the lariat. "Yes. We're still getting in your hair. I
want to see Pauline, that is if nothing has happened to her
yet. Your sergeant-at-arms isn't any too efficient."

"Pauline?" Mac asked. "But she—" He looked at the sleeping jig. "Didn't she go to the hospital this morning, Tex?"

Mayo got off his horse and answered, "No. The doc said—"

Mac turned and ran for the trailer. As he passed the sleeping guard, he hooked his foot in the chair and pulled. Whatever dreams the darky was enjoying came to an abrupt end
as he hit the ground. Mac disappeared within the trailer.

Tex confronted Merlini. "Just what the hell are you talking
about? Who tried to kill who?"

But Merlini lit out after Mac without answering. His
second attempt at entering the trailer was also thwarted. Mac
stepped out just as Merlini got there, and pulled the door to
after him.

"No you don't," Mac said gruffly. "Tex, what did she do?
Talk the doctor out of it?"

Tex scowled. "Say, do you mind telling me what this is
all about? Who is the magician? Why did you have a guard
on Pauline? What—"

"I'll get to that in a minute. Answer my question, will
you?"

"Yeah. The doc showed about six-thirty, but she was conscious and she told him to scram. After he heard her cuss
him out, he admitted she was some better. He argued her into
letting him give her a shot of morphine. She slept most of the
way over. I drove her. But she didn't say anything about all
this—"

Mac growled. "Damn the woman anyway. I've a good notion to blow the show and let her do her own worrying."

"Mac," Merlini said, "it's all so simple. If we find out what it was she was going to tell the Sheriff last night before she fell, that might end it."

"That's what you think," Mac said. "But she just now told me that she wasn't seeing anybody—you in particular."

"Sorry, Mac," said Merlini, "but I'm going to have to hear her say that. That could be a stall on your part."

"It looks like one of her own. I don't get it at all. Last night—"

"She was about to blow the gaff. Now, according to you, she isn't. You asked me to give you notice before I called any cops. You're getting it now, but it might be a lot smoother all the way round if we saw her first. Since you haven't seen her before this morning, perhaps she hasn't heard what went wrong with the lights last night. Knowing that, she might not be so reticent at this point."

"You and the light man are the only ones who think someone monkeyed with the lights. But *he* would."

"You still think her fall and the Major's smash were accidents? I noticed you jumped for her trailer awfully fast when I pointed out that the jig was sleeping."

"Anybody'd get the heebie jeebies with you around." Mac looked worried. "I still—"

Keith came up just then, and Merlini queried him silently with a raised eyebrow.

Keith shook his head. "All present and accounted for," he reported.

Mac gave us a puzzled look but didn't interrupt his argument. "I still think that if you haven't got any more than you had last night—"

"But I have," Merlini said. "Lots more. I'll give it to you; but, first, one question. The Headless Lady's trailer—is there supposed to be a small throw rug on its floor?"

"A rug?" Mac frowned. "Yeah. I bought that trailer for the Major in Bridgeport. Picked it up second hand—with furnishings. There's a rug—but what of it? Why—"

"There *was* a rug," Merlini corrected. "That's item one. The rug is gone. Item two: The Headless Lady is also a vanishing lady! Ross and I found her trailer abandoned by the roadside this morning. Engine in good running order, key in car, door unlocked—but no occupant. Clothes gone. Item: Hidden in the trailer we found a glass cutter, a pair of rubber gloves which might have made the whorlless fingerprints you saw last night, and the torn pieces of an envelope. Item: The envelope was the same one in which I placed the pieces of broken glass we found. Item: The hat, photo, and envelope with glass were stolen and the fingerprints wiped out last night during the excitement when Pauline fell."

This extra-large helping of information set Mac back on his heels for a moment. Then he brightened and said, "Well, what are you bothering me for? It's obvious as hell, isn't it? Go get the troopers and have them pick up the Headless Lady."

"It's not as simple as that. They'll have to know who they're looking for, or at least have a decent description. No one seems to be able to give me either. Maybe you can, but don't tell me her name is Mildred Christine."

"Why not? That's what's down on the pay roll."

"What's she look like?"

"You've seen her act, haven't you?"

"I haven't seen her face. Now look, Mac, if you want the cops to chase off after the Headless Lady and not bother the show, you'll have to stop being difficult. I must see Pauline."

"What makes you think she knows any more about it? The Major hired the girl. It doesn't follow that Pauline—"

"It does, though. You see, the illusion apparatus happens to have come from my shop. Pauline was the person who—well, 'bought' it from me last Friday. She told me her name was Mildred Christine, and Millie-Christine was an old-time circus freak, a two-headed girl."

Mac gave in. "Oh, hell!" he growled. "This would have to happen in this burg of all places. The shakedown money I paid out this morning is just plain loss. When Chief gets a load of this . . . Come on. She'll probably bite my head off, but you can see her."

Chapter 11

Elephant Trainer

"Things are seldom what they seem,
Skim milk masquerades as cream;
High lows pass as patent leathers;
Jackdaws strut in peacock feathers.
Very true
So they do.

—H.M.S.PINAFORE

THE STILL form of the girl beneath the covers on the bed had the disturbing, lifeless appearance of a mummy. She was too quiet, too rigidly motionless; and her face, surrounded on the pillow by a mass of dark hair, was white and blank, its features, under the bandages and adhesive, only half suggested, like an unfinished sculpture. There were two openings in the masking shell of gauze—one at the mouth, where the pale lips made a tight straight line, and a wider slit above, from which two black angry eyes regarded us with cold dislike.

Mac started to speak, but her words cut him off at once. The voice was low and strained as if speech were painful, but it was still commanding.

"Get out! At once! I told you, Mac—"

"Now wait, Miss Hannum," Mac protested hurriedly. "We're in a spot. My job is to keep this show moving in spite of hell, high water, and cops. I've had the day's ration of cop trouble already, but we're heading for more. And you're the only one who can do anything about it. I can't go up against a murder investigation by state troopers unless I know some of the answers. What was it you were all set to blow to the Sheriff last night?"

She was silent for a moment, her eyes leveled steadily on Mac. "Nothing," she said finally, her voice little more than a harsh whisper. "I was wrong. You'll have to do the best you can, Mac. Now clear out!"

Merlini, who had been watching her with an annoyed scowl

spoke quietly. "Miss Hannum, who is the Headless Lady?"

This resulted in another long silence. Then she turned her head and stared upward at the ceiling. Her lips moved just enough to allow the words to pass.

"Why do you ask that?"

"Because," Mac said quickly, "Merlini thinks she's the murderer he's howling about."

"But why her?" the girl said evenly. "Last night he accused me."

"Because she took a run-out powder this morning. There was a glass cutter hidden in her trailer, and a pair of rubber gloves that Merlini says could have made those fingerprints. And last night when the lights went out somebody swiped that photo, the Major's hat, and those bits of glass Merlini found. It looks as if she—"

Pauline cut in sharply at that. "I thought you were a fixer, Mac. If that's true, Merlini hasn't a thing to give the cops. Get him out of here and leave me alone! I'll talk to you later."

"Evidence or no evidence, Miss Hannum," Merlini said insistently, "suspicion of murder, an attempted murder, and a missing suspect is a train of events that will make any cop curious. And we *can* get another print of the photo, you know."

"Attempted murder?" She asked in a tight voice, turning her eyes to look at Merlini for the first time.

"Yes. Yours. The light failure wasn't an accident. The cable to the big top was deliberately disconnected. When the lights went out you fell, and the ensuing excitement supplied a lovely opportunity for making away with the evidence we had. Any murderer who is clever enough to use, quite impromptu, such a diabolically simple, practical, and indetectible means for gaining not merely one, but two, simultaneous and different ends is going to give trouble. He won't stop at that. In fact, Miss Hannum, I'm surprised that you lived through the night."

"I—I don't believe it," she said, but her voice lacked conviction.

Merlini followed through quickly. "You know who killed your father or, at the very least, something that is dangerous to the murderer. The only sort of life insurance that will

do you a bit of good is to tell us now what you know. Mac
had a guard on this trailer last night, and he's going to post
a better one now. But, if this murderer is the sort his performance to date indicates, a guard won't bother him much—
a bank vault wouldn't be any too safe. What was it you were
going to tell the Sheriff last night?"

She shook her head. "Nothing, I tell you! I was wrong."
There was fear in her voice—but it was balanced by an equal
amount of determination.

Merlini scowled and tried once more. He leaned forward
as if putting his physical weight behind his words.

"Who is the Headless Lady?"

He failed. She shook her head again. "I don't know."

"Do you expect me to believe that?" Merlini asked. "You
came and got the headless illusion for her. You gave me the
same phony name she has been using. You know why the illusion was wanted in such a hurry, why you were willing to
pay so—"

"I *don't* know," the girl insisted. "Dad hired her. He gave
me the money and sent me to get the apparatus. That's all I
can tell you. I gave you her name because it was the first that
occurred to me. If it's not her name, I don't know what it is."

"And you don't know why she disappeared this morning,
nor where she is, I suppose?"

"No."

Merlini looked at her for a moment and then gave up.
"You'd better post a couple of guards, Mac—wide-awake
ones. Though I doubt that it will do the slightest good. We
do need troopers now. Lots of them. I'm going to—"

As the trailer door swung open, Merlini stopped and turned
apprehensively. Irma King stepped through from outside and
slammed the door behind her with a crash that made us all
jump. She wore the red and gold uniform of her elephant act,
and she carried a heavy elephant hook. She was obviously
as mad as all hell—and enjoying it.

She looked at the girl on the bed and laughed, a queer thin
sound as though she were just a bit high. She glanced once
at the rest of us and then ignored us completely.

"I've got a surprise for you, Pauline. *Such* a nice surprise."

There was a full measure of concentrated venom in her

voice. The surprise was, very obviously, going to be anything but nice.

"You thought you could fire me, did you, Pauline?" She laughed again. "That's very funny. Only no one knows what a good joke it is but me. And I think it's so much more amusing when everyone knows. It's about time—"

"Mac!" Pauline's voice cut in. "Get her out of here!" Mac moved, but Miss King's next words stopped him.

"Mac Wiley, if you want to keep your job you'll stand where you are and listen. Pauline doesn't own this show now that her father is dead. *I do.*"

She stopped dramatically. Pauline was unimpressed. "She's tight, Mac. Do something about it."

But Mac, for some reason, wasn't so sure. He hesitated. Miss King drew a folded legal-looking document from her tunic and thrust it at Mac.

"You're the lawyer," she said. "Tell us what that is." Mac gave it a swift once-over. "Sure," he said. "So what? You were the Major's wife before he married Pauline's mother. I know that; we were on the same show together."

I had a hunch that *this* was news to Pauline. She was half-sitting up in bed now, the dark eyes in the bandaged face staring at Irma with horrified fascination.

"But that doesn't get you anything," Mac went on. "He divorced you." He glanced at the document again. "In 1913. These are your papers. *Rutherford Stark* vs. *Irma Stark.* What—"

"Stark?" Merlini asked.

"Yeah. That was the Major's name before he married into the Hannum family. He landed the owner's daughter, and when her father died he managed the show. When she died, about '25, she willed it to the Major. The show's name was worth dough and he couldn't change that, so he changed his own." Mac scowled heavily at Irma. "What the hell makes you think you get a cut? A divorced wife hasn't any claim—not unless . . ." Mac's voice played out for a moment, and then he added suspiciously. "So that's it! There *is* a will then, and you're the one who swiped—"

But Irma was full of surprises. She did not, as I expected, make another grab at her tunic and produce the document

there had been so much argument about. She grinned malici-
ously, watching Pauline.

"No," she said confidently, "that's just it. There isn't any
will. If there was I'd be out of luck. But there isn't, and I
collect! And it's Pauline," her voice rose higher, "who gets
canned—starting now."

"Dammit!" Mac demanded. "Talk sense, will you?"

Pauline shouted, "Mac, get that woman out of here! She's
drunk, I tell you!"

"No, Pauline." Irma was enjoying herself hugely. "I'm
afraid not. The name of the lawyer who got the Major that
divorce was Leo J. Snyder." She turned. "Perhaps you understand the joke now, Mac?"

Apparently Mac did, though he didn't laugh at it. He appeared, instead, to have been hit on the head with something
hard and heavy.

Merlini also seemed to be seeing the point. "Oh, Lord!" he
said weakly. "Now we pick up the pieces and start all over
again!"

"Leo Snyder," Irma explained with relish, "was before your
time, Pauline. A shyster lawyer with a lovely little racket. For
a couple of years, until the postal authorities finally caught up
with him, he did a land-office business in mail-order divorces.
Very handy for circus people, who are always on the road
and have no legal residences. His fees were very reasonable,
but his divorces weren't worth it. They were completely
phony." Irma laughed again.

"Your mother's and father's marriage was quite illegal;
your father was still married to me. He always has been! I'm
his widow now, and I get the estate. And you're an illegiti-
mate—"

"Mac!" Pauline's voice cut in like a whiplash. "Is this true?"

Mac didn't answer that. His voice snapped at Irma incredulously. "You mean to tell me that the Major never heard
about Snyder and had it straightened out? His conviction was
in all the papers and in *Billboard!*"

"It was during the winter season, and the Major was tour-
ing a unit through Mexico. Luckily he missed it. I'd married
again—Terry King, the animal trainer—and I was scared to
death the Major would hear about it. I couldn't let Terry

know. He had religion bad, and he'd have raised hell if he ever found out I'd been married before, much less that I was a bigamist. Naturally I didn't tell *him*."

"So now that his lions have canceled him out, you blackmailed the Major into giving you a job on this show again, refusing to give him a divorce and—"

"Don't be silly, Mac. I didn't dare tell him I was still his wife. Divorce or not, he *would* have made a will then, cutting me out. And he could have adopted Pauline. Not to mention what he'd have done to me for not telling him before Pauline's mother died so he could have married her properly and made his children legitimate."

"Children?" Merlini exclaimed.

"Pauline and her twin sister, Paulette," Irma said.

Merlini looked at Pauline and then at Mac. "Twin sister," he said ominously. "Why hasn't this been mentioned before now?"

But they paid no attention to him.

"Mac," Pauline said hoarsely, "then it is true. Can she prove it after all this—"

"She'll have one hell of a job," Mac said. "We can carry a case like that clear to the Court of Appeals, and I don't think Irma can afford it."

"There are lawyers," Irma countered, "who'll handle an inheritance case for a percentage of the take."

Pauline said, "Send him around, Irma. We'll take care of him. In the meantime, get the hell off this lot and stay off!"

"Sure. I'll go. But this show doesn't move an inch. There'll be an injunction on it before tomorrow morning that'll keep every last tent pole on this lot until I start giving orders. Think that over."

Irma gave Pauline one last venomous glance, snatched the divorce papers from Mac's hands, and went out, slamming the door violently behind her.

Mac shuddered. "Calamity was right," he groaned. "Suppé's goddamned 'Cavalry March' is poison. This is worse than murder. All we need now is a blowdown or a fire!"

Chapter 12

Eyewitness

"Twins have probably intruded—
Quite unbidden—just as you did—
They're a source of care and trouble—
Just as you were—only double."
— UTOPIA, LIMITED.

I AGREED with Mac. Whether or not the Suppé music was the cause, the Mighty Hannum Combined Shows was certainly having more than its share of grief. For that matter, the Merlini-Harte Murder Investigation wasn't treading what could be called a rose-strewn path. With one well-aimed shot Irma seemed to have made scrap of nearly every motive for murder that we had discussed. Merlini was right; this was the place where we got off and started walking back.

For a moment after Mac's outburst no one spoke. Merlini's half-dollar was motionless in his fingers, its intermittent vanishing stilled. Merlini regarded it gloomily.

Then Pauline said slowly, "It's not quite that bad, Mac. Irma is the murderer Merlini wants. It's obvious now. She had to get Dad before he should make a will. She—"

Merlini looked at her sharply. "Is that what you were going to tell Sheriff Weatherby last night?"

"Yes."

"But you didn't know until now that she had a motive—or am I wrong?"

"I didn't know. But I saw her enter the trailer last night after I had left."

"*That* does it!" Mac said excitedly. "I'll have her in the can on a murder rap before she can think twice about an injunction!" He started for the door.

Merlini stopped him. "Not so fast, Mac. I'm not so sure. Deep-Sea Ed says she was with him, lining up the bulls to go on after Tex's announcement. That's an alibi both for the lights and for the stolen evidence."

122

"Break it," Pauline snapped. "She's bribed him or told him that when she owns the show—"

"Maybe," Merlini said. "But I doubt it. I know Ed, and it doesn't sound like him. Does it, Mac?"

"Well—" Mac hesitated. "Maybe not. But a lot of people that you wouldn't suspect have tin mittens." [1]

"Suppose we put him through the wringer before you do anything rash. Send someone for him."

Mac put his head outside and called, "Joe, round up Deep-Sea for me. Tell him I want to see him here right away."

Then Merlini said, "While we're waiting I want some Hannum family history. More of this Irma Stark-King story. Quickly."

"It's a mess," Mac explained. "And if it ever does hit the courts it'll make legal history or something. Mr. and Mrs. Stark—the Major and Irma—joined the Hannum show in 1911. I was in the flying act, and our catcher cracked up right at the start of the season. He'd been swinging around in the top of a tent for years, and then he gets a broken arm in a clem. [2] The Major joined up to replace him. Irma did an equestrian routine and worked a ring of zebras. Before the season was half over, he'd fallen hard for old man Hannum's daughter, Pauline's mother. Her name was Lucille.

"Just about then I left the show. I was doing a two-and-a-half to a catch by the legs for the first time that season. One day I missed the Major *and* the net. When I got out of the hospital I had this game leg, and I've never been up on a trapeze since. The season after that I read in *Billboard* that the Major and Irma had split up, and it wasn't long before he married Lucille. They had twin daughters in '14. The Snyder case was reported just after that, but I never suspected that's where the Major's divorce came from. Even if I had, I'd have assumed he must have heard about it and straightened it out. There was a girl on the Hagen show who

[1] Tin mittens: Anyone who will accept a bribe has tin mittens; he likes to hear the money clink in his hand.

[2] Clem: A fight. The now seldom-heard call, "Hey Rube!" was the battle cry that rallied the show people when a clem was imminent.

got two divorces from Snyder and remarried after both of them. She found herself married to three men and had to get legal divorces from the first two."

Merlini turned to Pauline, "And your twin sister, Paulette, Miss Hannum?"

"She died two years ago."

Mac looked surprised. He said, "I didn't know that, Pauline."

"I know. Dad very seldom mentioned her after she married."

"Who did she marry?" asked Merlini.

"Fellow Dad didn't like. They eloped in '33, six years ago. He had been the patch on the show, and it was when he left that Mac joined on."

Mac nodded agreement, and Merlini started to ask, "What was his name and where did they—"

But Pauline folded up on us. I wasn't surprised. She hadn't been in any condition to withstand the shocks she'd been exposed to in the last half-hour. She seemed suddenly to go very limp. In a weak voice she told Mac to get a doctor, and once more requested that we get the hell out and leave her alone. This time we did.

Walter Jennier, the equestrian director, stood just outside the performer's entrance with an annoyed look on his face. "Mac," he called, seeing us, "where's Garner? Have you seen him?"

Mac shook his head. "No," he said rather curtly and turned his attention to Deep-Sea Ed, who had just arrived. "Stick here," he said, "I'll be right back. See about that doctor." He hurried off toward the front door.

"Who is Garner, Ed?" Merlini asked.

"Clown," Ed said. "The tramp. He disappeared right after the spec. It's upset the clown routines. Jennier's sore and—"

"Wait," Merlini said, "I want to catch Miss King before she—" He moved off quickly in mid-sentence. Irma King's car was moving away from the others and turning to leave the lot.

I lit out after him.

"Miss King—or Mrs. Hannum or whatever it is—just a minute."

She stopped the car and looked at him suspiciously.

"Yes?"

"Where were you night before last during the concert?"

"What's that to you?"

"Nothing," Merlini said. "But it's important to you. If you don't know, there was a murder committed on the lot during that time. There'll be troopers here any minute now investigating it and—"

"Murder? During the concert? Who?"

"Can't you guess?"

"No." She looked worried all the same.

"Where were you?"

"In bed."

"Anyone drive over with you from Waterboro when you came this morning?"

She answered almost hypnotically, as if she couldn't help herself, "No. No one."

Merlini kept the questions coming fast. "Have you lost a bull-hook?"

She nodded, wide-eyed. "But who—"

"Merlini," I broke in, my voice none too steady, "look!" I pointed toward Pauline's trailer. The slovenly, baggy-trousered figure of the tramp clown had just descended from the door of the trailer. He moved quickly, in a furtive manner, and ran hurriedly toward the entrance to the tent.

"You and Mac forgot all about the guard you were going to post. So I've had one eye on the trailer. That guy didn't go in since we left. He must have been in there all the time!"

Merlini very seldom used profanity, but he did now. "That wardrobe closet again!" he added, and then we were both sprinting wildly for the trailer.

But Pauline Hannum was apparently leading a charmed life. She lay on the trailer bed as we had left her, her eyes closed. She turned her head inquiringly at our entrance.

"Are you all right?" Merlini asked breathlessly.

"No," she said. "Is Mac getting a doctor?"

"Yes. What was that clown doing in here?"

"What clown?"

"Garner."

"There's been no one in here since you left."

Merlini turned and pulled the wardrobe door open. The hangers within held circus tights and brightly spangled costumes. Merlini looked at them for a moment and then closed the door again.

"My mistake," he said. "Sorry."

But when we'd stepped outside, Merlini, his voice lowered, said, "He overheard all that conversation. He was in the wardrobe. Must have gone in while that jig guard was having his siesta. There are smears of clown-white on several of the costumes and a streak of it on the inner surface of the door."

"Suspects popping up all over the place," I commented. "Irma, and now a mysterious clown."

Merlini frowned. "Yes, a mysterious clown who has a full set of alibis. He was waiting in the back yard to go on when the lights went out; and he was working that impromptu act in the ring after Tex carried Pauline out, when the evidence was stolen. If he traveled with the other clowns in the sleeping car this morning, then he had nothing to do with the Headless Lady's disappearance, and if . . ." Merlini raised his voice. "Ed, know if Garner worked the concert night before last like he did last night?"

Ed nodded. "Yes. I saw him. I was—"

Mac, returning hastily, barked at Ed, "Did you tell Merlini that Miss King was with you last night when the lights went out just before Miss Hannum fell?"

"I did. She always is. Tex's announcement only lasts a minute or so, and we have to be ready to swing in."

"You're real sure of that, are you?" Mac asked quietly.

Ed gave him a slow once-over, threw Merlini a puzzled look, and then answered curtly, "I am."

"Are you prepared to stick to that statement under oath in a murder trial, remembering that a perjured statement on your part will make you liable to a charge of accessory to murder?"

Ed seemed quite sincerely bewildered. "Murder?" He said, "Say, what the hell is this?"

"It's beginning to look as if the Major's death the other night wasn't an accident after all, nor Pauline's fall either. Someone put those lights on the blink purposely. Are you still sure that Irma King didn't pay or promise to pay you for an alibi?"

"Oh," Ed said interestedly, "trouble! I've been expecting it. Only this is more than I figured on. I'm glad I put a few lines out, because I think this is about where I get off. Nobody's offered to pay me a nickel; I have a job as it is collecting my pay envelope on time. I don't like—"

"You've been expecting trouble, have you?" Mac cut in. "Why?"

"Same reasons everyone else has. The boys on the advance have gone nuts, and the Major—well, he used to know how to route a circus, but the way we've been jumping all over the map and making all the wrong stands doesn't make sense. Something damned fishy's been in the wind for a couple of weeks now. If it's murder, I'm counting myself out. That accident in Bridgeport—" Ed stopped uncertainly.

Merlini, smelling a rat, pounced on it. "Bridgeport accident," he said. "I'd almost forgotten that. The elephant car piled up in a ditch and two of your bulls escaped. What was fishy about that?"

"The whole damned thing," Ed replied. "It wasn't an accident at all. I put that car in the ditch and saw to it the bulls got out, under orders from the Major himself!"

Mac blinked, started to say, "Well, I'll be—" then stopped, apparently at a loss for words, and just stared at Ed.

"It wasn't easy, either," Ed added. "Modoc didn't want to go. I had to prod her a bit. If shenanigans like that make sense, you tell me."

"Major Hannum," said Merlini, "told you to fake an accident and see to it that the bulls escaped?"

"He did, and it wasn't no publicity stunt either. Atterbury says he didn't run a word on it. And the Major told me I'd lose my job instanter if I opened my trap. But now that he's dead and you say maybe he was murdered, I don't like it around here anyhow, so—"

Mac said simply, "I don't believe it. It's screwy."

Merlini seemed readier to accept it. "I think I do, Mac. Screwy things, like birds of a feather, flock together; and this is just more of what we've got already. He didn't give you any sort of an explanation, Ed?"

"No. He told me I didn't need to ask questions before I got a chance to open my mouth. He said all I was to do was follow orders. Just trail his car with the bull truck, and when he gave me the high sign, run it in the ditch and see to it the door came open and at least a couple of bulls got out. After the way he yelled about the high price of elephants when he bought Rubber just before we started out, he must have gone completely loco."

"Where did it happen?"

" 'Bout a mile and a half outside Bridgeport. And that's funny, too. I know that part of the country pretty well. Bridgeport's famous for Barnum, of course, and I lived there for four or five years when I was a kid. And I know that the jump we made out of Bridgeport that day was a good ten miles longer than necessary. We headed west out of town instead of north. For some cockeyed reason he wanted those elephants to escape in a certain place. I don't expect you to believe any of this. Maybe I did dream it."

"What was the place like where it happened?"

Mac answered, his unbelief still strong, "You've been hitting the bottle, Ed. It was like any other along the road. Couple hundred yards from a farmhouse. The bulls took to the woods; and the man and his wife, who acted as if they owned the place—didn't look like farmers, though—city people—came out and raised hell. But it didn't do 'em a lot of good. There was quite a crowd trespassing all over their place before we got the truck back on the road and the bulls in it again."

"Kellar," Merlini muttered cryptically. "I wonder if it's his elephant story in reverse?" Then he addressed Mac seriously. "We've got to get the cops in on this, Mac. It's way out of hand. I'm going after them. Just one more thing I want to know first. Can Irma really collect on a story like the one she gave us? It sounds a bit thin to me. If the Major remarried in good faith, not knowing—"

"That's the catch," Mac replied. "How the hell do I prove that? It's a heller all the way around. Enough to give the whole damned Bar Association kittens. We've got to sort out how many different states it all happened in for one thing.

The laws all vary. In this state she's still his wife, and even if he'd made a will leaving everything to Pauline, she could still collect a third. Unless there's a statute of limitations. I don't know; I hope so. Or the Court of Appeals might decide Pauline was legitimate because of the length of time involved, or maybe the fact Irma married again is sufficient proof of infidelity. It's a rip-snortin' mess."

I could see that, though Mac's legal remarks didn't interest me greatly at the moment. Whether Irma could collect or not, she obviously thought she could and that was the important thing; she had a motive—two in fact: money and revenge. And, besides, I had just thought of something else. It classed as a brainstorm. I proceeded to let it loose.

"Mac," I asked, "did you ever see Pauline's sister?"

"Yes," he nodded, "once. When they were about sixteen."

"They were twins. They look a lot alike?"

"In a way, yes," he said. "They weren't identical twins, though, if that's what you mean. Pauline took after the Major, and Paulette looked more like her mother. Pauline's no slouch as a looker, but Paulette was a lulu. Regular movie star for looks."

I said, "I see."

Merlini, catching the inflection I couldn't keep out of my voice, gave me a quick curious glance. I tried to keep a poker face. I had just discovered that I was pregnant—with a theory. But I wasn't going to give yet. I wanted time to think about it. I was asking myself if Pauline might not have been lying when she said that sister Paulette was dead. Suppose sister was alive and kicking. She'd have one nice simple Grade A motive for eliminating both the Major and Pauline—the inheritance. And Pauline could know it—but, in spite of the attempt on herself, have some reason to cover up. If I could prove that assumption, the next step was as obvious as the Atlantic Ocean—sister Paulette was the Headless Lady.

Then Merlini, blast the man, grinned widely. "Ross Harte, I'll bet you a ten-gallon cowboy hat that I can read your mind right now."

He turned to Mac, and his abrupt change of subject from Paulette to Headless Lady made me glad I hadn't taken the bet and sore as a boil because my theory wasn't exclusive.

"I'm afraid this is going to hurt a bit, Mac," he said. "But I'll bet you another hat that the Headless Lady is dead, and it's high time we did something about it."

Mac nearly had apoplexy.

"You aren't going to tell me she was—was—" The word nearly got him down. "—*murdered too!*" he finally finished.

"I don't think she left that trailer willingly," Merlini answered. "Ross here has lately been theorizing high, wide, and handsome to the effect that whoever the Headless Lady is, she committed the murder and took it on the lam. That hypothesis completely disregards the fact of the arrow on the pole. The arrow quite obviously indicates that she was deliberately sidetracked—misled into thinking that she was following the proper route to Norwalk."

I didn't have a good objection ready for that. "Why was the arrow covered with the poster?" I asked.

"So that the other circus people who came along afterward wouldn't all come traipsing down the side road and interrupt whatever was going on. Someone cut in ahead of the Headless Lady, placed the arrow, and after she had made the turn, covered it with the poster and streaked out after her. Then he stopped her, and the rest is pure guesswork. Of the clues at the trailer, the really ominous one is the missing rug."

"Missing rug?" Mac asked, bewildered.

"Yes. My hunch is that it was carried away because its presence would have contradicted the theory that she had simply ducked out."

"How?" Mac asked. "I don't get it."

"Suppose," Merlini said, "that it had blood on it."

"No, dammit!" Mac exploded. "This is too much! You see murder in everything. That's the flimsiest—"

Mac's expostulations ran suddenly aground. He stopped dead, his mouth still open. Then suddenly he emitted blue flames, swearing like—well, like an old circus man.

Two state troopers in their spruce gray uniforms, Stetson hats, Sam Browne belts, and shiny boots were coming toward us across the back yard with purposeful determined strides. Somehow they didn't look as if they merely wanted passes; they acted as if they were on a job—a serious one. With them there was a round-eyed excited boy of about twelve and a middle-aged nervous man whose appearance was that of a farmer. Another man, Stuart Towne, followed interestedly in their wake.

The trooper with the captain's stripes, a bronzed, square-jawed individual with a direct no-nonsense air about him, addressed Mac.

"We're looking for a man named Wiley. They said he'd be back here."

"Wiley?" Mac asked innocently. "Wiley. Oh, yes, saw him an hour or so ago over by the cookhouse. That way. Tall man with a squint."

"Mac," Merlini objected, "for Pete's sake! That won't—"

The boy who accompanied the troopers was pointing at Merlini and myself and saying, *"That's them!* The ones I saw in the trailer after we heard the shot!"

Chapter 13

Clown Alley

> *The river must be dragged—no time be lost!*
> *The body must be found, at any cost.*
> *To this attend without undue delay;*
> *So set to work with what despatch ye may!*
> —YEOMEN OF THE GUARD.

"THE MARINES have landed," Merlini said wryly. "And with the usual fanfare. Mac, where can we hold a conference?"

Mac knew when he was licked. His scowl was black, but he gave in like a good loser. "Major's trailer," he said helplessly. "Come on."

On the way Merlini asked, "The shot. What time did that happen?"

"No you don't." The trooper shook his head. "Your story first."

At the trailer Merlini made a few introductions, and we discovered that the trooper was Captain Schafer, of the New York State Police. His companion was Trooper Palmer.

Rapidly Merlini gave them the works. His swift summary was concise, stripped of irrelevant detail and yet complete in all the essential points. Mac listened wearily as Merlini paraded one suspicious circumstance after another, pyramiding the little evidence we actually had, but cementing it with enough deduction to make it hold together remarkably well. Well enough so that Captain Schafer's eyes were popping before Merlini was half finished. The Captain interrupted just once, to send Palmer on the run for the nearest phone and reinforcements.

Merlini held back only one thing, the mysterious clown; evidently with the intention of saving that piece of investigation for himself. He soft-pedaled the objections Mac and. Pauline had raised at nearly every turn and offered the lack of concrete evidence as an excuse for not informing the authorities sooner. The Captain wasn't greatly impressed.

When Merlini had described our discovery of the trailer that morning, told where it was now, and handed over the garage ticket, Schafer let us hear the boy's story. Buddy and his father were brought in to repeat it. At seven that morning the boy had been doing his chores on the farm which lay behind the hill out of sight of the road. He had heard what he thought was a shot and, since it was not hunting season, had wondered about it. His father, less romantically inclined, had reckoned it was a car backfiring and made the boy finish his work. But as soon as he was free he had set out, a Buck Rogers disintegrator pistol in hand, to investigate. He had found the trailer, occupied a strategic position in the woods on the hillside above, and was holding a council of war with himself when Merlini and I arrived. We discovered now that all the time we were there we had been covered by Buck Rogers' deadly weapon of the future and in constant danger of instant annihilation. The kid was completely disgusted with himself for his error of the dislodged stone and his subsequent hasty flight, though I'm sure that if I had been faced with a couple of charging interplanetary outlaws I'd have done the same.

"They looked like murderers," he said, finishing.

His father had again expressed his skepticism, but the boy was persistent. Captain Schafer, recently married to the boy's sister Ann, ran Buck Rogers a close second in Buddy's esteem; and finally, behind his father's back, he had phoned the barracks with his story. The Captain had agreed that it was odd enough to investigate, had checked on the license number the boy had given him, and discovered that the owner of the vehicle was the Mighty Hannum Circus Corporation. The Captain hadn't, however, expected to scare up anything quite like this. He was by now nearly as excited as Buddy, though he did a fair job of hiding it.

Merlini, as Buddy and his father started out, leaned forward and took a half-dollar from the boy's ear. "Take that," he said, "and buy a circus ticket. I'd get you a pass, only I don't stand in so well with the management just now."

Merlini finished off his story then and was just laying out the rubber gloves, the torn bits of envelope, and the glass cutter for the Captain's inspection when the called-for reinforcements arrived, Chief of Police Hooper among them. The Chief, I discovered later, was a deacon on Sundays, a sideline that Mac insisted was merely a vote-getting ruse. I rather agreed with Mac; Hooper was an officious, blustering, overly confident small-town official, quite convinced that any persons without a permanent address, circus folk in particular, were likely candidates for his jail. The sidewise glance he gave Mac when he first came in warned that there'd be trouble if anyone referred to the shakedown of the morning.

Schafer gave him a hasty résumé of the situation, sent a man out after Irma King, and announced that he was going to begin at once to verify Merlini's story by getting the facts from the people concerned at first hand. He started us on our way out.

Merlini, however, had one final suggestion. "Those rubber gloves," he said. "I wonder if you have facilities for giving them the nitrate test? If you do, I think it might be a good idea."

"Nitrate test?" Schafer asked. "What's that?"

"The ballistics man at Center Street told me about it," Merlini explained. "It's a test, introduced in this country by the Mexican criminologist, Gonzalez. Once it has percolated through enough police departments, as it is beginning to do, it will make shooting with criminal intent a considerably more hazardous proceeding for the gunman than it is now. The test can tell you which of your suspects has recently fired a gun. The 'invisible backfire' of the pistol blows minute particles of nitrate, part of the residue of the powder combustion, back into the skin of the hand.[1] The application of Lunge's Reagent, dephenylamine and sulphuric acid, makes the nitrate specks, if any are present, visible, turning them a dark blue in color. Since the acid can't be applied directly to the hands, a paraffin cast is made first, and the reagent applied to that. The paraffin lifts the nitrate specks off the hand. You could do the same with these gloves. I'd like to know if they've been worn by anyone firing a gun."

"Say," Hooper asked. "Who the hell is this guy?"

"He says he has an in with the New York Homicide Department. I'm checking it." Schafer turned to Merlini. "Might be a good idea at that. I'll see what can be done. What's the reagent formula?"

"I can't give you that offhand, but almost any library will have a copy of Robinson's *Science Versus Crime*. You can find it there."

Hooper said, "I don't see that knowing whether or not these gloves were worn when a shot was fired is going to be a damn bit of help. But if you want to get fancy, give them to Burns to play with. Ever since he went to Washington and took that three-month F.B.I. course, he's been yelling for microscopes and ultra-violet lamps, and smelling the station house up with chemicals. The cases we get around here don't need all that embroidery, and I don't think this one does either."

"Got it all figured, Chief?" Merlini asked politely.

"No, but I've got ideas."

I noticed that the look he gave Merlini when he said that also included me, and I didn't think I was going to like the ideas.

"Wiley," Schafer said as we went out, "I'll take you first. Then I'll want to see Miss Hannum and after that the others Merlini has mentioned, and probably some more."

---

[1] This may not happen with some guns, particularly automatics —but you're always taking a chance!

I steered Merlini toward the grab joint on the midway and insisted stubbornly enough that he wait while I surrounded two hamburgers and some coffee. He ordered one himself, but didn't pay much attention to it when he got it. This outdoor life seemed to be giving me a country mouse's appetite, and I was ordering a refill when he said:

"What are you doing? Studying up to be the fat man in a side show?" He started off impatiently. "I'll see you later."

Hastily I grabbed the final sandwich and hurried after him. He was making tracks for the back yard. The afternoon performance was by now nearly ready to blow off. The band music, a waltz, indicated that the flying act was in progress, which left only a clown number and the chariot races to follow.

"We've got to work fast," Merlini said as I caught up with him. "We've got competition now, and I'm afraid that once they've sorted out the alibis there will be an arrest. I'm not so sure that the person with the least number of alibis is necessarily it. We may have to set some alibis up on a cat rack and throw baseballs at them until we knock a few off—if we want to win any cigars. And that may not be so easy if the joint is gaffed."

"Gaffed?" I asked. "As in fishing?"

"No," he replied. "Like 'gimmicked' in conjuring. A joint is any game concession. When it's gaffed, strong or French, it's set up so that the player can't possibly score enough to win. Most of them are two-way joints that can be operated either gaffed or fair. They are run fair when the operator or his shill is demonstrating how easy it is to cop a big prize. The signs reading: *This is not a game of chance* are literally correct. The chump has no chance."

"That the sort of thing the Major's Carnival Equipment Co. manufactures?"

"Yes. Also gambling supplies. A couple of dozen varieties of loaded dice, phony roulette wheels and chuck-a-luck cages, marked cards, holdouts, shiners, even punch boards with the winning numbers keyed so the operator can punch out the big winners before he sets it up.

"Some of the people who buy these sometimes get an unpleasant surprise when they find that the two-way games can also work three ways! I know a grifter who got his hands on the gambling accessory company's list of customers. He made the rounds and, knowing what sort of crooked set-up was being used, swindled the swindlers! He'd switch the loaded dice for a set that were loaded differently—that sort of thing. When the other man thinks he has the best of it, that's the time to take him over; he is in no position to beef to the fuzz."

Merlini stopped by the clown car and waited as the clowns, having just finished their crazy walk-around, came toward us from the big top carrying their props. The tramp wasn't among them.

"Where's Garner?" Merlini asked as they came up.

An extremely obese clown who bulged alarmingly both fore and aft started to pull off his costume. As the balloon-padded garment dropped from him, it disclosed a remarkably skinny man who growled:

"That's what I want to know. He blowed right after the spec, and we haven't seen him since." He turned to one of his colleagues, who had also started to disrobe. "Keep your pants on, Mike," he said. "You'll have to take his place in the concert."

Merlini scowled at this information. "How long has he been on the show?" he asked.

"He's a Johnny-come-lately," was the reply. "Three weeks or so." Our skinny friend stood before a cracked mirror that hung on the truck door and swabbed a towel across his face. The transformation that occurred was as astonishing as if he had removed a mask. His grotesquely grinning caricature of a face was wiped away, and a quite ordinary, rather sour face left in its place.

"Was he in the car with the rest of you when you made the jump from Waterboro this morning?"

The clown looked at Merlini curiously. He shook his head. "I guess so. He usually is."

"But you don't know for sure?"

"No. I didn't wake up until we got on the lot here. Why?"

"Anybody else know?" Merlini looked around, but the other answers were all like the first one.

"Thanks, boys," Merlini said. "If he shows up, let me or

Wiley know about it, will you? Some state troopers out front looking for him. Come on, Ross."

"One alibi down," I said. "And two to go. He was working the concert when the Major got his, and though he might have doused the lights, he was out in the ring again when the evidence was stolen."

Merlini didn't answer. His long legs carried him quickly back the way we had come. At the front door Calamity was sputtering to himself.

"State troopers," he muttered glumly. "*And* cops. I knew something like this was going to happen." He saw us. "Superstitious, am I? That boss windjammer and his 'Cavalry March'! Might as well have played 'Home Sweet Home.' "

Merlini didn't argue that. "Calamity," he said, "send someone around to see if they can find Garner. If you can locate him, maybe your troubles will be over."

Calamity nodded. "You're probably right about that. I think he's a Jonah too. All the funny business on this outfit started right after he joined up."

"Another thing," Merlini added. "Who did Paulette Hannum elope with?"

"Press agent who was on the show then. Young fellow, by the name of Andy Myers. The Major didn't like him much. And neither of them been on the lot ever since as far as I know."

"Pauline's mother," Merlini asked, "Lucille. What sort of an act was she doing when the Major married her? Do you know?"

"Sure. She was the other flyer in the act with Mac and the Major. Damn good aerialist. One of the first women to do a double somersault."

"Thanks, Cal." Merlini started off. "Don't forget Garner. Oh, by the way—any Western Union messages come for me?"

"No."

Merlini made for the Major's trailer again. Mac, Keith, and Joy stood outside talking. Stuart Towne emerged just as we arrived, and one of the assistant troopers put his head out and said, "Miss Pattison, you're next." The inquisition was in full swing.

Merlini said, "Wait, Joy. I've got news for the Captain."

He shoved in past the trooper at the door and announced, "One thing I forgot to tell you. A tramp clown by the name of Garner needs some questioning. He was hiding in the wardrobe last time Wiley and I talked to Miss Hannum, and what he overheard seems to have scared him off. No one's seen him in the last hour or so anyway. Looks highly suspicious. He hasn't been with the show long, and I've noticed that his ring presence is none too professional. He doesn't know how to fall on his face properly, for one thing. Pagliacci's costume might hide a joker, and that's not intended as a pun. I—"

"Description?"

"That's the catch. I haven't seen him except in his make-up. Better ask Wiley."

"Palmer, you see to it."

Merlini was eyeing a revolver that lay on the desk before the Captain. "Atterbury's?" he asked.

The trooper nodded. "Yeah. And he had no permit, so I guess the Sullivan Law'll take care of him unless I find something better."

"The gun's no help, then? It hasn't been fired lately?"

"Doesn't look it. Could have been cleaned, of course."

"Turn up any other firearms?"

Schafer nodded slowly. "Towne has one. Same condition like this. But he has a permit. And there are quite a few irons in the Wild West department. One of the boys is checking those."

Chief Hooper had a suggestion. "We didn't frisk the magician."

Merlini turned to him. "It's all right with me," he said.

He held his arms out, and the Sheriff did a thorough job of slapping his pockets. As he finished, Merlini put two fingers into the Sheriff's breast pocket and drew out a half-dozen playing cards. He fanned them with an expert gesture.

"Well," he grinned. "Aces. All aces! You play poker, Chief?"

Hooper merely growled, "Wise guy!" and set about fanning me, but without any better luck.

Merlini asked the Captain, "No news of any bodies on the teletype?"

"No. But I sent out some men to look over the woods near

where that trailer was parked this morning."

"Good. And what about your inquisition? Is my story holding up?" Merlini glanced at Hooper.

Schafer said, "Yes. It's doing all right so far. No contradictions. But you certainly had all the dope there was. We haven't gotten a thing that's news yet."

Hooper chimed in. "In other words, *you* know a hell of a lot too much."

"No, Chief," said Merlini. "Not yet. But I hope to before long. Have you quizzed Miss Hannum yet?"

The Captain growled this time. "No. Doctor she had in awhile ago got to her first. He said we'd better hold off awhile. But I wonder. Think she could be playing 'possum?"

"It's quite possible," Merlini said. "She alternates between talkativeness and dead silence. When you get at her, put the screws on. Particularly see if you can uncover anything about the mysterious angel who paid off the six weeks' worth of back salaries here last Saturday. Find out what she knows about the two runaway elephants and the phony wreck near Bridgeport, and why the show's three-card-monte man was told to lay off. It wasn't because Tin-Plate-Johnny here"—Merlini nodded at Hooper—"was causing any heat. He got his."

With that parting shot Merlini started out, and Hooper, with an ugly look on his red face, moved toward him growling something about libel.

But Shafer halted him. "Skip it, Chief," he snapped. "You're on the sidelines this trip. *I'm* running this. And I know all about the shakedown this morning, so get the ants out of your pants."

Hooper's voice followed us through the door. "Okay," he snarled, "but I'm going to get something on *that* guy!"

Chief Hooper would have disclaimed any imputation that he was clairvoyant or possessed of second sight, as a lot of damned nonsense. Nevertheless, his prophecy, as we were to find out in short order, was one that Nostradamus himself would have been proud to own.

Chapter 14

Stolen Sword

". . . all the human freaks and wonders just the way they are pictured, painted, and described along this long line of pictorial paintings. Twelve big acts and oddities all inside, all alive, and all on the one ticket . . ."

FOR THE next hour or two Merlini dithered nervously, his usual oriental calm more than a little upset. He wandered with apparent aimlessness about the lot as if waiting for something to happen; he side-stepped all my attempts at conversation. We side-walled in to the kid show again and caught the final afternoon performance. Merlini glumly eyed the armless knife-thrower, the snake woman, and "the Human Salamander who actually eats, drinks, and swallows living flame."

Finally, however, I struck a spark that caused him to brighten momentarily.

"You remember the old chestnut about the boy who found the strayed horse by imagining himself to be a horse and asking himself where he would stray to?"

"Yes, of course. The horse chestnut." Merlini regarded me curiously. "You aren't suggesting that I imagine I'm a missing body and ask myself where a murderer might hide me?"

"Something like that, yes. Imagine you are the murderer. Personally, I think I might figure that the innards of a phony mummy on exhibition—the mummy of a murderer at that —would be the last place anybody'd look."

Merlini gave me a sour glance. "That just goes to show what writing for the pulps will do to a man's imagination. You need a cold compress in place of your hat. *This* imitation cadaver is pretty well shriveled up. It would have to be an awfully small missing body."

"I'd cut it up into smaller pieces for easier packing."

Merlini shivered. "Okay, Butch. If the body's there, you've convicted yourself. Then I'll imagine I'm Chief Hooper and arrest you."

He went over to the mummy, lifted it slightly, and gave it a shake.

"No," he decided. "Light as a feather and nary a rattle. He's empty enough. I wish you'd take that morbid imagination of yours out for a walk—and lose it."

Farmer came up just then, and before you could say "Hey, Rube" he and Merlini were involved in a technical discussion of three-card-monte, and were trying their damndest to fool each other with it. Merlini demonstrated a positively diabolical magician's version in which a corner of the Ace bearing a pip was torn off and left lying face up. Then he threw out the three cards face down and asked me to put my money on the Ace. Like a chump I chose the torn card and lost. It proved to be the three-spot, while the Ace, its corners all intact, was one of the others!

Then Farmer started what Merlini tells me is known as "cutting up old scores"—talking over old times.

"I was tossing broads on the backstretch at Saratoga," he said, apparently not realizing that the Romance languages I'd been exposed to were all the orthodox sort. "There was a fly gee in the tip with a big mittful of folding scratch. He thought he could pick me up, so I let him see me take out the crimp. Then I crossed him up by putting it back in the same broad! He was all set to spring when Paper-Collar Ed, who was weeding the sticks, rumbled the gaff trying to duke the cush back to me. Another savage blowed it, sneaked out, and beefed to the fuzz. The mark knew the big fellow, and the coppers had to turn on the heat. Ed and I were sneezed before we could slough the joint, and then the fix curdled. The robe was all set to hand us a ninety-day jolt when . . ." [1]

[1] Merlini later furnished this translation: I was running a three-card-monte game at the races in Saratoga. There was a wise guy in the crowd who knew how the swindle was worked. He had a fistful of paper money. He thought he could beat me at my own game, so I let him see me straighten out the bent corner. (In monte one of the operator's assistants in the crowd bends the corner of

I was interested, but I don't like foreign films without English subtitles dubbed in, so I wandered off and took in the freaks. My association with Merlini had taught me just enough about the principles of misdirection so that I caught one thing some of the other onlookers missed. Swede Johnson, the sword-swallower, handed out a razor-sharp sword for examination. After it had been returned, he laid it aside for a moment while he swallowed and regurgitated a lemon and a live white mouse. Then, when he picked up the sword again, he really took another apparently identical, but much duller, one. When he had finished his act, I saw him duck out under the side wall and head toward the cookhouse in search of something more digestible.

I also caught the Headless Lady again. It was operating now with one of the cooch dancers doubling for the missing girl. After that, as the lecturer was about to blow the performance off with the last presentation, the Oriental Dancing Girl Review, for men only, and just as I had paid out the extra quarter that entitled me to an eyeful, Merlini and Farmer announced their intention of putting on the feedbag. I was still full of hamburgers, but I was afraid that if I didn't stick to Merlini I might miss something even more interesting than "the little lady's graceful and astonishing exhibition of muscular control." I wrote the two bits off as a loss and went with them. Joy Pattison joined the party when we met her in the back yard.

According to custom, the performers and white-collar

the winning card slightly so that the sucker thinks he can spot it and is betting on a sure thing. Knowing how the swindle usually worked, the sucker would expect the operator to put it in *another* card.) Then I double-crossed him by replacing the bend in the *same* card! He was all ready to bet when Paper-Collar Ed, who was retrieving the money that other members of the mob had been allowed to win as a come-on, wasn't successful in concealing the fact that he was passing the money back to me. Another sucker saw it, sneaked out, and called the cops. The sucker had a pull, and the police were forced to take action. Ed and I were arrested before I could stop the game and clear out, and then the protection money that had been paid out to the authorities didn't do its work. The magistrate was about to give us a ninety-day sentence when . . ."

workers were seated before the long oilcloth-covered tables at one end of the cookhouse, the workingmen at the other. An excited conversational buzzing arose from both groups. The activities of the troopers had let the cat out of the bag. The Major's murder, Pauline's fall, and the missing lady were being given a thorough going-over.

Merlini said little as he ate, his attention directed at the fragments of talk that floated our way. We were having our coffee when Keith made a belated arrival and announced that the troopers had just started on a search of all the cars and trailers.

"Mac's sputtering about it some," he said. "But not too much. He knows he has to play ball, or this show'll never get off the lot in the morning. Schafer holds the high card there. By the way, Merlini, I hope you and Ross have a full set of ironclad alibis?"

"The Chief still after our heads?"

"Yes. I heard him say that he wouldn't like *any* alibi that you turned in. When I said that you and Ross were with me when the lights went out, he told the Captain, 'So what? The guy's a magician. He could rig up some sort of hocu-pocus that would douse the lights when he was some place else!"

Merlini frowned. "They're concentrating on the alibi situation, then?"

"Looks that way," Keith replied. "And I don't like it at all. The only person who doesn't have a single solitary corroborated alibi—" His voice came to a slow stop, and he scowled angrily at his plate.

"Yes?" Merlini asked.

"Well, it's Joy, isn't it?" Keith looked across at her. Joy's fingers playing with her cheap spoon had bent it into a complete circle. "If they try to arrest her I'll probably go along too, charged with assault and battery. It looks as if someone was fixing it for her to take the rap. I'm going to know who or—"

"No," Merlini contradicted, "I don't think suspicion is being directed at her—if it were, we'd probably have found the rubber gloves planted in her trailer instead of where we did. Besides, you know that the person who doesn't have any alibi at all is usually an innocent bystander, while the murderer always tries to be prepared with one or more nice slick ones."

Joy asked, "But is the Captain going to figure it that way? Sounds a little advanced for the ordinary copper."

"I've a notion," Merlini said, "that Schafer isn't just an ordinary cop; and Hooper, who is, seems to be concentrating on me. Perhaps we'd better run through the alibis once, set them up, and see if we can crack any. Ross, you've been taking notes on this affair, I hope. How do they stand?"

The back of an envelope in my pocket carried a chart with just that information on it. I got it out.

"There are three separate items that call for alibis," I stated. "The Major's murder in his trailer and the subsequent moving of his body to the scene of the phony accident—time: between 10:30 and 11:30 Monday night. Two: the monkey business with the lights that caused Pauline's fall and the swiping of the evidence immediately afterward—time: 9:30-9:45 last night. We can omit for the moment the eavesdropping at the hotel, since we can't prove that person and the murderer are the same. Three—"

"I'll take an exception there, Judge," Merlini said. "We'll discuss it later. Proceed."

"Eavesdropper at the hotel?" Keith wanted to know. "What's this? I hadn't heard."

"Someone snooped around our door," Merlini explained, "and listened to Ross and myself discussing the case after we'd gone to bed last night."

"Oh," Keith said with a flat sound. "That's why you were quizzing me about staying at the Hotel Chesterfield, was it? I see. But if you think that was the murderer, then it lets Joy out, doesn't it?"

Merlini shook his head. "It's not that simple. The desk clerk was in bed. Anyone could have walked in from outside, taken a peek at the register to see what room we had, and put his ear to our keyhole."

Joy looked at the spoon she had now pulled back into something approximating its original shape. "Keith, my boy," she said quietly, "if you and I went into conference with that Justice of the Peace, as you've been suggesting, maybe, next time there's a murder, I'd have a witness to my innocence;

I wouldn't be sleeping alone."

"Sounds like a contradiction in terms," Keith grinned, "but I think I get what you mean." He took a folded paper from his pocket. "I've had this license nearly six months, and because the Major was afraid marriage would interfere with your career, I was beginning to think I'd never get to use it." He stood up and looked at the rest of us. "Who wants to do the honors? We both need a couple of witnesses for this."

"But, Keith," Joy protested, "I've got another show yet tonight. We can't—"

"No you don't, baby. No excuses accepted at this date. Do your show, if you like; but there'll be a wedding between the acts. I'm going to corral a minister and get him here right now." He leaned across the table, kissed her, and reached for his hat.

"No," Merlini objected, "what you'll get is trouble. The Captain has sentries posted and, when they nab you trying to leave the lot, the scene of the wedding will have to be transferred to Chief Hooper's clink. . . . I'd appreciate it if you two kids could restrain yourselves until later. Sit down and help me with these alibis. Weddings are supposed to come *after* the murderer is unmasked anyway. Go on, Ross."

Joy signaled Keith to follow directions. He said, "Well, I'll postpone the match temporarily, but you'll have to work fast." He circumnavigated the table and took a seat beside Joy.

I picked up where I had been interrupted. "Three: innocent parties would do well to provide themselves with an alibi for the time of approximately 7:00 o'clock this morning. The Headless Lady, according to witnesses, drove off the lot in Waterboro shortly after 6:45. I'd say that it should have taken her about fifteen minutes to reach the spot where we found the trailer. That all right by you, Merlini?"

He nodded. "Yes, that sounds reasonable enough."

"The score, then," I went on, "stands as follows: Joy Pattison, as has been mentioned, leads the field, from the cop's angle, with no runs, no hits, no alibis. Difficulty: no witnesses to corroborate her statements as to where she was at the crucial times. Keith Atterbury places second with one alibi. He was talking to us in the Major's trailer when the lights went out, so, unless we assume some mechanical contraption—"

"He doesn't know one end of a screw driver from another," Joy said with emphasis. "I doubt if he knows how to wind a clock. I put a patent bottle opener in his stocking last Christmas along with some Scotch. He'd still be thirsty if he hadn't had help."

"The deposition of the character witness will be filed," Merlini said. "Next."

"Irma King," I replied. "She scores twice if we accept Ed's testimony at face value. She's in the clear on Pauline's fall and on the stolen evidence. But she has a definite black mark chalked up against her by Pauline's assertion that she entered the Major's trailer at just the wrong time. Tex Mayo does better. Three solid-gold alibis. He was working in the concert before a tentful of witnesses when the Major got his; he was in the back yard when the lights went out; and he was busy carrying Pauline out to her trailer when the evidence vanished. Garner ties with him for fourth place, since he also was performing on three occasions. None of the other clowns can swear he was in the sleeping car with them when it made the trip over this morning; that's his only blank. Irma, Tex, and Garner also seem to have another alibi because, barring clairvoyance, they could hardly have been aware last night, when Pauline fell, that any investigation was going on or that any evidence worth swiping had been discovered. Mac says Pauline told no one what had been going on in the trailer, and it's not exactly the sort of thing he'd broadcast. As for Mac's alibis, he's the worst suspect of the lot. Four good alibis without a miss. Calamity was with him on the front door when the Major went West, and en route with him in the ticket wagon this morning. In the matter of the lights and the evidence, he was conversing with Sheriff Weatherby. Of course, if the fix was in . . ."

Farmer shook his head. "Maybe," he said doubtfully. "Fixing a murder rap has been done often enough, but it takes lots of folding scratch. It looks as if you'll have your dukes full cracking any of *those* alibis, Merlini."

"Offhand, I can see three of them that aren't much good," Merlini said. "That isn't the lot, is it, Ross?"

"No. There's Towne, and I think some of my money goes on him. Where has he been when things happened? Nobody's thought to ask him for alibis."

"I have," Keith put in. "I've been doing a little detective work. He doesn't have any. He says he was watching the concert Monday night when the Major was killed—no corroboration offered. He says he was sitting on the blues watching the show when the lights failed last night—still no witnesses that he can produce."

"And he was in the hotel," I added, "when we got up this morning, but that was later than seven by a good bit. With the desk clerk oversleeping as he did, Towne could have gone out earlier and returned. His only gold star is that, so far, he has no apparent motive, whereas all the others have." I paused a moment, then finished, "I've got one other name on the list and I think the rest of my bet goes there. A person with absolutely no alibis at all!"

Merlini looked at me oddly. "Oh, so! A premium in the crackerjack box! Now who—"

It wasn't until considerably later in the evening that Merlini got the answer to that question. The lack of rapid-fire during the past couple of hours was only the lull that preceded the storm. The barometer now began a rapid descent as the sword-swallower, who had gone out a few minutes before, hurried back in. Mac was with him. Swede's Scandinavian stolidness had vanished; his excited jabbering was strangely accompanied by a flock of Latin gestures. Mac's face held a look that was worried even for him.

Swede lapsed with every few words into his native Swedish, so Mac made the announcement.

"One of Swede's swords has disappeared!"

"When?" Merlini asked instantly, his voice startled.

"Yoost now," Swede answered. "It was there when Ay come to eat. Ay go back. It's gone!"

"And it's not one of those dull shivs he sticks down his gullet," Mac added. "It's one of the nice razor-sharp ones he hands out for examination."

"Did you report it to Schafer?" Merlini asked.

"Yeah. He doesn't like it either."

"It's not a comforting occurrence," Merlini admitted.

"Those guards of yours that are casing Pauline's trailer—are they all wide awake?"

"Yes. I added a couple more for good measure. That's the idea I had, too."

"Hmm. I wish I knew if it was the right one!" Merlini glanced at Joy. "If you're doing that ankle-drop tonight, I think I'll personally give your rigging a once-over just before you go on. And all of you better steer clear of dark corners for the time being. Mac, that telegram you have there. For me?"

"Oh," Mac said, "yeah. Boy brought it just now."

As Merlini ripped it open, a bugle call sounded outside. Joy said, "Damn! First call for spec. I'd better get going." She rose and waited a moment as if hoping that Merlini would read his wire aloud; but, when he made no move to do so, she started out. Keith, obviously on the horns of a dilemma, hesitated a moment, and then hurried after her.

"Wait, Joy," he said. "You're going to be supplied with a witness for the duration."

Merlini addressed Mac. "Where's Towne? Seen him?"

"No. Not lately."

"Round him up for me, will you?"

Mac eyed the yellow telegram form. "Got something on him?" he asked hopefully.

"Yes, I have. I'm going to town on Towne."

Mac, brightening a bit at this, hurried out. Swede, still scowling, followed.

Merlini gave me the wire. "We ought to hear something really interesting now—from our detective writer. And we'll hope what he gives us isn't fiction, for a change."

The telegram had been handed in at Mamaroneck, New York, at 5:10 P.M. It was addressed to Merlini, care of The Hannum Circus, Norwalk, N.Y. It read:

"FACT THAT I AM TRAVELING ON CIRCUS NEWS TO ME. THOUGHT ALL THE TIME I WAS HERE. SUGGEST YOU CASH NO CHECKS FOR MY ALTER EGO."

It was signed: STUART TOWNE. NONE GENUINE WITHOUT SIGNATURE.

"So," I said, blinking a bit, "that's why our Mr. Towne doesn't know proofreaders' symbols when he sees 'em. And he's not an ex-convict after all. How'd you know where to locate the real article?"

"I didn't. I wired his publishers, Coward-McCann. Told them a man representing himself to be one of their authors was circulating in this vicinity, and that I had doubts. They passed it along to him."

"You suspected he wasn't the ex-professional thief because he didn't know any of the pickpocket lingo? And you checked up with the proofreader's symbols and the hobo signs?"

"Yes. That and some other things. Remember that the Captain said 'Towne' had a pistol permit? The real Towne couldn't have one—at least none that was legitimately obtained—because he has a felony conviction chalked up against him. And, since the Captain is satisfied, the photo on the permit must match our 'Towne.' And apparently the name that goes with it, though not Towne, doesn't bother the Captain. He knows who 'Towne' really is, and his lack of excitement over the knowledge intrigues me no end."

"I suppose it must," a quiet voice behind us said. 'Towne' stood there, a sober expression on his dark face. He took the red wrapper from a stick of gum which he popped into his mouth. "You're doing all right," he added. "I hunt you up because I've got a confession to make and I discover you're already hep. Takes some of the wind out of my sails."

"Mac find you?" Merlini asked.

"Mac? No, haven't seen him. This is my own idea. Mind telling me where the impersonation fell down?"

"Lack of proper background," Merlini said. "You should have brushed up on the subjects of proofreaders' symbols, hobo signs, and pickpocket argot. You—"

"Proofreaders' signs? Is that what the rest of those hen tracks were in the note you gave me this morning?" Towne frowned. "I guess that point goes to you. I knew the tramp symbols, but I didn't want to admit it at the time. Besides, I didn't see why Stuart Towne should know them—I still don't. Nor the gun talk either. Why would *he* be up on that? Most detective-story authors still use the old-fashioned lingo, and about all they know of that is the word 'dip.' "

"You're not only not Towne, you don't seem to have read many of his books either."

"No, I haven't. Just the last one, *The Empty Coffin* thing. Read it a few nights ago before I started passing them out. But he doesn't—"

"Not so much in that one, no," Merlini said. "He's using a new locale. But in most of his others there's plenty of underworld dope, and it's all the quill—the real thing. If you had read the book reviews or the jacket blurb on his first book, you'd have known that."

Towne gulped and swallowed his gum. "I'll be damned! I'm ashamed of myself. My only excuse is that the impersonation was damned impromptu. Oughta read more, I suppose. You see, when I decided to be an author, I hardly expected to run smack into a couple of mystery-story addicts. Should have pretended I was e. e. cummings, or do you read him, too? I've known I was on damned thin ice ever since you arrived, and the first crack out of the box you started talking about *The Phantom Bullet,* which I haven't read."

"Neither have I," Merlini said. "There isn't any such book, or at least no such title on the Towne list. But you still bother me, Mr. X; you're not the ex-convict and yet you say you do know the gun talk and the tramp signs, though you hadn't realized that you should have admitted it. Could I see that pistol permit you showed the Captain?"

"Uh huh," Towne assented. "High time I ran up my true colors. The pistol permit will do for identification as well as anything."

He took it from an inner breast pocket and tossed it on the table before us.

As he talked, I had been rapidly trying to fit together a deduction or two in the classic Holmes manner and construct a theory as to his identity, or at least his occupation. I had a couple of guesses all formulated, but it's just as well I didn't have a chance to go on record with them. The name on the pistol permit was one that, in all the excitement, I had nearly forgotten.

"Stuart Towne" was our old friend Martin O'Halloran, the private dick who had been tailing Pauline and who had subsequently followed us last Friday evening.

"This is a nice tidy development," Merlini said in a relieved tone. "The O'Halloran loose end has been buzzing about annoyingly in my subconscious. I'm happy to see it gathering itself up. I wired Inspector Gavigan of the New York Homicide Department asking him to send me a dossier on you. No answer as yet. The Inspector's probably up to his neck in a hatchet murder or something of the sort."

"He's *plenty* busy," O'Halloran said. "Haven't you two seen any papers lately?"

"Circus people don't read newspapers. Except when they're in winter quarters, they don't have time. That's been *our* trouble the last few days. Have we missed anything?"

"You certainly have. But I'd better start at the beginning. The reason I was tailing Miss Hannum Friday afternoon—"

Detective O'Halloran's revelations suffered a sudden postponement. At that moment Captain Schafer strode into the tent, moving with that determined steam-roller way he had. His face was grim. Patrolman Crossen, who was with him, was also grim, and in addition somewhat white about the gills.

Schafer's voice was hard. "Tonight seems to be bank night," he said. "We just finished searching all the cars on the lot. In the last one—we found things."

The statement was directed at Merlini, and he stopped there as if waiting for comment.

Merlini raised one eyebrow and said, "Yes? You found something?"

Schafer's square jaw protruded slightly. "I'll say we did. You'd better come look."

A distinctly uneasy feeling settled around me as we followed him out. It was caused by the fact that the Captain and Patrolman Crossen had dropped into step, one on either side of Merlini, and by the fact that they both had their hands on their guns.

We walked the length of the lot past car after car and stopped outside the side-show top at Merlini's car itself. The trunk compartment at the rear was open. Chief Hooper and several other cops stood beside it holding flashlights.

"Don't tell me," Hooper said, "that you've got a nice pat answer for *this*."

He stopped and suddenly jerked away the canvas that

covered the shape on the ground. I saw Merlini's jaw tighten. Slowly he said, "No, Sheriff. I'm afraid I hadn't counted on this."

The girl's body was dressed in blue slacks and a bright yellow sweater. Laid out beside it, I saw a blood-stained rug, a cowboy hat, and a bright two-edged sword with an ornamental hilt.

The body had no head.

Chapter 15

Murder Charge

THIS TIME there was no trick or illusion to it. One quick look at the severed stump of white flesh projecting from the open shirt collar was more than enough. I raised my eyes and kept them up.

Derisively Hooper said, "And I thought you were going to be a tough baby. Not so blamed smart for a city slicker after all, are you?"

"Apparently not," said Merlini. "I should know better than to leave my trunk compartment unlocked, even when it's empty." He turned to the Captain. "Find anything else?"

Schafer regarded him darkly. "This is plenty, isn't it?"

"That depends on the point of view. If you think this proves I'm the murderer, then it's quite a bit. Otherwise not."

Hooper's snort was pure disgust.

The Captain asked, "You aren't going to tell me it means anything else?"

"Afraid I am," said Merlini. "I've been dealt a cold hand. And I'd like to know just how many jokers there are in the deck."

"So that's going to be your angle, is it?" Schafer said truculently. "Yes, I've got more—a damn sight more than I need. The missing photo of the auto smash for one thing, and a couple of suitcases and a hat box full of clothes. The side-show manager says they're the Headless Lady's. There's also a .32 Smith and Wesson automatic."

"Oh?" Merlini said interestedly. "One shot fired, I suppose? And no fingerprints."

"I don't know about the prints yet. You were probably careful about that. The gun's fully loaded and, offhand, it doesn't look as if it had been fired lately. You either cleaned it or used another." Schafer took a forward step toward Merlini. "You haven't got the chance of a snowball in hell, so why don't you spill it? Leibowitz and a dozen more like him couldn't get you out from under *this* rap."

"Did you ever hear that one about appearances being deceptive, Lieutenant?" Merlini smiled a bit wryly. "Someone seems to have given me a good dose of my own medicine. Was there any identification on the body or clothing that tells us who the Headless Lady was?"

Schafer looked at him silently for a moment. Then he said, "You're a cool one, all right. Yes, there are clothing labels from a couple of New York shops. Classy ones. We'll have her name in a couple of hours. That'll give me your motive. Palmer, put the cuffs on him. We'll go into town and have this out."

Palmer slipped a bright steel bracelet around Merlini's right wrist, pulled the ratchet tight, and locked it. The other cuff he snapped on his own arm. Merlini, thoughtfully surveying the objects at his feet, the open trunk compartment, and the car hardly seemed to be aware of the action.

"Do me a favor, Captain," he asked. "Dust my car for prints—around the compartment lid there. I doubt if you'll find any but mine. The person who's responsible for this isn't likely to trip up over anything as primary as fingerprints. Just the same, it's high time he turned in at least one error. His batting average is way too high to last. Even a tight-wire walker takes a tumble once in awhile."

I had just decided it was time I put my oar in when O'Halloran beat me to it, and with the same idea.

"Captain," he said, "don't you think this is all a little too obvious?"

Schafer scowled at him nervously as if the thought had crossed his mind and, though not acceptable, was still a nuisance, "I'll ask you one," he replied. "Why'd he slice her head off?"

"Well—" O'Halloran began uncertainly.

"It wasn't to keep us from identifying her. He'd have ditched the clothes. Even cutting out the labels would have been lots simpler and a helluva lot less gruesome. I know the answer too—he's off his chump. Not enough that he can duck the chair, but just nuts enough to keep a body in the wrong place. They do things like that."

"I think you're wrong there," O'Halloran said, "And, crazy or not, I've got a hunch that if he committed a murder you wouldn't find evidence by the bushel like this. You got enough exhibits here to outfit a complete crime museum. Besides, he wasn't even on the show when the Major had his accident. Or are you figuring someone else for that?"

"No. He'll do."

I did come to bat then, indignantly. "He was with me in Albany eighty miles away Monday night. I told you that."

"Yeah, I know," Schafer said obstinately. "And the two of you were holed up all day working on some manuscript— so you say. You're his only witness. That's why you're coming along to the station house, too."

"Charged with what?" I asked, trying to make it sound confident and having to fake most of it.

"Nothing—yet. You're being held as a material witness. There'll be a charge quick enough—as soon as I get a confession. If you'd like to talk now, it'll save a lot of wear and tear and maybe draw you a couple of years less. I can't make any promises, but I'll see what I can do. How about it?"

Before I could reply that in that case I guessed I'd have to take the full stretch, Merlini spoke. "Mind explaining how I removed the head with that sword when I was in the cook-house all the time it was missing?"

"I been waiting for that," Hooper snapped instantly. "You weren't! You could've swiped the sword. That Swede left the side-show tent a few minutes ahead of you. Maybe you didn't have time to use it, but that don't mean a damn thing. You had already cut her up—with something else. You're playing the sword for an alibi, but it limps like hell!" His voice rose as he demanded, *"What did you do with the head?"*

Merlini's poker face only increased the Chief's irritation, and his calm, unruffled voice added still more fuel to the fire. "When you get your teeth into the seat of someone's pants you hang on like grim death, don't you, Hooper? Very commendable trait. But if I knew where that head was, I wouldn't have a worry in the world. When you do find it, you really will have a case."

"We've got one now," Hooper growled. Then, noticing the crowd that was rapidly collecting around us, he stooped quickly and drew the cover over the body again. "Let's take them in, Schafer," he added. "This is no place to chew the fat."

Schafer nodded and ordered, "Palmer, frisk Merlini and get his car key. Give it to the Chief. He'll see to bringing in the body, and the other stuff and the car. Stevens—"

Merlini turned quickly and said, "O'Halloran, you had a story up your sleeve back there. I'd like to hear—"

"Forget it," Schafer commanded sharply. "You're under arrest if you didn't know it. I'll look after O'Halloran. He's coming, too. I think he's got more story than he gave me this afternoon, and I'm still checking his credentials. Get going, Palmer. Stevens, take Harte and come with O'Halloran in his car. Robbins, you go with them. Chief, have some of your men stick around here and keep an eye on this circus. It doesn't move until I say so, and nobody with it leaves the lot."

As Trooper Palmer started off with Merlini at his side, the latter did something that I think would have convinced the Chief and the Captain more than ever, had they heard it, that he was completely loco. He looked straight ahead at nothing and, as if talking to himself, said in a quick low voice:

"Cop a heap, Farmer, and case the can. I'll light a rag!"

Palmer gave him a puzzled, apprehensive look. Then, as one of the flashlights sent its beam across the crowd that was moving back to let them pass, I saw the faintest ghost of a smile flicker briefly across Farmer's lean face. Promptly, unobtrusively, he edged backward among the others and vanished.

I gathered that the maestro was not going to be caught short without a trick up his sleeve; this was obviously a bit of off-stage preparation. I decided that, once out of the Cap-

tain's clutches, I had better query Columbia University as to
whether their Romance Language Department offered a seminar in advanced Grifter's Argot, and, if so, what the pre-
requisites were. Foreign languages have always been my *bête
noire* (except for a few residual phrases like that one); but if
Merlini was going to make a habit of consorting with underworld folk, it was obvious that I would have to go back and
get more education. "Cop a heap and case the can. I'll light
a rag" might just as well have been idiomatic Sanskrit. It
was nearly as clear as mud.

O'Halloran's car was parked near by, and as we went
toward it he whispered in a low voice, "You and Merlini
may have to spend the night in jail, but I think I can spring
you by morning. I've got some ideas about this case."

"You know who the murderer is?"

"If you'd read the papers the last few days that might not
bother you so much. He—"

"What are you two chewing the rag about?" Stevens, who
had come up behind us, demanded heavily.

Neither O'Halloran nor I made any answer. O'Halloran
got into his car behind the wheel and put his ignition key
in the lock.

Stevens said, "No you don't, Mister. I'll drive. Robbins,
you take the other one in back, and keep your eyes peeled.
If you ask me, these two look suspicious as hell."

Under the circumstances our conversation from there on
didn't amount to much. I saw the Captain's white patrol car
swing in behind us as we left the lot.

We drew up a few minutes later on a quiet elm-shaded
street before a brand-new jail, a hoosegow so neat and fresh
that I looked down the street half-expecting to catch a glimpse
of the masons as they left for home. Although the workmanlike solid construction of the walls and the heavily barred
windows weren't exactly inviting, I was reassured by the
newness of the building because I had had visions of a jerk-
water jail with hot and cold running rats in each cell.

Even the interior hadn't yet attained the official coating
of dust and grime which is standard decoration in jails, court-
rooms and statehouses.

The Captain arrived a moment later, took over the Chief's office and said, "You first, Towne."

Merlini and I remained in an anteroom under the eyes of Troopers Palmer and Stevens and Officer Robbins. Palmer had removed the cuff from his wrist, and Merlini now wore them both. He was practicing his vanishing half-dollar trick and appeared pleased that he was still able to accomplish it though handcuffed. The law eyed him with more suspicion than ever. He vanished the half-dollar for keeps, twisted his arms about, and succeeded in reaching a back pocket from which he drew a deck of cards in a case.

"Palmer," he said, "name a card. Any card in the deck."

Palmer asked, "Why?"

Merlini gave him a startled glance. "Come to think of it, I don't know," he said. "But take a chance."

Palmer scowled, and his tone of voice was the one he saved for humoring nuts. "The Jack of Spades," he said.

Merlini took the cards from their case and started to run through them, backs up.

"I'm not sure why this is, either," he said, "but a magician always does things the hard way. When he wants to find a card he does it by looking at the backs rather than the faces. Sometimes it works."

As he said that, one lone card suddenly showed face up among all the other face-down ones. It was, of course, Palmer's Jack of Spades.

Merlini's audience had started to sit up and take some notice. They sat all the way up a moment later.

"And to show you," Merlini continued, "that I didn't, in spite of these handcuffs, use some sort of invisible sleight of hand to turn that card over as I came to it—to show you that I knew what card you would choose *before* you named it, when I put it in this deck face up the day before yesterday, I used a Jack of Spades from another deck!"

He removed the Jack from among the others and turned it over. The design on its back was red, that on all the other cards was blue.

"That's known to the trade as the 'Brainwave,' an invention of my friend, Dai Vernon. It's a magician's dream."

Palmer and Robbins both had dreamlike expressions on their faces. Stevens did too for a moment. Then, suddenly, he woke up.

"It's a gag," he said deprecatingly. "You had Palmer primed to call for the Jack. You fixed it on the way over."

Palmer's face gave the lie to this; but Stevens, a realistic soul, insisted that it wasn't magic, only a low sort of practical joke.

"I've heard that one before," Merlini countered. "And I know the answer. Suppose you name one, Stevens. Take your time about selecting it, and make it tough as you can for me. While you're doing that I'll discard the Joker. It sometimes causes trouble."

He turned the cards, faces toward himself, went rapidly through them, removed one, and dropped it face down on the floor. Then he waited for Stevens to name his card.

"The four of clubs," Stevens said skeptically, choosing one of the more undistinguished cards in the deck.

Without saying anything Merlini ran through the face-down cards once more. This time none showed up reversed. Stevens grinned.

So did Merlini. "The four of clubs," he said, "is face down like the others. But it's not where you think." He turned up the deck's top card and showed it. *This* is the Joker. The card I pretended was the Joker and discarded *before* you named your card is the four of clubs!"

Using the Joker as a lever so as to avoid touching the card on the floor with his hands, he flipped it over face up. It was, as he had said, the four of clubs. "Never try to outguess a magician," he advised. "If he performs much, he's sure to have met the situation before, and he is consequently prepared for it."

I've seen him do that trick at least a dozen times; it has never failed yet and the cards named are invariably different. I've tried to solve it using bribery and threats; but with no success.

"That's an additional wrinkle of my own," said Merlini. "Here's another."

For the next fifteen minutes, in spite of his manacled condition, he entertained the cops. There was only one interruption. Chief Hooper arrived while Merlini, his hands clasped to his forehead and his eyes tightly closed, was summoning up his powers of clairvoyance in an endeavor to discover what card it was Sergeant Robbins had, while out of the room, secretly selected and sealed in an envelope.

Hooper glowered at Merlini as he went on through to his office. "Watch him closely, boys," he ordered, not knowing that the closeness of attention Merlini had been receiving made him perhaps the most carefully guarded prisoner of all time. As he went through the door, he added, "He's the kind who's likely to try suicide."

"Cheerful man, your boss," Merlini commented, coming out of his trance. "And you're an ornery cuss too, Robbins. You didn't put a playing card in the envelope as I asked. It's a traffic ticket."

A few minutes later a call came from within the office. "Stevens! Bring Harte in here."

Stevens led me up to the lion's cage, shoved me in, and closed the door firmly behind me. The Chief, with his heavy face and his shock of sandy hair, looked remarkably like a lion—and a hungry one. Had he been equipped with a tail, it would have been switching angrily. Captain Schafer was more like a Bengal tiger—ambushed and waiting. There wasn't as much roar to him, but his teeth were just as sharp and when he pounced you knew something had happened.

O'Halloran was still there, and there was another man, a lean little fellow with spectacles who turned out to be the scientific fly in the Chief's ointment, Lester Burns. He began the proceedings by taking my fingerprints. Then he started to get intimate. He asked for my name, address, place of birth, age, sex, color, height, weight, color of eyes, and for any identifying scars or marks.

I told him that I was a female, colored, and had a three-inch scar that hurt me when I sat down. "I had a scissors lock on an F.B.I. agent," I said. "He bit me."

This was not, I well knew, the proper approach for a wild-animal trainer to take, but I was annoyed. I wanted very much to be out there on that showground when what was going to happen next happened—and I could plainly see that my chances were not good.

Schafer said, "All right, Burns; that'll do. Harte, Chief Hooper wants to test out a new rubber hose he has. If you keep that up, I'll let him."

"Sure," I replied. "Go ahead. But when your names hit the news teletypes tomorrow morning, I'll see to it that they're spelled wrong. And *that* won't be all."

The way Hooper jumped from his chair, I thought it must have kicked him. The lion's tail switched in earnest now. "Are you a goddamned reporter?"

"In my spare moments I do little pieces for the papers, if that's what you mean, yes. I've got a Guild card and I usually get a by-line. What's the matter? Have you been bitten too—by a newspaper?"

"Hell!" he said disgustedly and sat down again. His broad fingers nervously hefted the inkwell on his desk; a psychoanalyst would have diagnosed a repressed urge to throw it.

Schafer said, "That complicates matters some, but not as much as you'd like to think. I want some straight answers out of you—now!"

"Shoot," I replied. "But skip the questions you asked this afternoon. The answers you got then were straight—all of them."

The Captain didn't act as if he had heard me. He started in right at the beginning and slowly and carefully worked his way down to date without skipping a thing. He asked all the questions he'd asked before and twice as many new ones. I gave him the same answers as before, though I had to say "No" and "I don't know" and "Okay, I'm lying then" to some of the new ones—too many of them to suit him.

The Chief and O'Halloran listened to the inquisition without speaking. They both scowled a good bit, though not always at the same things. Burns, with a notebook at a desk in the corner, industriously transcribed our talk into rows of little pothooks. He glanced up now and then and fixed me with a bright, beady eye as if I were some new and especially virulent species of bacillus.

The Captain's supply of questions finally gave out. He had obtained very little new information, considering the large amount of expended effort, and his manner was getting harsher by the minute.

"Stevens!" he rapped. "Send in the other one."

As he entered, Merlini dropped his cards into his pocket and asked, "May I smoke?"

"Yes," Schafer growled. "If it'll make you more talkative. Take his prints, Burns."

Merlini drew a cigarette from his breast pocket. O'Halloran started to toss him a paper of matches, but Merlini shook his head.

"No, thanks." He put the cigarette to his lips, inhaled and blew forth a cloud of smoke. The cigarette seemed to be already lighted!

Quickly then, while the Captain and the Chief were a bit off balance, he said, "I'd like to hear that story of yours, O'Halloran. I suspect it's important."

"No," Schafer contradicted. "We're going to hear yours—the revised version."

Merlini let Burns take his fingers and roll them across the inked sheet of glass. "I haven't made any revisions," Merlini said flatly. "I don't intend to."

"Maybe not," Schafer said, "but I think you will. Why did you show up on this circus in the first place?"

Merlini shrugged. "Because, as I've told you, Miss Pauline Hannum took a Headless Lady illusion from my shop under very odd circumstances. I wanted to know why."

"And you found out—?"

"I haven't yet. Miss Hannum hasn't been exactly cooperative. I've got a theory, but there's too much plain and fancy guesswork built into it, so I won't bother you with it yet."

"Merlini"—Schafer's voice suddenly had a knife-edge sharpness—"did you ever hear of Duke Miller?"

"Duke Miller?" Merlini gave a perceptible start. "Yes, of course. Maxie Weissman's lawyer. But what—"

"Oh, you know Maxie? Rather well, maybe?"

Merlini gave him an intent look; then his eyes shifted toward O'Halloran. "I'm completely floored," he said, in what sounded to me like genuine surprise. "What would the Racketeer King and his mouthpiece have to do with me or this case? Is this some of your story, O'Halloran?"

"You're overdoing the surprised innocence," said Schafer icily. "It won't wash. What's your real racket? A magician might be a handy guy to have around to juggle policy numbers or betting odds. You might as well tell us about it."

Merlini made no reply. He stood very still, and I had the feeling as I watched him that inside his head a multitude of little wheels and curiously shaped gears were spinning rapidly in a busy whirl.

The Captain, catlike, extended his claws in a threatening gesture. "Sitting tight won't do you any good," he added. "Inspector Gavigan is coming up here himself with all the dope. We'll have the goods on you as soon as he arrives. You might just as well give."

Merlini looked interested. "You've talked to him?"

"I have. Long distance. Bridgeport, New York. He's on his way now."

"Oh, at Bridgeport, was he? Did he say anything about removing these shackles and letting Harte and myself go?"

"Yes, he did. And you had a nerve this afternoon to tell me he'd vouch for you! He said we were to throw you both into the best cell we had. He's been hunting you ever since Sunday."

If Burns had tried to express in his notebook the speechless looks on both Merlini's and my faces, he'd have had to use a double row of exclamation marks and a colored pencil.

"Blast the man!" Merlini exploded, and followed that with several heated remarks about certain medieval customs that had to do with boiling oil, drawing and quartering, iron boots, the rack, and the thumbscrew.

The Chief, watching Merlini as a young doctor watches his first patient, issued a terse clinical bulletin.

"More homicidal tendencies!"

Chapter 16

Cells for Two

THE CHARACTER or, perhaps better, the lack-of-character reference supplied by our old friend Chief Inspector Homer Gavigan was obviously less than no help at all. Detective Lester Burns, who had disappeared with Merlini's fingerprint card, came back into the room and made a report that didn't improve matters.

"The prints on the trunk compartment lid," he said, "are being photographed now. As soon as I can get them developed and have some enlargements run off I can give you a final report. But I just gave them a quick once-over, and I haven't any doubt that they'll check with these." He indicated the black smudges on Merlini's card. "And there are a couple that fit Mr. Harte."

"Good," Schafer said. "What about that glossy photo of the accident? Any prints there?"

"No. That's clean."

Merlini asked, "Did you make that nitrate test on the gloves, Burns?"

Burns didn't reply, but Schafer said, "Show him."

The detective went to his desk in the corner and came back with several paraffin molds which he placed before the Captain on the blotter. Merlini and I stepped forward to look. O'Halloran and Chief Hooper, the latter somewhat skeptically, did the same.

"I put the gloves on and made paraffin molds in the usual manner rather than apply the reagent directly to the gloves," Burns said, displaying his technical knowledge rather proudly for the Chief's benefit. "Rubber contains some combined nitrate that might, just possibly, react positively and spoil the test." [1]

He had gotten his positive reaction on one of the molds. A dozen or so nitrate specks which the invisible backfire of the gun had deposited on the glove had been lifted off by the mold and now, due to the application of the reagent, showed as blue specks against the milky white paraffin near the crotch of the thumb and along the upper edge of the forefinger.

Merlini looked at the mold a moment, then said, "Funny,

[1] Melted paraffin is dropped over the fingers and hand until a thick coating is obtained. This is slightly reinforced by a thin layer of cotton, which in turn is covered with hot wax. After the paraffin has set, it is cut around the sides and removed in two halves. The resulting negative cast or mold is then tested for the presence of nitrates.

isn't it, that, if I used gloves when I shot the girl and when I handled the photo, I was so careless when I loaded the body and the other stuff into my car?"

"I don't think so," Chief Hooper put in. "In the first place, you'd already given us the gloves to test. And besides, you'd know that if anyone found the body in the car, the lack of fingerprints on the lid wouldn't make a damn bit of difference. You're guilty as hell either way."

"If my prints weren't on the car," Merlini insisted, "I might have an easier time selling you on the idea that someone planted that stuff there. Not much easier, but some."

"No," Hooper contradicted, "not even some."

Merlini fished for some more information. "The glove-wearer fired a shot, all right. But we still don't know if the Headless Lady was shot—or do we? Are there any bullet wounds on the body?"

"The medical examiner is having a look at it now," Schafer answered. "I doubt if he'll find any. I think you got her in the head."

"I hope you're going to make a strenuous effort to find that head."

Schafer nodded. "The boys I left at the lot are doing that, and there's a search in progress where you found the trailer. But you don't really want us to find it, do you?"

"Yes, I do," Merlini said earnestly. "Because once you find it, you'll know that I'm not the murderer. And without it, unless the medical examiner does find some evidence of violent death on or in the body, you or anyone else is going to have the devil's own time proving that she was murdered."

"Now I know you're nuts," the Chief said. "Her head was sawed off, wasn't it? You don't think that was an accident, or suicide, or death from natural causes, do you—for God's sake?"

"The fact that her head was removed certainly doesn't *prove* murder. There was very little blood on either the body or the sword. I think your medical examiner may tell you that the head was removed quite a while after death. My guess would be about twelve hours—death at 7 A.M., head removed at 7 P.M. You *can* prove mutilation of a dead body;

you *can't positively prove* that her death was not accidental, natural, or suicidal."

"It ain't very likely to be one of those, is it?" the Chief said.

"Maybe not," Merlini said. "But 'It ain't likely,' won't be good enough when you get into court. You'll do a lot better if you hunt like hell for that head and hope it'll give you the evidence that *will* prove cause of death."

The Captain reached for the phone. I'm still wondering why the phone's mouthpiece didn't shrivel up or at least blister when he spoke into it. The exchange operator was startled enough so that she gave him his number in record time.

"Byrd," he howled. "What have you done on that autopsy so far?"

We could hear the doctor's voice coming angrily in reply. "For God's sake, man! The body just came in. What do you think I use, a high-speed buzz saw?"

"It'd help," Schafer said. "Are there any surface indications of the cause of death?"

The doctor's voice was sarcastic. "Why, yes," he said. "There's one little thing. Her head's missing."

Schafer glanced at Merlini and spoke again into the phone. "That what killed her?"

"I don't know. Didn't I tell you the body just got here?"

"Well, go look, dammit," Schafer said. "I'll wait."

We all waited. Schafer's left hand played with a pen on the desk and dug savagely with its point into the blotter. Hooper took an angry bite from a plug of tobacco. No one spoke.

Finally the Captain dropped the pen and said, "Yes?"

We heard the doctor's first words. "There is no exterior indication of what caused death. The head was removed several hours after death." Then, more puzzled now than angry, he stopped shouting and the rest of what he said came to us as an indistinct muttering.

In the middle of it Schafer suddenly sat bolt upright and barked. "Say *that* again!"

He listened very briefly; and then, while the doctor's voice still continued faintly, Schafer reached out and slammed the receiver back on its hook. He swiveled around in his chair to face Merlini.

"For a murderer," he said in an awed and baffled voice, "even a batty one, you do some of the god-damndest things. Burns, get me those hair samples I gave you."

Burns at his desk produced the envelope containing the hair combings Merlini had found in the trailer that morning. Schafer hurriedly opened the envelope, tipped the contents out onto a sheet of paper before him, and pulled the gooseneck desk light down close above them. He stared at them a moment, then slowly looked up. "Merlini," he said, "how do I know you found these in that trailer?"

I answered him: "If you look at the envelope you'll see my initials. I was around when he found the hair."

"You see him take them out of the wastebasket?"

"I—" Then I remembered. I had been outside the trailer when Merlini had made the discovery. "Well, no, but—"

"What the hell is this?" Hooper growled. "And what if Harte had seen him? Merlini's a sleight of hand expert. He takes rabbits out of empty hats. He could pretend to take some little wisps of hair out of a wastebasket without any ever having been there. I could get by with that myself. What—"

Merlini went to bat. "Don't you two gentlemen ever look before you leap? Perhaps if you examined the trailer yourself you might find more of the same. I didn't go over the interior with a vacuum cleaner."

"Always got an answer ready, haven't you?" Schafer said belligerently. "What did you do, plant more blond hair around the place?"

Merlini raised an eyebrow. "Oh, I see. It's the blondness of it. Hold your hats, everybody; we're going to do a loop-the-loop. The doctor says the body is a brunette. That it?"

"Yes, dammit, he did! If this case doesn't take the cake—"

"That's mild," Merlini commented. "It gets the bale of blue ribbons and several gross of loving cups. If the clothing labels do identify the brunette corpse, you've still got a blond, vanished, and unknown lady to worry about. We both do, for that matter."

I suddenly caught a curious look on O'Halloran's listening face, something that was almost a smile; but he hastily concealed it. None of the others had noticed.

"Chief," the Captain said, "lock 'em up. This guy will drive me nuts too if I have to listen to him much longer. We'll keep him on ice for Inspector Gavigan and hope he's got something that'll help. And in the meantime we're going to be busy as all hell."

Merlini said, "You're charging me, then?"

"Yes." Schafer eyed him calculatingly. "I won't make it a murder charge until Gavigan gets here and I find out what he's got. For the moment, we'll make it breaking and entering Major Hannum's trailer last night. You picked the lock, you know."

"Won't do, " Merlini objected. "Miss Hannum won't back you up. If she does, I'll prefer a similar charge against her. Besides, it hasn't been established yet that she owns that trailer. Miss King insists that she does. You can't get the owner to prefer a charge until you know who the owner is."

The Captain, however, still held an Ace. He turned to O'Halloran, who stood leaning against the wall at his right. "Merlini picked your pocket yesterday. You're charging him with that. Understand?"

"But I returned his property to him," Merlini said.

"Maybe so," Schafer returned, "maybe not. If you've got any evidence or witnesses to prove it, you can produce them before the judge tomorrow. In the meantime—"

Merlini faced O'Halloran. "Well," he said, "whose side are you playing on?"

O'Halloran took his cigarette from his mouth and tapped the ashes into a tray on the desk. He gave Merlini a wink as he did so and crossed the first two fingers of his right hand, which was on the side away from Schafer, but visible to us.

"I can't help myself very well, can I?" he answered.

I decided then to make a last stand myself. "You aren't locking me up as a material witness without a court order," I stated.

Schafer said, "A sea lawyer, eh? Okay, then I'll get one. Hooper, get Judge Ewing on the phone."

As the Chief reached for the instrument, Merlini took a step forward, gave me a dig in the ribs with his elbow and said, "I guess he wins this round, Ross. Come on. Let's see your dungeon, Hooper."

Hooper put the phone down. He and Stevens started to take us out. Schafer said, "Don't forget those picklocks of his, Chief. Inspector Gavigan said it would be a good idea to strip them both. He says Merlini knows how to escape from packing boxes that have been nailed up and dumped in the river."

Hooper snorted. "*This* jail ain't no packing box. He'll find that out."

The prospect of jail hadn't bothered me much until I heard this. I'd figured that Merlini might be able to roll up his sleeves and pass a minor miracle that would circumvent the stone walls and iron bars. I was beginning to have doubts, and in a few moments I had more of them.

If Merlini was bothered, however, he pretended not to show it. As our guides ushered us into the jail proper, he said lightly, "I'd like a nice roomy cell with a southern exposure, please."

"You'll take what you get," Hooper growled. "And none of the cells have any windows, so if you're thinking of sawing your way out, forget it. Every bar in the place is case-hardened steel, and if I gave you a hacksaw you'd still be trying six months from now."

The cells, a dozen barred steel cages, were arranged in two rows on either side of a corridor within the cell-block that ran the length of the long cement-floored room. Another exterior corridor, ten feet wide, completely circled the cell-block, so that it was a steel-ringed island completely isolated from the outside walls. There were a half-dozen smallish windows in one wall, but from the interior of the cell-block they were completely inaccessible, and the grating of thick, close-set bars that crossed them looked distinctly formidable.

Hooper opened the door of an electrical control box on the wall and pulled a switch. "Each cell has its own individual lock," he said proudly. "And this switch operates an additional bolt on all the cells simultaneously, double locking them. Your arms are plenty long, but they'd have to be about ten feet longer yet to get at this switch. A ghost couldn't get outta here unless I let him."

"Very nice," Merlini commented. "And you don't believe in ghosts, I suppose?"

Hooper didn't think that merited an answer. He took a ring of keys from Stevens and fitted one in the lock of the single door that opened into the cell-block corridor. "We'll put Merlini in Cell Two with Harte across from him, well out of reach of that switch even if they had a twenty-foot pole, but in sight of the door so I can look in now and then and keep an eye on them." He turned to Merlini. "I guess we can take them cuffs off now."

As Stevens removed them, Hooper added, "And your duds too. Peel them off."

"All of them?" Merlini asked.

"Yeah, you ain't too modest, are you?"

"I'm very susceptible to colds, Chief," Merlini replied. "And, warm as the weather is, these cells are built so as to allow the maximum number of drafts. If one of your prisoners dies of pneumonia you'll have a newspaper scandal on your hands. What's more, I'll come back and haunt you."

"Stop jabbering and undress. Stevens, there are a couple of old uniforms in the locker room. Have Robbins get them. They won't fit so well, but these guys aren't going any place."

The Chief investigated the pockets of Merlini's clothes as they came off. He found, among other things, a couple of decks of cards, a red and a green silk handkerchief, several vari-colored thimbles, a spool of black silk thread, and two or three queer-looking gadgets of an indeterminate nature.

"Lunatic," Hooper said. "If you get violent you can try our padded cell. First chance I've had to use it." Then he found a key ring that held a dozen oddly shaped angular bits of metal—the picklocks. "That's that," he grinned. "I'll let Burns add these to the Crime Museum he's collecting."

"Not unless they execute me," Merlini objected. "I want those returned when I leave here. Some of those picks are collector's items. They were once Houdini's."

"Okay," Hooper said. "*If* you leave."

"Any objection if the condemned men keep their cigarettes?" asked Merlini, indicating his pack of Camels and a cigarette lighter the Chief had taken from his pockets.

Hooper looked at him suspiciously, carefully examined the two articles in question, and then handed them over. "I guess not," he said, and, turning, gave my discarded clothes equal attention. When we had completely disrobed, he eyed us both inquisitively as if he were making sure that neither of us were equipped by nature, like kangaroos, with pockets in our skins.

Merlini, however, was irrepressible. As he got into the uniform which was none too adequate for his lanky figure, he sang lightheartedly,

> *"When I first put this uniform on,*
> *I said, as I looked in the glass,*
> *It's one to a million*
> *That any civilian*
> *My figure and form will surpass."*

Hooper, satisfied but wary, ushered us into our respective cells and locked the doors behind us himself.

The metallic clang of my door as it closed and the shooting over of the heavy bolt were final, irrevocable sounds that were anything but reassuring. Chief Hooper's satisfied smile was even less so.

He and Stevens went out through the cell-block door; and, as Stevens was locking that, Hooper threw the switch in the wall. I heard the extra bolts click over solidly all down the line.

Hooper gave us a last malevolent grin and then went out. He slammed the door behind him.

Chapter 17

Fond Farewell

> *Warders are ye?*
> *Whom do ye ward?*
> *Bolt, bar, and key*
> *Shackle and cord,*
> *Fetter and chain,*

Dungeon of stone,
All are in vain—
The prisoner's flown!

Spite of ye all, he is free—he is free!
Whom do ye ward? Pretty warders are ye!
                    —YEOMEN OF THE GUARD.

THE COT in my cell was a wooden shelf with a leather-covered mattress on it. I sat down and lit a cigarette. Then, for the first time, I noticed that we had company. Further down the line of cells toward the rear of the cell-block, two cells were occupied. One held a heavy-set, blue-jowled individual whose round bulbous nose shone like a red danger signal. I guessed that he might be the town drunk. He stood at the door of his cell watching us interestedly. The other man, lying on his cot, also regarded us, half-raised on one elbow. His languid posture, his sleepy drawling voice, and his ill-kempt clothes suggested a knight of the road who was doing his thirty days for vagrancy.

Weary Willie, when he saw me light up, asked, "How about a smoke down this way, buddy? We ran out a coupla days back and we're both too flat to buy more."

I took two cigarettes from my pack, put my arm between the bars and pitched them one at a time down the corridor. They managed to reach them and snake them in. I looked across at Merlini, who was absorbed in an examination of the lock on his cell door.

"What I can't understand," I told him, "is why you didn't shuck those handcuffs long ago and make a break for it instead of waiting until we landed in this pocket edition of Alcatraz. Don't tell me the Chief has a new style of cuff that you can't beat?"

"No," he answered. "They were a cinch. But I didn't want to impress our hosts with any escape tricks too soon. They might have made it really inconvenient."

I stared at him. "Inconvenient? Don't look now, but we seem to be pretty completely surrounded by case-hardened steel bars and an electrically controlled double-lock system. Even if you still had your picklocks and could beat that first lock on your door, you'd still have to project some ectoplasm or something to reach that wall switch that controls the other bolt. It's a good twenty-five feet from us both and ten feet outside the cell-block itself."

"But it could be worse. Hooper might have left Stevens in here to watch us. About the only way out then would have been to hypnotize him, and he doesn't look like a particularly good subject."

"We're so lucky!" I said. "That leaves us three or four ways out, I suppose."

"Well, it leaves one good one at least, and we're taking it. I've got to get a look at those newspaper stories O'Halloran has been jabbering about. I want to know what Maxie and the Duke have to do with this case. Somehow I don't like not knowing. It's something Gavigan apparently doesn't want us messing around in. And I want to mess. If I don't, and quickly, the devil might find more work for the murderer's idle hands to—" Abruptly he stopped, gave me a queer, thoughtful look and added, "Idle hands—idle hand— Ross, *that* does it!"

"Does what? Get us out of here?"

"It tells me my hunch about the murderer's identity is correct. I think we'd better go away from here right now."

"Good," I cracked. "After you, Gaston."

Merlini all this time had been fiddling with the lock on his door. He fiddled a moment longer, then suddenly straightened up and said, "Okay, Ross, I'm set. Now do exactly what I tell you and don't argue. We're in a hurry. Take this cigarette lighter"—he scaled it across the floor and under the bars into my cell—"rip that mattress cushion on your cot a bit, light the kapok inside, and as soon as you have a fair blaze, holler, 'fire.' And rattle your tin cup against the bars. That's the customary prison etiquette."

I would have agreed then that Hooper was right and that Merlini was off his chump except that I'd heard him issue cockeyed orders before—orders that later proved fairly sensible. I obeyed.

Our jailmates down the way watched me wonderingly. Red-nose said, "Hell, those two have gone stir-bugs already."

Weary Willie said, "Look like a couple of dope-hops to me." [1]

When I had fanned up a little blaze and a good deal of smoke Merlini said, "That's fine. Your story is that you dropped your cigarette. Now turn in the alarm."

I sang out and got action immediately. The very thought of fire in his nice new jail brought Hooper on the double-quick, and nearly everyone else—the Captain, O'Halloran, Stevens, and others.

Hooper fumbled and swore at the lock on the cell-block door. As he got it open and came on the run toward me, he yelled, "Somebody throw that switch, for Christ-sake!"

Stevens reached it, and a moment later Hooper pulled my door open. Robbins ran in with a sloshing water bucket and threw the contents on the cot. Hooper poured a lavalike flow of language at me that was so blistering I was afraid it would touch off a much larger conflagration. I wondered if Merlini was hoping that the Chief's wrath would melt the bars off the cell. It nearly did.

"You'd better throw another bucket of water on the Chief," I told Robbins, "before he goes up in smoke."

"We've got a charge on *you* now, Harte," Schafer said. "Willful destruction of county property. Laugh that off."

Hooper relieved me of the cigarettes and the lighter, placed me in the next cell down the line, and slammed the door angrily. This time the sound seemed more irrevocable than ever.

Merlini, standing close against the bars of his cell door, watched us and made no comment. Hooper gave him a piece of his mind in passing, for good measure. He relocked the cell-block door and threw the switch. Then, with the others, he went out again, still muttering.

"Well," I said then, "here we are again. Why didn't you do whatever it was you had in mind?"

"I did," Merlini said quietly.

He pushed gently at the door of his cell. It opened and he stepped out.

He went immediately to the cell-block door, thrust his hand

[1] Stir-bugs: Prison crazy. Dope-hop: Drug addict. (Prison argot.)

between the bars and, from the outside, inserted an angular buttonhook-shaped probe into the lock's heyhole.

"Where the devil did you hide that picklock?" I asked, my mouth ajar. "Swallow it?"

"No. When we first came in I took a good look at these locks. They're Courtney-Brema Company's latest model. Then, my hand in my pocket, I slipped the picklock I figured I'd need off the key ring and palmed it. Perhaps you've noticed that all my picks have a small sharp hook on their upper end. There's a reason. While we were undressing I edged up near Hooper, used a little primary misdirection to keep his eyes front, and hung the picklock on the back of his coat. It's slender and black and wouldn't have shown up much against his dark-blue uniform even if he had turned around. When he ushered me into my cell I lifted it again. I used the Chief himself as a gimmick. It's a simple dodge and an old one. It's highly recommended and endorsed by leading professionals in *Jail, Bank-Vault, and Underwater Escapes,* issue number 16 of my dollar booklets, 'The Strange Secrets Series.' "

"Stop advertising," I said. "What about that electrically controlled double lock? I saw the Chief throw the switch." I glanced at the door of Merlini's cell. The heavy switch-controlled bolt was projecting in the locked position. In opening his door, Merlini had apparently caused solid steel to pass through solid steel!

The cell-block door opened as I spoke, and Merlini went quickly to the wall switch and pulled it down. The bolts on all the cells slid back. He returned and got to work on the individual lock on my cell.

"I had my door unlocked, except for the electrical device," he explained, "before you called Hooper in with your fire alarm. As soon as Stevens threw the switch I was free of my cell. When they left, and just as Hooper reached up to throw the switch again, I pushed my door open half an inch. The bolt on my door slid over without engaging. Hooper's clink would be a mite harder to leave if that cell-block door was on the electrical hookup too. Courtney-Brema Company gave him short weight."

Merlini's attack on my lock was swift and sure. As he

finished his explanation, the door swung wide and I stepped out into the corridor with him.

From down the corridor a voice said, "Say, old-timer, don't forget us."

"I haven't," Merlini said, going toward them. He began to work on Weary Willie's door.

"You're a right gee," that gentleman said appreciatively. "This is really swell of you."

"Don't jump to conclusions," Merlini replied. "You aren't going far. Just down to my cell. You and your friend are going to take our places so that if the Chief gets nosy as he promised, he'll think we're still here and sleeping. Keep under your blanket and keep your faces out of sight. He may not notice your absence because right now *we're* on his mind almost exclusively."

"Yeah? Do we look like chumps? If you don't take us with you, we'll sing out right now. His Nibs might give us a few privileges if we prevented a couple of big-shots like you two from lamming. He might even fix it so's our lags were cut." [2]

"Well," Merlini said, "you know him better than I do. But I doubt that. He's more likely to throw you into solitary for life so you won't be able to spread the news that it's so easy to cop a sneak out of his pride and joy of a jail. Besides, if you boys play ball it will be worth a double-saw apiece. That'll fix you up for smokes and a few other luxuries. Ten now and ten later if you keep him thinking we're still here as long as you can get away with it."

Rednose was interested but skeptical. "Yeah, but if you get out, what the hell would you be coming back for? How'd we get that other ten?"

"I'll be back. If not, I'll mail it. You'll have to take a chance there. Though if the Sheriff has anything to say about it, I won't be gone long. He wants me for *murder*." Merlini put the word in verbal italics.

Our friends looked at each other uneasily. This was out of their class.

Willie said then, "Okay. You're the boss. I'd sorta like to

[2] Lags: Sentences.

stick around to see dribble-puss' face when he discovers
you've crashed outta his nice, shiny new can."

Quickly Merlini transferred the men to our cells and began
locking them in.

"Why bother with that?" I asked. "If we just throw the
switch that'll be enough."

Merlini shook his head. "You've no feeling at all for the
finer points of jail breaking, Ross. We must emulate Colonel
Fairfax in *The Yeoman.*

> *"Of his escape no traces lurk!*
> *Enchantment must have been at work!"*

"Much more artistic. Maybe Hooper *will* believe in ghosts
then. That is, he may, if we can get the rest of the way out
without being seen. The tough part is still to come. There's
only one way—out the front door, and we've got to—Ross!
Quick! Someone coming."

I had heard the footsteps, too. I ran for the door on my
toes, making as little sound as possible. I got there just as
it opened. Robbins' astonishment was all that saved us. My
haymaker arrived in the nick of time—just as his mouth opened
and the warning cry rose in his throat. The punch landed
square on the point of his chin; his jaw closed with a sharp
dental click; and Merlini, arriving as though it had been re-
hearsed, caught him as he fell.

"I was afraid we were having it too much our own way,"
Merlini said. "Now we are in for it. They'll be looking for
him when he doesn't come back and, even if we do get out,
we won't have any time to ourselves at all. There's only one
thing to do. Take his feet."

We carried Robbins into cell number three and laid him
out on a cot. Merlini relieved him of his gun and moved back
toward the outer door again. "I'm afraid we won't leave a
mystery behind us after all," he said. "It's going to be only
too obvious to Hooper how we—"

More footsteps approached the door from the other side.
When it swung open, Hooper was saying, "Robbins, just in
case that magician still has any funny—"

"—ideas about escaping," Merlini's voice finished for him.

"Sorry we must be going, Chief. We've had a lovely time, but it's getting late. Take his gun, Ross."

Even without the gun I don't think I'd have needed to give Hooper a sock on the jaw to quiet him. The very sight of us was having all the effect of a mule kick.

"Now, Hooper, if you'll just ask Captain Schafer and Stevens to step in here, I think we can handle the rest of the boys two at a time. And careful of your voice."

Since he thought Merlini was a murderer and crazy to boot, he was far more impressed than I would have been at the sight of Merlini's gun. The Chief didn't know that Merlini had a positive dislike for firearms of any sort, and had no intention of actually using one now.

He gulped a bit, got his vocal chords under control, and called out as directed.

"Thanks," Merlini said. "This way, Chief. You watch the door, Ross."

Hooper started a protest, but Merlini cut him off. "No arguments. March!"

The Chief's expression was a really interesting sight. Baffled bewilderment and griping rage played across his face like the shifting flicker of an Aurora Borealis. His face, also like the northern lights, was green, and I hoped fervently that when the incandescent gases that were beneath its surface finally erupted I would be miles away.

Merlini's attitude wasn't calculated to soothe the Sheriff much. He was humming Captain Spalding's song from *Animal Crackers*.

> *"Hello! I must be going.*
> *I came to say—I cannot stay;*
> *I must be going.*
> *I'm glad I came,*
> *But just the same*
> *I must be going."*

Merlini put Hooper in a cell and I threw the switch. Then the Captain and Stevens arrived together. Expressions exactly similar to the Chief's blossomed on the faces of everyone who walked through that door in the next few minutes.

I collected a couple more guns; Schafer called and kindly decoyed his two troopers and the remaining three of the Chief's men into our trap; we filed them all neatly away.

Merlini told Schafer, "I'm sorry about this. You can blame Inspector Gavigan. If he hadn't double-crossed me I wouldn't have needed to take such extreme measures. Is O'Halloran still around?"

"No," Schafer snapped, "he's gone. And if you think you can get away with this—"

"Let's go, Ross," said Merlini. "But quietly. I don't trust the Captain much."

We had nearly reached the door of the Chief's office, when hell broke loose in the cell-block behind us. Quickly Merlini kicked in the Chief's door. O'Halloran stood at Hooper's desk, examining the paraffin molds Burns had made, his back toward us. He pivoted instantly, and, in turning, started to say, "What's all that racket out—"

Then he saw Merlini's gun and his eyes narrowed.

"Don't move your hands, O'Halloran," the latter commanded. "Give me his gun, Ross."

O'Halloran was as puzzled as the others, but as I went toward him he laughed. "All you need is a cutlass between your teeth, Ross. I'll be damned!"

I'm afraid I did look rather like Sir Henry Morgan preparing to repel boarders. I had a .45 in each hand and two more tucked into my belt. I transferred one to my coat pocket and took O'Halloran's .32 and passed it to Merlini.

"I collect firearms too," I said. "Official police weapons mostly."

"How the hell did you get loose?" O'Halloran asked. "And what did you do to Hooper? That sounds like his bellow out there."

"It is," Merlini said. "He, most of the Norwalk police department, and a detachment of state troopers are signed up for a little night course in applied penology. Class won't be dismissed for some time yet, I hope. To make sure of that, we've got to do something about you. You can either join them or sign articles with us. Which will it be?"

"You do things up brown, don't you?" O'Halloran said, regarding us thoughtfully.

"It's my favorite color," Merlini replied. "Make up your mind. We're getting out of here before something else delays us."

"What are you going to do?"

"I'm going back to that circus lot and polish off some unfinished business before I get tangled up in more official red tape. You're getting an invite to go along because I want that story of yours. What about it?"

O'Halloran grinned. "Let's go," he said, starting for the door.

The angry roaring from the cell-block outside reminded me greatly of the Bronx Zoo at feeding time.

O'Halloran added, "Boy, oh, boy! I hate to think of what will happen when Hooper, Schafer & Co. catch up with us. I hope you'll remember that I came with you because I had no choice. You sure you haven't bitten off more than you can digest, Merlini?"

"I don't know." Merlini was trying on a uniform cap that lay on Burns' desk. "I expect there'll be signs of a stomach ache. But if we can bring back the real murderer, Hooper and Schafer will have to take it and like it."

"I warn you, he won't take anything less than that. You two have chalked up a whole damn police blotter full of offenses; and, if you wear those uniforms out of here, they'll jump you for impersonating an officer. But"—O'Halloran paused—"I'll give odds of two to one that you pull it off."

"You will?" Merlini asked. "Why?"

"Because," O'Halloran smiled, "I'll make you a present of the murderer. I know who he is! I've got this case on ice!"

Chapter 18

Headless Man

MERLINI'S FACE didn't wear the dismayed look I half expected. Instead he said, "That's fine. I'm glad to hear that there's one detective in the immediate vicinity who doesn't think that I'm the culprit. Now, let's blow before we meet someone else we'll have to lock up. We'll hear your story on the way."

"Okay," O'Halloran agreed. "Can I have my gun now?"

"No. I'll keep it for the moment just in case you should get the urge to revert to the side of law and order. I don't want to see any more jails tonight. They slow me up. Come on."

As we left the building O'Halloran said, "My car's right here."

"Our transportation," Merlini replied, "is all arranged for. You can get your car later." Rapidly he led us down the street to where a Ford sedan was inconspicuously parked a block away. There was a man at the wheel.

Merlini's appearance as an officer of the law wouldn't have won him any commendations at police inspection; too many extra inches of wrist and ankle projected from beneath his uniform's inadequate coverage. But this unnatty appearance wasn't greatly noticeable in the darkness; and, in any case, the bullying, officious voice he suddenly assumed more than made up for it.

"You can't park here," he said sternly to the figure in the car. "I'll have to give you a ticket."

Farmer's voice answered, "Now listen, Officer—" Then at Merlini's chuckle he stopped. "Oh," he said, "it's you. What kept you so long? You must be slipping."

"We were busy delaying the pursuit," Merlini explained. "The showground, James."

As we piled in, I said, "I'm beginning to get it now—or part of it. *Case the can* means 'watch the jail,' and *I'll light a rag,* I suppose is 'I'll escape.' But what's the translation of *cop a heap?*" [1]

"The verb *cop* means to take. Some people might call it stealing. A *heap* is a car. O'Halloran, start talking."

"Okay," O'Halloran said. "Here's where you find out who your Headless Lady was. I'd better go slow, start way back at the beginning and break it to you gradually. Three weeks back a couple of gorillas walked into Maxie Weissman's country hide-out near Bridgeport and let a lot of daylight through him with Tommy guns. You know that. What wasn't in the

---

[1] Light a rag actually means: to leave. Synonymous with *cop a sneak, take a powder, lam.*

papers was the fact that Maxie's pals, mainly his mouthpiece, Duke Miller, and Bo Lepkewitz started scrapping about who was going to take over. In the mixup, somebody with an ax to grind spilled a lot of first-class beans in the D.A.'s ear. He had himself a picnic. He had Judge Commager and Judge Parton busy issuing warrants in shifts. But they needed just a little more than what they had to really pin down the big shots. They figured that the right kind of pressure on the Duke would do the trick, but he got a tip-off and turned up missing just as they reached for him.

"The Crime Prevention Association and the Merchant's Bureau put up rewards that added to ten grand. The agency business hasn't been too hot lately, so I thought maybe I could, with luck, cut myself a piece of that. When the D.A. found the Duke had gotten off the hook, he got Inspector Gavigan assigned to special duty and they got busy. First thing they did was put tails on Paula Starr."

I groaned. "So that's it. Paula Starr, café society's darling. El Algier's acrobatic dancing sensation, Broadway's cutest nudist. The Duke's gal friend. And you're going to tell us that she—"

"Is Pauline's sister, Paulette Hannum; that she was the Headless Lady; that she's not only the Duke's girl friend—they've been married for five years; and that Duke Miller is the ex-circus legal adjuster, Andy Meyers, that she eloped with. You begin to see light?"

"The dawn came up like thunder," I said. "But what—"

"Ross," Merlini cut in impatiently, "shut up and let him talk. Gavigan's men were tailing Paula, hoping that she'd contact the missing Duke. Then what?"

"Well," O'Halloran went on, "I hung around her apartment some, too, looking for a break. Last Friday I got it. Paula left her apartment in the East Fifties and ankled into the classiest eating joint on Park for lunch. One of the city dicks, Mike Brady, followed her in, flashed his shield, and got a table in the corner and a glass of water. The cover charge alone in that place almost runs into three figures, and if he'd ordered anything more than water Fiorello would have started an investigation. That was where I had the edge on him. I took a chance, pushed in enough blue chips to buy me meals for a week, greased the headwaiter with a fin, and got a table next to hers. So, when it happened, I was close enough to get something Mike missed. I caught her giving the wink to another dame a couple of tables away. What made me sit up and take notice was the fact that they looked a hell of a lot alike. The other gal wasn't the 14K looker that Paula was, but she'd get by all right. The main thing was I had a hunch that kept getting stronger all the time that they were sisters. Then what happens but Paula gets up and heads for the nearest ladies' can and a minute or so later the other gal does the same. It was a smart dodge—Paula knew Mike was tailing her, and she knew he couldn't follow her in there, not unless he was carrying a disguise kit with a wig and a set of skirts in it, like these pulp-magazine dicks do.

"I was damned sure now that the lunch money I'd risked was going to pay off, and when Paula left with the boys after her, I hung around and gave attention to sister. You know what happened then. It was Pauline, and she ends up at your shop and disappears on me. I still want to know what happened. Secret passageway you have built in, I suppose?"

"No," Merlini replied. "She got a glimpse of you and left via the fire escape. Then you followed us, thinking we were Duke Miller in disguise, probably."

"Well, I admit I didn't know what the hell to think. If you were friends of the Duke's you were new ones on me. But he had funny friends. And anyway, all I could do was check on you. I followed you downtown to the Square, and then I phoned one of my men and, when he took over, I went back to the office and started checking on sister. She'd made a stop at Billboard Magazine before coming up to your place, so I phoned there and found out that she'd come in to pick up some mail, that her name was Pauline Hannum, and that she was with the Hannum Circus, which was showing in Bridgeport the next day. The first names, Paula and Pauline, clicked; and I knew damn well they were sisters and had had a conference in the ladies' room and that something was on the fire. I figured this could be the contact with the Duke, and I decided to make tracks for the circus. And then that night, while you two were driving up from Albany, hell busted loose."

"Your man was still tailing us?" Merlini asked.

"Yeah. He stayed on until Sunday when I called him off. He'd been sending in some of the dizziest reports about a convention of crackpots you were attending. What made him sure you were all fresh out of a loony house was when some guy‚ who had been talking to you marched over and calmly cut off most of his necktie with a pair of scissors. Anyway, it didn't sound much as if you were tied up with the Duke, so I called him off."

"That joke," Merlini said wryly, "seems to have turned and bitten me. If the O'Halloran Detective Agency had only decided I was a more sinister character, you'd have kept the man on and Ross and I would have had a witness to the fact that we were in Albany when the Major was killed."

"Teach you a lesson, maybe," O'Halloran said. "And you owe me two bucks. My man put the cost of the tie on his swindle sheet. What the hell was the gag anyway?"

"Swindle sheet is right," Merlini replied. "The tie came off Gimbel's dollar counter. I had just sold a customer a trick pair of scissors with only one blade. Magicians use them for a laugh, handing them to a spectator who's assisting on stage and asking him to cut the rope the performer will later restore again. The scissors look all right and sound all right, but they don't cut. I demonstrated them, and then, because my customer was a little tight and I suspected he'd go right to work with them, as a joke I secretly switched them for a good pair. And he cut the tie that was worn by the dick that worked for O'Halloran who called him off and left me without an alibi on account of which I landed in the jail that the Chief built!"

"And now," I objected, *"you're* delaying the next installment. What happened while we were driving to Albany Friday night? You said hell broke loose."

"Paula Starr," O'Halloran explained, "dusted the D.A.'s men off her tail with a vanishing trick of her own. Those two gals should be billed as the Vanishing Twins. That half-dollar of yours doesn't do any better. She popped in at the stage door of El Algiers a few minutes before her act was due on. Knowing she'd be busy giving the customers an eyeful for the next twenty minutes or so, the boys relaxed a bit. And

Paula dolls herself up in an ermine wrap and a prop tiara, picks up Tommy Mannering at the bar for color, and slithers out the front door as if she was the current No. 1 glamour girl. She had her nose so high in the air even the news photographer out front who got a shot of them didn't realize who it was until he'd developed his film. She led Mannering to the Crystal Club, knowing that the powder room there has two entrances. Powder rooms seem to be her specialty. Mannering hasn't seen her since, except in the papers. Saturday morning every sheet in town had her publicity leg art all over the front pages—those they could run and still send the edition through the mails. In the tabloids, you couldn't see the war for cheesecake. Here"—O'Halloran pulled a clipping from his pocket—"this is a sample of the text that went with 'em."

He shoved it at me and I read it aloud.

WILBUR WILTON
ON THE MAIN STEM

COPS AND ROBBERS

We knew it would happen. The Dicktracys from the D.A.'s office are still holding the sack down at El Algiers, cafe society's smartest hotspot. Duke (Ten Grand) Miller's ever loving mamma, Paula Starr, the Nightspot Queen, topped her near nude dancing routine with the neatest trick yet when she turned her beauteous self inside out and disappeared as completely as vaudeville. . . . Chief Inspector Gavigan invented some new cuss words (naughty naughty) and transferred two not so bright-eyed sleuths to the back side of Staten Island.

The boys have been living in hopes our Paula would lead them to the missing Duke, the liquidated Maxie Weissman's hotshot mouthpiece. She had been stripteasing the force for three weeks, and, just when they decided to pinch her (!) and find out what she was hiding, she does a fadeout. . . .
The D.A. had kittens all up and down Centre Street—the cutest things!

Tommy Mannering, nitery addict and blond fiend, was also stood up. Rumor has it that he is still waiting outside the powder room at the swank Crystal Club, and there is some talk of applying gilt and keeping him on as a permanent exhibit. . . . Your correspondent also hears that the Duke was the finger man in the matter of his boss' late demise via the Chicago typewriter route with Bo Lepkewitz cast as the trigger man.

Things we won't know until tomorrow: How does Paula hope to hide the phiz that launched a thousand champagne buckets? . . . Has she joined the Duke, and where? . . . What happened to Maxie's do-re-mi, and why have two of Gavigan's pet gumshoes been living at Bridgeport in the house where Maxie got it in the neck? . . . And will the D.A. recover?

I'll be seein' yah!

When I had finished, O'Halloran added, "Wilbur is still wondering how Paula expected to be able to hide out without being recognized. Her face has been on the cover of every picture magazine in town more than once, and a couple of years back she was in Hollywood. Her shape had so much oomph that it took the producers three pictures to find out she couldn't act. But as soon as I hit the show I knew the answer. Somebody was using his head and she was minus hers. She was the Headless Lady. And when she was off duty and had a head, she wore blinders, and—"

"And," Merlini interrupted, "she'd done a color change from brunette to blonde. She'd bleached her hair. Why, if you told Schafer this story, was he so upset when he discovered the corpse was a brunette?"

O'Halloran said, "I'm afraid I didn't tell the Captain everything. I told him I was following a hunch of my own on the Duke. I told him I'd discovered he used to be with a circus, and I thought it was this one. Now I know where the Duke is; and, after all the spade work I've done, I don't see why Schafer and Hooper should reach out and grab a fistful of that reward."

"The Duke, then—" Merlini started.

"Now wait," O'Halloran objected. "Let me get on with my story. I found Paula, and then I discovered that the show's route had been juggled around, that nobody seemed to know why, and that they all thought it looked queer. Knowing what

I did, I thought I saw some sense in it. The show has been heading in one hell of a hurry for Canada. By the quickest route; that explains the long jumps and the fact that they've been dating some towns that are way too small. It looked a hell of a lot as if the Duke might have gotten out of the country; and that Paula, with her Dad's help, was on her way to join him. I decided to tag along, nab him when she connected, and collect the reward. But it didn't pan out that way. Next thing I knew the Major dies in what everyone thinks is a car smash. Then you two guys show up and things really do begin to happen."

"You didn't suspect the accident was a phony?" Merlini asked.

"No. Why should I? I wasn't interested in the Major particularly. I was busy keeping both eyes on the Headless Lady. But your arrival had me worried. I'd discovered that circus people practically never look at a newspaper and that Paula, with a little care getting to and from her trailer, could probably pull it off and reach the Duke in Canada before she was recognized. When you showed up I wasn't so sure. I didn't know that you two hadn't read the papers either. And I was still wondering what Pauline had gone to your place for. I see now I should have figured it was the Headless Lady apparatus, but at the time I didn't get it. So I gave you some attention, hoping you'd drop a hint that would give me a lead.

"You ducked out on me after we had seen Pauline and Joy do their tight-wire act, and so I trailed along in the background, keeping my eyes and ears open. I saw you meet Keith, overheard part of what he told you about his suspicions, and was right behind you when you broke into the Major's trailer. When you found that broken windowpane you almost found me too, because I was just outside getting an earful. Then, when I heard you decide that the Major had been bumped off, I figured Paula for the rap, though I couldn't see much motive unless maybe the old man had renigged on helping her and was going to turn her in. And when Pauline said that what she had to tell would hit the front pages of every paper in the country, I knew she was thinking of Paula and had picked the same horse. When she went out for her perch act and somebody cut the lights, it looked like Paula more than ever. Particularly since she had no alibi. She was apparently working in the Headless Lady apparatus, but there was no way of proving it was her and not someone doubling for her."

"And you didn't arrest Paula then because you were still hoping she'd lead you to the reward?" Merlini asked. "That makes you an accessory after the fact, doesn't it? You concealed the fact that you had reasonable grounds to believe her guilty."

"Yeah, it would, if I'd had any real evidence to back up my theory. I didn't have, of course, because, as Paula's own murder has proved, she wasn't the guilty party after all. And then when she didn't show up in Norwalk this morn—"

"Hold it," I broke in. "You're skipping. You eavesdropped at our door in the hotel last night too, didn't you?"

"At the hotel? No, sorry. Did someone—"

"Someone got an earful," Merlini said. "But go on. When Paula didn't arrive on the lot this morning . . ."

"Well," O'Halloran continued, "I began to think I'd pulled a bloomer, that she'd lammed and that I was out of luck all the way around. I was parked behind the side-show tent, chewing my nails and waiting for her to show, when you and Harte got there. I'd been worrying some about where you'd got to, too. I must have passed you on the road when you were finding the empty trailer. You pulled in and parked your car right alongside mine. I was on the floor by that time, and I overheard your talks with Joy and Keith. That didn't make me any happier—but right there was when I got my break."

"But I didn't mention murder then," Merlini said. "Only that we'd found her empty trailer."

"I know, but the important thing was that I discovered somebody else listening in on your broadcast. I heard somebody sneak up on the off side of my car and squat on the running board. When he heard you say you'd found the empty trailer, he scrammed quietly. I edged my car door open a crack and got a look at his back. Then when you and Keith moved off I came out of hiding and went after him. He made a beeline for Pauline's trailer. The coon Mac had on guard was snoozing, and this guy ducked in."

"Garner!" I said.

O'Halloran nodded as Farmer drove our car onto the circus lot.

One of the Chief's men on duty at the entrance stopped us. Merlini put his head out enough so that the man got a quick glimpse of his uniform cap. "Special detail, New York Police," he said gruffly. "When Chief Inspector Gavigan arrives tell him I'd like to see him in Miss Hannum's trailer."

The cop nodded and Farmer stepped on the gas. "Take us around by the cookhouse," Merlini ordered. "And we'll park there until we've heard the rest of O'Halloran's yarn. There'll be cops by the side-show top where we were before." Then he asked O'Halloran, "A point of information: Was Garner wearing his tramp make-up when you caught him eavesdropping?"

"You're catching wise, aren't you?" O'Halloran said. "Yeah, he was. And since then I've done a little nosing around, and I've discovered he never did wash his face much. He wore his make-up around the lot much more than was necessary. While you were arguing with Mac about seeing Pauline, he was inside having a heart-to-heart chat with her, mostly in whispers, so I couldn't get much of it. But I did hear him threaten Pauline. He said he'd kill her if she gave him away. He had a gun, and when you two and Mac barged in, he backed into the wardrobe. You know now why Miss Hannum wasn't saying very much. He was right there with a heater all set to go. I began to have hunches fast along about then, and I started checking his alibis."

"So Paula did lead you to the Duke after all?" Merlini said. "Garner is the Duke. He came from a circus originally and, when he wanted to hide out, he came back to one. His manner of concealing himself is identical with Paula's, perhaps because he thought of them both. A man wearing the heavy, grotesque grease paint of a clown is hiding behind the best disguise in the world. He might just as well not have a head at all. So we have a headless man as well as a headless lady. And his alibis . . ."

"Aren't any of them worth a continental damn," O'Halloran said. "When Major Hannum's 'accident' occurred, Garner was supposed to be working in the Wild West show. Any one of the other clowns could have taken his place, and his own mother wouldn't have caught it. Same thing when Pauline fell and the evidence was stolen from the trailer. Someone else subbing for him in the tramp getup. I questioned the other clowns this afternoon, and I couldn't find anyone who'll swear positively he was in that clown car when it made the trip over this morning. Most of them were asleep, and the others didn't notice. The Duke is the guy you've been hunting who is so smart about not leaving any decent clues—a hot-shot mouthpiece like him knew enough to try to make his killings look like accidents. And he came within inches of getting away with it. He's your murderer. But *I'm* going to be the one to pick him up. I'll give him to Hooper, and you two will be in the clear."

"Why, for God's sake," I asked, "didn't you spill that when Schafer and Hooper arrested us?"

O'Halloran grinned. "Couple of reasons. First, I had to take time out to do some heavy thinking. There was so damned much evidence in that car of yours I began to wonder for a minute if maybe I wasn't slipping some. I wasn't completely sure that maybe you two hadn't done it after all. And besides, the Captain had a whale of a lot more evidence for his theory than I did for mine. If I'd a popped with my dope on the Duke, they'd have arrested you just the same, picked up the Duke because he was wanted, and grabbed off the reward. Maybe I'd got a piece, maybe not."

"O'Halloran," Merlini said quietly, "I'll have to admit that you've solved the case. You've supplied the one bit of information I've been wanting desperately ever since Monday night. But there's one small error in your theory that you should fix."

"What's that?" O'Halloran looked at him apprehensively.

"The murderer's identity," Merlini said. "You've put your money on the wrong horse. The Duke is not the murderer."

"The Duke isn't—" O'Halloran's voice was flat and empty like a busted balloon. He stared at Merlini. "You got a better guess?"

"I think I will have," Merlini said. "Some of the most surprising ideas are beginning to occur to me."

O'Halloran gave him a hard, incisive stare. "I don't know

what bee is buzzing in your bonnet, but I'm still betting on the Duke. And I'm picking him up right now."

"I don't think—" I began, got an admonishing poke in the ribs from Merlini's elbow, and changed the ending to read: "—that he'll like that much." What I had intended to say was, "I don't think that's going to be as easy as you think. Last we knew Garner had disappeared."

"I know he won't like it," O'Halloran said. "And he's got a gun. Before I tackle him I'd like mine back."

Merlini produced it and gave it to him. "Yes. I guess you had better have it."

O'Halloran said, "I want to hear those surprising ideas of yours, but I'll just attend to this first. Even if he shouldn't be the murderer, there's that ten grand." He left on a run.

Merlini turned to Farmer, who had been quietly taking it all in. "Let him find out for himself that the Duke-Garner is A.W.O.L. We've got O'Halloran's story, and I'd rather not have him around for the next few minutes. He's too set in his ideas. But you might mosey along after him, Farmer, and report on what happens. I don't know where the Duke is, and if he should still be around, O'Halloran might find him."

Farmer said, "Okay. What about letting me have one of those 'Forty-some-odds' just in case?" [2]

"He's asking for one of your guns, Ross," Merlini translated. "You come with me. We're going to see Pauline Hannum."

I gave Farmer a gun, and we separated. Merlini and I made for the back yard. The performance in the big top was nearly over. I could hear the raucous amplified voice of the announcer saying, *"Ladeez and gen-tul-men, please remain in your seats until the show is all out and all over! The arena track must be clear for our final presentation, The Chariot Races! The first event—a thrilling exhibition of dare-devil equestrianism, the Five-Horse Roman Standing . . ."*

Merlini's hand was closing around the doorknob of Pau-

[2] Forty-some-odd: A gun, so called by con-men who seldom, if ever, use them and pretend, as the phrase indicates, not to know even the proper caliber designations. The Farmer, Merlini tells me, gives himself away on several occasions by using rather more big-con argot than a short-con grifter should.

line's trailer when the door suddenly opened. Mac Wiley ducked and came out. He was closely followed by a figure whose square shoulders, determined chin, and bright blue eyes were all too familiar, as were the perturbed scowl and the sharp bite his words held.

"Merlini," he barked. "What the everlasting, blazing, blue hell are you and Ross doing in those uniforms?"

It was Chief Inspector Homer Gavigan.

Chapter 19

Who's Who

MERLINI LOOKED at me. "Lieutenant Harte," he said, "this man is a dangerous character. If he makes trouble place him under arrest." Then he faced Gavigan. "I'd rather be arrested for impersonating an officer than for exhibitionism. What do you want us to do—turn nudist? You had your colleagues deprive us of our clothes. And how'd you get here so fast—did you charter a witch's broomstick?"

"No—a plane." Gavigan's frown was still forbidding, but his eyes twinkled. "I might have known jail wouldn't stop you. What did you pick the locks with—your teeth?"

"That's such a prosaic suggestion, Inspector. I said 'Open Sesame' three times, and the walls of Jericho fell flat. Mind telling us why you had us thrown into durance vile?"

"I didn't think you'd stay there long," Gavigan admitted. "But I thought it might keep you in a safe place long enough so that I could get here and take over. This isn't your sort of case. It's full of gangsters and gunmen. I was afraid that that sort of professional criminal might reply to your subtle and fine-drawn methods of detection with a machine-gun barrage. I thought you might be more comfortable in Hooper's jail than on a morgue slab."

"The morgue slab would be lots cooler than the fire Ross and I have jumped from the frying pan into. Your wellmeant solicitude has resulted in our breaking half the penal laws of the State of New York. When Schafer and Hooper catch up with us, you're going to have to go to bat for us—

that is, if you want this murder case solved."

"That's what you think," Gavigan said. "I've got it solved!"

"Oh," Merlini said sharply. "Arrested the villain?"

"I'm going to just as soon as I've heard your story."

"He's still on the lot, then?"

"He's still on the lot?" Gavigan asked. "Who's still on the lot?"

"Why, the Duke, of course. Isn't he the man *you* want?"

"The Duke? How did you know he was anywhere around here? Miss Hannum says she didn't tell you."

"He's the bee in O'Halloran's bonnet. We've just heard all about the Duke and Maxie and the Vanishing Lady."

"O'Halloran?" Gavigan said. "Martin O'Halloran? Has *he* got a finger in this pie?"

Merlini nodded. "Both fists. And he seems to have stolen a march on you. He's scouring the lot for the Duke now with visions of a ten-grand reward under his hat."

"He won't find him," Gavigan stated. "The Duke's lammed. And I sent Brady in to put a four-state alarm out on the teletype. He and Keith Atterbury's car have been missing ever since the matinee. I want him, all right, but not for a murder rap. The murderer is still around. Say, where are Schafer and Hooper? Haven't they discovered you're gone yet?"

"Well," Merlini said a bit uneasily, "I imagine they are beginning to get the idea. I think you'd better make your arrest before they show up. They've some awfully biased ideas on the subject, all of which concern Ross and myself. And I doubt if our escape is any contribution toward establishing our innocence. So Pauline finally admits that the tramp clown, Garner, is the Duke and that the Headless Lady was her sister, Paulette Hannum, café society's Paula Starr?"

"Yes. When we told her the Duke had run out, she talked. She says she was afraid to before because he threatened to kill her. She also accuses him of the murders and causing her tumble last night."

"Yes, I thought she might," said Merlini. "But you don't believe her. Why? What color rabbit is it you've got up your sleeve, Gavigan?"

"You'll find out," he promised. "But I want your story. I got a lot of it from Wiley here. I want more. How did you find out about this case in the first place? And don't tell me it was crystal-gazing!"

"Inspector," Merlini said insistently, "that's not important just now. We've got to roll up our sleeves and work fast. If you questioned Mac, you've got most of the story. Did Pauline tell you why the Major was helping Paula and the Duke get out of the country? We've heard a couple of times that he actively disliked the Duke and was none too pleased with Paula for eloping with him. What motive did he have for routing his show through a lot of unprofitable tank towns in order to get them to Canada the quickest way? I smell a rat. How much did the Duke pay him for the ride?"

"Pauline says he did it for love—on sister Paula's account," Gavigan answered. "But she's lying. I think she's scared I'll make her kick the money back. I think I know the answer, though. It's no secret that Maxie Weissman cleaned up a fortune in the policy racket before somebody put the finger on him. What isn't so well known is that, when we went through his bank accounts and the like, we didn't find nearly enough. A measly ten or fifteen thousand. I had a damn good hunch that he had his nest-egg in cash and that he had hidden it somewhere in or near the Bridgeport hide-out where he was killed. We tore the place apart, and we didn't find it. I had two operatives, a man and a police-woman, playing the part of man and wife, rent the house from the owner and stick there, hoping that some friend of Maxie's who knew its location would be up there after it. He must have had a tin box so full of cash that I was sure, if anyone knew where it was, they wouldn't be able to resist it for long. Sooner or later they'd come snooping."

"That," Merlini said, "is what I call needed information. It explains the unexplainable—the fantastic incident of the elephants that escaped on purpose. The Duke, though he has tried to hide it behind clown white, certainly does have a head on him. Kellar once said, and without any exaggeration, that he could stand facing you and so misdirect you that if an elephant walked past, behind Kellar, you wouldn't be aware of it. The Duke has worked that stunt in reverse. The elephants themselves were the misdirection! It's a classic. One of the most massive bits of misdirection in the book."

"Never mind the blurbs." Gavigan glowered. "The Duke's a slick article right enough, but he'd have been lots smarter to stay on the right side of the law. You've figured it right, though. While the front yard was full of auto wreck and the flower beds full of elephants and animal trainers, the Major —the Duke would probably have kept out of sight—fished up the boodle. I think now it was in the well. We found a few traces. I'll have to admit that an elephant-truck accident was so damned unusual that I didn't think it could be a phony. And I'd just dug up the fact that Paula Starr was originally Paulette Hannum and figured what had happened when Captain Schafer phoned me about you."

"And now the Duke is on the run with the dough. O'Halloran will be glad to hear this—because it gives the Duke a motive for eliminating the Major. He didn't want to split with him. And Paula might have boggled at murder—while the attempt on Pauline was to prevent his discovery. But if Pauline accuses the Duke without mentioning the money, what motive does she give him?"

"One of those jaw-breaker ones like we had in that Skelton Island case. She says he's a claustrophobe—that he'd commit a dozen murders to avoid landing in a prison cell, and that the phobia worked on him so strong he got to the point where he wouldn't trust a soul. He began to suspect that the Major and, after he'd killed him, even Paula, were going to turn him in. But that's eyewash. Because the Duke isn't the murderer."

"And who is?"

Gavigan shrugged. "Why should I tell you that until I've made the arrest? Do you ever tell me?"

"I'll make an exception this time," Merlini said. "If your candidate is not the same as mine, I'll trade you. I think I'm going to need your help putting the cuffs on anyway."

"Thanks for nothing," Gavigan said. "Okay. It's a deal. And Ross is a witness to that promise, remember. If you try to welsh, you'll have another chance to try getting out of Hooper's jail; and this time I'll make it really tough for you."

"Cross my heart, hope to die," Merlini said.

Gavigan scowled at him, suspicious of this unexpected

open-handedness. "Okay. I don't see how you can have any other answer anyway. The murderer, as usual, is the most unlikely person. How the hell you manage it I don't know, but you always seem to get mixed up in just the kind of a murder case that gives Harte here material for a book. No waste motion with you two."

"The most unlikely person?" Merlini asked. "Sure you know who that is, are you?"

"I don't see how anybody could be more unlikely," Gavigan came back. "It's the old, old gag—so old that I'm afraid for once Ross will say it's too trite to write. The murderer is the invalid who's flat on her back and apparently can't move hand or foot—*Pauline Hannum!*"

I wasn't too surprised at that, because I'd been considering the idea myself. I couldn't make out whether Merlini was surprised or not. But Mac Wiley wasn't having any.

"You're crazy," the latter exploded. "Pauline wouldn't—"

Merlini broke in, "You don't think her injuries are real then, Inspector?"

"They're not as bad as she makes out by a long shot. She may have some cuts and bruises, but she took that fall on purpose for an alibi. You told me yourself once that acrobats know how to fall with lots less chance of injury than other people. They land relaxed instead of all tightened up, and they go into a roll. And since it wasn't unexpected, since she knew exactly when she had to take the drop . . ."

"Then you're holding off on the arrest until you can check back on Dr. Tripp in Waterboro?"

"Yeah. And *he's* going to get a good going-over. If he says she's really badly injured, it's possible she paid him off with some of the cash. I'm pretty sure the Duke already handed over a first payment because of that salary payoff last Saturday."

"I see," Merlini said. "And her motive?"

"She inherits the show, doesn't she?"

"I wish I knew," Merlini said. "Though of course when the Major was killed she may have thought she did."

"But she does. She just showed us the Major's will. There was one all along. She sneaked it from the Major's trailer right after his accident. It leaves Pauline, Paulette, and Joy

Pattison each a third interest. The show's to go on with Pauline as manager and the profits to be split three ways. Pauline held back the will because it mentioned Paulette under her real *and* under her stage name, Paula Starr. She didn't want the cops to pick up Paula before she'd had a chance to eliminate her, and she wanted the Duke to get clear so she'd collect some more of the Weissman dough that he'd promised to pay. The circus needed cash. Joy was next on her list. Pauline's always been burned up because of Paula's more glamorous success and has been angry as hell that Joy should chisel in on what she figures should be hers. When she killed the Major, I don't think she knew he'd actually left Joy anything, but she did it partly because she was afraid he would. She planned the Major's death to look like accident. When you got nosy, she knew Paula's death, accident or not, would look suspicious; so she arranged that fall of hers as an alibi and planned to make Paula's death look like a disappearance by concealing the body. She was going to take it along for a day or so and ditch it a hundred miles or more away. When Schafer started his search, she had to get rid of it quickly, and she passed it to you to queer your investigation. And now, because she knows that won't really stick, she's got the Duke picked for the fall guy."

"Tex Mayo assisted her, I take it?"

"Yeah. They worked together on Paula's death, and maybe he did more than that; though if necessary, being an athlete herself, she could have moved the body."

"And the missing head?" Merlini asked. "Was that removed so as to prevent discovery of Paula's identity and avoid any suspicion that the Duke might be lurking on the lot?"

"Anything wrong with that reason?"

"I don't think I care for it particularly," Merlini said. "Our murderer has been so careful all along, I can't quite see him —or her, as the case may be—failing to remove the clothing labels."

Gavigan wasn't greatly impressed. "When you've known as many murderers as I have," he said, "you won't give them credit for so damned much intelligence. They make mistakes like anybody else, and some of the smartest killers make the dumbest ones."

"Yes," Merlini said, "I know that. Just the same—"

I took a chance and stuck my neck out. "I know another reason why that head might have been removed," I said. "And the murderer, though trying to hide the identity of the body, would have left the clothing labels on purpose and for a damn good reason."

Gavigan said hopefully, "Well, let's have it."

Merlini looked at me narrowly and said, "Wait a minute. Ross, I noticed that you carefully avoided using the murderer's name. I've a feeling that you are not talking about Pauline."

"No," I said, "I'm not. I've got a much better candidate for the job. And boy, has she given us the run around! The murderess—"

Merlini looked behind him and said softly, "Oh, oh! This would happen! It's pay day. And we collect the wages of sin. Brady has opened Pandora's box!"

Several running figures came at us out of the darkness, Schafer and Hooper in the lead.

Hooper spied us first and, though the bellow he gave vent to didn't sound like "Tally-ho!" by a long shot, that's what it meant.

He had a gun in one hand and a pair of handcuffs in the other. He didn't waste any words until one cuff was on Merlini's wrist and the other on his own. Then, still puffing, he said, "From now on we sleep together!" He added a few epithets that aren't particularly decorative in type. Schafer grabbed me.

Merlini said unhappily, "That's an indecent proposal, Chief. There's a law—"

Inspector Gavigan stepped forward. "Just a minute. I'll vouch for this man. He—"

Hooper turned on him. "You?" he growled. "Who the blasted hell are you?"

"Now you've gone and done it, Hooper!" Merlini said. "May I present Chief Inspector Gavigan? Chief of Police Hooper and Captain Schafer."

"Oh. Ha. Humpf. I'm sorry. Glad to meet you." Hooper was flustered, though not nearly as much as I had hoped.

Schafer asked heavily, "What do you mean, you'll vouch

for him? *You* told me to lock him up!"

"Yes, I know," Gavigan said, and rapidly gave Schafer the reasons he had given us.

Chief Hooper, however, wasn't going to play. "I don't care if he's your brother, Inspector. I don't even care if he's not a murderer. I've got all I want on him. Pocket-picking, breaking and entering, willful destruction of county property, jailbreaking, assaulting officers in the performance of their duty, impersonating an officer! Most of that goes for Harte, too. Stevens, get the patrol wagon around here! They're going in now!" [1]

Schafer regarded Gavigan. "The Chief's right," he said. "I don't know why you've changed your mind, but we're not taking any chances. And we have got enough on them to keep them behind bars for a good long time. Take 'em away, Hooper, and for God's sake watch them."

"Are you telling me?" Hooper growled. "All right, you two, march!"

Chapter 20

Chariot Races

Misdirection is a short-circuiting of the mind. Mother Goose supplies an admirable example with the man who, going to Saint Ives, met a polygamist with seven wives, each of

[1] Chief Hooper even missed a charge. I've since discovered that Section 899 of the New York Code of Criminal Procedure includes in its list of disorderly persons, "Jugglers, common showmen and mountebanks, who exhibit or perform for profit puppet shows, wire or rope dancers, or other idle shows, acts, or feats," and "Persons who keep, in a public highway or place, an apparatus or device for the purpose of gaming, or who go about exhibiting tricks or gaming. . . ." Though my friend, Merlini, would object to being called a *common* showman, he might have trouble proving it, and his deck of cards is certainly a gaming device with which he goes about exhibiting tricks!—R. H.

Double crosser! For that matter, if you ask me, a free-lance writer is "a person without a visible profession or calling by which to maintain himself." See same section, paragraph 5.—Merlini.

whom carried seven sacks that held a total of 343 cats and 2,401 kittens. The misdirected mind multiplies to discover how many were going to Saint Ives. Since the puzzle is a sort of practical joke on paper the misdirection has to be considerable. In practice, so much misdirection is unnecessary. A few well-chosen, well-timed words can, and have, vanished an elephant!
         —A. MERLINI: THE PSYCHOLOGY OF DECEPTION

HOOPER STARTED forward abruptly. He stopped even more abruptly when Schafer suddenly let loose with a fusillade of profanity that was every bit as good as anything Hooper had yet emitted. Hooper looked around, startled, and his eyes popped. For the moment he was at a loss even for cuss words.

Merlini walked away from them; and we saw that Hooper's cuff, which had been on Merlini's wrist, now encircled Captain Schafer's arm outside his coat sleeve. Schafer and Hooper were linked like the Siamese twins. Merlini held a key at his fingertips, and as Hooper saw it he said "Goddammit! He picked *my* pocket!" Then he grabbed at the key. But as he did so, it flickered like Merlini's famous half-dollar and vanished with the same dispatch.

"No you don't, Chief," Merlini said, spreading his empty palms. "I'm in Dutch so far now that it couldn't be much worse. That key won't appear again unless you and the Captain agree to calm down and listen to the Inspector and myself solve this murder. And furthermore, if you're real good, I might even promise not to let any reporters know what a pushover that nice new jail of yours is. The taxpayers of the county might think they had bought a turkey—or appointed one!"

Hooper was purple. "Stevens," he roared, "search that man and get that key!"

"It won't do any good," Merlini said. "When I vanish something it stays vanished, unless I want to—"

Inspector Gavigan had had enough. "Merlini!" He did some roaring himself. "Produce that key at once! And give it to Hooper. You hear me?"

"If you say so, Inspector," Merlini replied. "But you'd better figure out some way to call them off. The solution you've got for this case won't stand up under a good stiff push. And I can't give you a better one if I'm going to have to collect the evidence I need from a jail cell. If we don't get this murderer within the next few minutes we may never—"

Gavigan came through then. "Hooper," he said, "you're way late. These men, both of them, are in *my* custody. I arrested them last week. You can have them after I'm through with them. But, until I give different orders, they're staying here."

"That's more like it," Merlini said. He closed his empty left hand, made a pass over it with his right, and opened it again slowly. The key lay on his palm. He gave it to Stevens, who unlocked the cuffs.

Both Schafer and Hooper eyed Gavigan with deep suspicion, but they simmered impotently. Schafer released me.

Gavigan said, "Okay, Merlini. Wave your wand, but wave it fast and use your best spells, because you've got to produce something damn good."

"I know. And I could produce an elephant on an empty stage with more confidence." He turned to me "Ross—"

Detective Brady stepped from among the cops, dicks, and troopers who had followed in Schafer's and Hooper's wake. "Inspector," he said, "just as we left, a teletype message came in from upstate. The State Police picked up the Duke the other side of Utica. They tailed him for speeding, and when he started shooting they let him have it, and winged him."

Merlini turned to him. "Did he have the money?"

"No," Brady said, "He had a couple of grand in bills in his hip pocket. But he didn't have what we've been after."

Merlini looked at him a moment, without speaking. Then he said, "Inspector, I want a word with you in private."

They moved off to one side out of earshot, and for a good ten minutes Merlini poured words into the Inspector's ear. I tried to move closer, but Schafer gave me a warning glare and I gave it up. Schafer and Hooper muttered to themselves. Mac Wiley leaned against a stake and watched Merlini and Gavigan with the worried look that had come to be his usual expression. O'Halloran chewed dejectedly at his gum. The news of the Duke's capture by someone other than himself was obviously a disappointment.

I wasn't too cheerful myself. I had the answer of the case under my hat, a whirling, coruscating humdinger of a solution, and Merlini was over there spilling it into Gavigan's ear—grabbing off all the glory for himself. I gave my theory another once-over in my mind. I couldn't see any holes. Maybe I would come out on top after all. Merlini, I was beginning to suspect, had a theory that differed from mine, he hadn't picked the same murderer after all. If he had, why was he stalling, why had he said he needed more evidence? My theory was so easily checked. It stood or fell on one point—the true identity of . . .

Gavigan called, "Hooper, Schafer. Step over here a minute, please. And you, Brady."

At my elbow a voice asked, "What's happening? Have they found the murderer?"

I turned to see Joy Pattison. She had changed from her ring costume and wore a close-fitting sweater and riding breeches. Keith stood beside her, his arm in hers.

"There are four theories to date," I replied. "And I think we're going to strike fire with one of them any minute now. You'd better stick around. Did you know that the will had been found, Joy, and that you're a third owner of the show?"

They both stared at me. "Pauline have it?" Keith asked.

I nodded.

Joy said, "After what has happened, I don't think I want it."

"It's yours anyway," I said.

Schafer approached us. "The Inspector wants to use your trailer for a few minutes, Miss Pattison. Some questioning."

"Why, yes," she said. "Yes, of course."

"You, Atterbury, and Wiley wait for him there. Harte, too." Schafer turned, jerked his thumb at me, and spoke to Stevens. "You go with 'em. Watch this guy. O'Halloran, Mayo must be nearly finished with his Wild West act. Wait for him and take him down, too."

As we started off, Schafer added, "Oh, yes, and Merlini wants to know if you can let him have a spool of white cotton thread, Miss Pattison."

"White cotton—"

"Do you have it?" Schafer asked.

"Yes."

"Okay. Robbins, you bring it back here." He turned on his heel and walked off.

As we moved away, Joy said, "Robbins, what does he want with white cotton thread?"

"I don't know, miss. He might be figuring to catch a murderer with it."

We followed orders. Joy's trailer was the last one in line near the further end of the big top. There were some camp chairs near it. We sat down and waited. No one said very much. I lit a cigarette and mentally polished up my theory, piecing in some additional facts and checking it over for weak spots. I couldn't find any. As far as I could see, the machinery turned over nicely on all eight cylinders.

Brady brought Irma King along a few minutes later; and then, when the concert performers had come out of the big top and the crowd inside was leaving, O'Halloran arrived with Tex Mayo. The latter produced a bottle, sat glumly on the grass, and proceeded with simple directness to make a start toward getting tight. He didn't offer to pass it around, which may have been just as well. The keyed-up nervous tension that held us all might have been produced by alcohol. Our voices when we spoke were a little too high and bright, our words slightly stilted as if their formation was a conscious effort.

Beyond the dark, lifted silhouette of the big top, I noticed a far-off flickering of light in the sky. Heat lightning. I paid little attention to it at first, but when it came again it was much nearer and brighter. Then I noticed that the hot breeze which had been blowing steadily for some time had increased alarmingly.

"We're in for a blow," Atterbury said. "By the looks of it, the sooner they slough that top, the better."

The wind increased as he spoke, and the canvas top bellied. This time, the flicker of lightning was a sharp bright gash in the dark and there was thunder behind it. . . .

Suddenly, from the dark beyond the edge of the square of light that fell from the trailer window, Merlini's voice came.

"Ross," he said, "you had the murderer all picked out. Who is it?"

"What are you asking for? Information or corroboration?"

"Are you going to be difficult, too?" he asked a bit wearily. "Come, let's have it."

"I'll make the same deal with you," I replied, "that Gavigan did. I'll trade even."

"That's fair enough. Talk."

"No. Just for once let's hear your answer first. We don't want to have an anticlimax. This time I think *I've* got the solution that fills in the last chapter."

"I wonder," Merlini said. "It's just possible that this is only the next to the last chapter. I warn you. If you want it to go on record at all, you'd better put it in now."

I fully intended to stick to my guns, but I didn't after all. I felt an underlying insistence in Merlini's tones that seemed to telegraph a warning. Something in the swift, sharp glance he threw at me contradicted his easy manner and told me that he had a definite and important reason for wanting me to lead first. I thought: Okay, Mastermind. Here goes, but don't say I didn't warn you.

The canvas superintendent hurried past, pulling on an oilskin. A single swollen raindrop plopped against my face and ran down the side of my cheek. Someone within the tent shouted, "Get those flats on that truck, dammit! I'm striking this top now!" The tent rigging creaked and groaned with the strain of the flapping, wind-swept canvas.

"Inspector Gavigan," I said quietly, "was half right. The murderer *is* the unlikely invalid. Only, it happens that the woman on the bed in Pauline Hannum's trailer is not an invalid—*and she's not Pauline!*"

The reaction that got me was pure disbelief all the way around—except for Merlini, whose poker face was about as revealing as those on the statues of Easter Island.

"That is the reason the head was cut off," I went on. "It was removed to conceal the fact that the body was *not* the one the clothing labels said it was. The headless corpse, like the invalid, is a timeworn fiction device too. Rule number four for readers says: 'When the corpse has no head, it's always the wrong corpse.' I should have thought of it sooner,

Merlini, but I didn't, somehow; not until you made the statement that this case had a headless lady *and* a headless man.
I realized then that it was far worse than that. There are
two headless women! Pauline's been as good as headless for
the last twenty-four hours. No one has seen the face beneath
those bandages. And she's upset as hell any time anyone
tries to set foot inside that trailer. It's as plain as a twenty-
four sheet.

"The woman on that bed is not Pauline, but her twin
sister, *Paulette*, the much-wanted Paula Starr!"

Keith Atterbury shook his head dazedly. "But, Harte, why
the devil would she—"

"She had plenty of reasons—good ones," I answered.
"Don't you see that if you can successfully impersonate the
victim of your murder—you've really got something? You
will have vanished, your victim appears to be still alive, and
no one even suspects that there has been a murder! Furthermore, Paula was in a spot. She was wanted by all the cops
from here to Cape Horn. And I think she'd recognized Stuart
Towne as the private dick who'd tailed her in New York the
afternoon she contacted Pauline. She knew he had penetrated
her Headless Lady disguise. It was her move. By changing
places with sister Pauline, she make it look as if Paula Starr,
the Headless Lady, had taken it on the lam. O'Halloran and
any other dicks who picked up her trail could be expected to
ride off in all directions on a wild-goose chase."

Joy objected, "Paula wouldn't have killed her sister for a
reason like that. I never met her—but it's——it's too cold-
blooded."

"All right," I said agreeably. "If you don't like that motive,
I'll give you another—the old standby—money. Pauline's
death automatically gives Paula a greater cut of the inheritance. And *you're* a very lucky girl not to have had an accident on that swinging ankle-drop of yours before now. It
would have come."

"Are you saying," Mac Wiley cut in, "that Paula gaffed those
lights last night, expecting Pauline would be killed when
she fell; and then, when that didn't work out, finished her off
at the trailer this morning?"

"Something like that, yes. Only she didn't expect the perch fall to kill Pauline. That's bothered me all along. But Paula and her intended impersonation explains it. It's the only way we can explain the fact that a circus person would know that a fall of twenty feet or so is not a sure-fire way to kill off an acrobat. No. The fall was to make the bandages necessary so that, with a little hair bleach, the impersonation would be possible. Though they were twins, their faces weren't greatly alike. But their voices were."

I paused a moment. The neatly dovetailing facts were beginning to bring some of my audience over. But there was one reaction I still wanted. I went on.

"The brain behind these accident-murders is a diabolically clever one—so much so I'm not sure Paula gets all the credit. Detail after detail has been carefully planned and executed. Every—"

That did it. Tex Mayo pulled himself to his feet. He wavered a bit. "I guess I know my name when I hear it," he said thickly. "I drove Pauline over from Waterboro this morning. But damn you, Harte; we didn't make any stops on the way!"

I pulled my feet back under my chair and sat up a bit straighter, ready for action. Tex started toward me.

"It won't do, Tex," I said flatly. "Paula Starr made a few movies in Hollywood two years ago. That's your bailiwick. Unluckily Paula was already married to the Duke. And you weren't going over so well in the horse operas any more. You can't sing or play a guitar. You needed money to keep Paula in the style to which the Duke had accustomed her. Just who thought of what and just who did what, I don't know; but between you, you rubbed out the Major so Paula would get a piece of the show. Then you went after Pauline so the piece would be bigger. And you finessed that gambit in such a way it served to get Paula out of a tight spot as well. When you two start throwing stones you always try to get the whole flock with one rock. You'd have taken care of Joy next, and the Hannum circus would have served you as old-age security. The Duke was on the list too, of course. I should have thought you'd have seen to his untimely end first. Or was it because a clown's job isn't so dangerous and you had to wait for a good chance to fake a plausible accident?"

Tex doubled his fists and came at me with his arms swinging. "Damn you to hell," he roared. "You don't frame me that way. I'll—"

Schafer suddenly stepped between us. "You'll what?" he asked, his jaw sticking out a mile.

Tex started a haymaker, but the arc was too long. The Captain's fist drove swiftly upward in a short, hard punch and hit bone. Tex folded up. Behind him the canvas spread of the big top mimicked his action. It settled quickly to the ground, the metal bale rings sliding rapidly down the center poles. Moving figures carrying lights ran in and began unlacing it.

"Thanks, Captain," I said. "I'm sorry about that little fuss at the jail. I don't deserve such—"

"This," Merlini said hastily, "is getting way out of control. I think we've had enough patchwork solutions for now."

I didn't like the confident way he said that. I could feel the watertight spread of canvas that was my solution sink and lie flat on the ground like the big top, ready to be rolled and carted away.

"It's good, Ross," he added. "Ingenious as anything. But it doesn't explain the arrow on the pole, for one thing. And besides, I've just come from questioning Headless Lady number two. Your theory had occurred to me as a possibility. Just to make sure, we had her bandages off and got a look at her face. The flaw in your solution is the fact that she *is* Pauline after all. And she's going to wind up this case. Her nerves are pretty well shot with what she's gone through today, and she passed out on us before we'd finished. But she has told us that she knows who killed her father! She listened at the broken pane of the trailer window when she saw Irma King go in. A little later, when the elephant goad struck the Major, she saw the person who wielded it. And she was watching when that person moved the body to the Major's car and drove it off the lot to set the accident."

Irma King's face was white. "But I tell you I didn't—"

Merlini disregarded her. "Pauline fainted just before she

could finish. There's a doctor working on her now. The murderer might as well turn in his chips. We've got an eyewitness. Anyone want to say anything?"

The silence was short, tense. Then Mac Wiley spoke. "I don't believe it. Why wouldn't she have told us that before now?"

"She had an excellent reason, Mac," Merlini said. "You see—"

Inspector Gavigan came out of the darkness. "Okay, Merlini. Let's go. The doc says we can see her now."

"Good." Merlini's eyes moved around the circle, resting for an instant on each of us. Then he turned abruptly and started off.

I slid out of my camp chair and went after him. "I'm in on this," I said flatly. "And don't give me any back talk."

"Okay, Ross," he said ominously. "But remember that you asked for it."

O'Halloran caught up with us. "You still insist it wasn't the Duke?" he asked.

"I'm not insisting on anything at the moment," Merlini answered. "The anti-aircraft guns have bagged too many high-flown theories in the last hour. I'm keeping my fingers crossed until after Pauline has said her piece. Inspector, I want a man at each window and one at the door."

Gavigan issued orders. "Windows. Brady, Stevens, and you," he indicated Robbins. "Schafer, where are the rest of your men?"

"Up front with Hooper. Working on the you-know-what."

"Okay. O'Halloran, you take the window on the other side. Schafer, take the door. Let's get this over quick. I don't like it."

He ducked his head and went through into the lighted trailer. Merlini and I followed. Pauline's figure lay stiffly on the bed with the covers pulled high about her neck. The new bandages on her face hid her features even more than before. There was the thin black slit where her eyes were, but their cool black stare was lost in the shadow which the edge of the near-by lampshade threw across the upper part of the white mask of gauze. The edge of the yellow light circle touched the bandage-swathed point of her chin as if the light man had centered his spotlight badly.

Merlini knelt at once by the side of her bed and as he did so her jaw moved slightly and her voice, half hysterical and thin with effort, said:

"I'm sorry. I'm better now. I'll try—"

Gavigan's hand fastened on my arm above the elbow in a tight, motionless grip.

Merlini said, "Your father opened the wardrobe door to get his raincoat. The elephant hook struck him and you saw—"

Again the bandage over her jaw moved. "Yes." Her voice rose in a high tone that I hadn't heard before, a frightened, horror-stricken tone. "The murderer is—"

I half expected it. From beyond the window above the foot of Pauline's bed a sharp cry came; then the words, "Damn you, get back. . . ."

Something bumped against the trailer's side.

The sound of the pistol shot within the narrow trailer room was deafening.

I saw the sharp spitting rush of flame that came through the window; and, when I jerked my head toward the direction in which it spurted, I saw the ugly black hole that had appeared as if by magic in the center of the white mask of gauze above the eyes.

I stared at it and wondered with a strange clarity of thought why I was having none of the sensations I would have expected.

The interval before Gavigan's hand yanked downward on my arm, pulling me floorward, seemed long. I know now that it was less than a second.

We hit the floor together; Merlini had moved like lightning back against the wall beneath the window. I waited for the second shot.

But the momentary stillness was followed instead by the sound of shouts and running feet. Then, with the sudden rush of a bursting dam, the rain came in earnest, pounding on the trailer roof.

Merlini started up, and moved quickly toward the door. "I think we can go now," he said.

Gavigan pulled the door open and tumbled out into the driving swirl of the storm. I plunged after him. Schafer was not at his post.

We circled the trailer. O'Halloran lay by the window on the ground, half propped on one elbow. Stevens' torch spotlighted him. Gavigan and Schafer stood over him. The blood on O'Halloran's forehead mingled with the streaming rain.

"He ran behind the trailers," O'Halloran said. "That way. For God's sake, get him! He took my gun."

Schafer, bellowing orders, ran. O'Halloran rolled over and lifted himself shakily to his feet. Gavigan put a hand under his arm and helped him.

Mac Wiley, Keith, Joy, and then Tex appeared on the edge of the circle of light. Others crowded behind them. Irma King pushed through.

"Sure it was a man?" Merlini asked quickly.

O'Halloran shook his head dazedly, "I—I think so. I couldn't see too well, but—"

Merlini said evenly, "It's all out and all over now. The person who fired that shot didn't go far. Misdirection again. But the gunman might be interested to know that the shot didn't do its work. The figure in the bed now is not Pauline Hannum! We substituted the mummy of John Wilkes Booth. With a length of white cotton thread to make the jaw appear to move and a little ventriloquism—*Gavigan, watch it!*"

Gavigan swung, his whole body behind the blow. The first blow landed in the pit of the stomach; and, as the murderer doubled up, Gavigan's other fist found the skull behind the ear.

Merlini bent above the figure on the ground. When he stood up he held an object wrapped in his handkerchief. He placed it under his coat quickly to shield it from the pouring rain.

"O'Halloran's gun," he said. "That does it. There'll be prints on that ivory handle."

Chapter 21

Blow-Off

"Ladeez and Gentulmen, the big show is all out and all over! We now present the last performance of the evening, the Oriental Dancing Girl Revue! They shake it in the East and they shake it in the West, and then they're going to shake it where the shaking is the best. If you can stand to hear the old cannon roar, smell the smoke, and see the flame, here's the place to go. It'll clean and press your suit, curl up the brim of your hat, restore your hair, and put ants in your pants. The boys like it and the girls learn. The red-hot jamboree is stahting ri—ght awaaay. . . . "

CHIEF OF Police Hooper was still not completely sold on Merlini's innocence. However, after he had been assured that the next day's headlines would give credit for the murderer's apprehension to the local authorities and would contain no whisper of anything concerning a jail-escape, he led his captive off.

The rest of us crowded into Pauline's trailer. We were a dripping, water-soaked crew; but the story Merlini had to tell made us forget that. He pulled back the covers on the bed and exposed the mummy of John Wilkes Booth. He showed us the length of white thread attached to the bandages covering the chin, and, kneeling by the bed as he had done before, demonstrated how the thread led invisibly down across the bed covers and ended in a loop around his right forefinger. When he pulled the thread the gauze over the mummy's chin moved and Pauline's voice, not nearly so illusive now that we knew it came from Merlini's mouth, said:

"The principle of the ventriloquial dummy. The thread pulls the bandage down, and a rubber band beneath pulls it back again so that in the half-light enough apparent chin movement is created to attract the attention and complete the illusion. Ventriloquists, as I've said before, don't throw their voices; they simply create that appearance.

210

"The joker in the whole business is, of course, the fact that Pauline never was an eyewitness to her father's murder. She didn't know who the murderer was until I told her when we were moving her over into Tex Mayo's trailer. She not only didn't stay behind to listen at the trailer window, but she admits now that Irma King did not go to the Major's trailer Monday night. When Pauline accused her of that, she did so because she was burned up by Irma's attempt to grab the show and by Irma's public accusations of illegitimacy."

"Well, anyway," I said disappointedly, "I was right about the girl in the bandages not being Pauline. If only she had turned out to be Paula instead of a mummy my theory would have crossed the finish line. I still want to know why you were so sure Pauline wasn't the culprit. Tex may not have been in love with Paula, as I had it, but he is in love with Pauline. Together they could have done it all."

Merlini shook his head. "They couldn't have accomplished Pauline's fall from the high perch, Ross. With Tex's presence at the back door established, it would have meant still another assistant to douse the lights. You can always solve a crime if you parcel out the various bits of dirty work to enough different people. But that's not only bad fiction; it's also bad practice from the murderer's viewpoint. Too many criminal accomplices are dangerous because one of them might trip and get caught out, or might break down and confess. If you want to see that murder is done right, don't delegate your dirty work—do it yourself."

"Maybe they didn't know that," I said stubbornly. "And besides, their motive is much stronger than——"

"No," Merlini contradicted even more stubbornly, "that's not so. I was suspicious all along that the inheritance of a circus—the outdoor show business being what it has been lately—was hardly motive enough for two murders and an attempted third. Circus management today is mostly a first-class headache—too much competition from movies and radio, I suspect—and no one in his right mind is going to undertake wholesale murder in order to inherit a headache. The real murderer's motive is right here."

Merlini turned the stiff figure of the mummy over on its face and exposed a gaping hole between its shoulder blades.

"You knew that the mummy was *papier mâché* and hollow," he said, reaching in and bringing out neatly banded packets of United States currency by the handful. "This particular mummy classes as one of the most valuable sideshow draws ever exhibited. He's nearly filled with cash, and I haven't seen a bill in the lot yet that is smaller than a C note. Most of them are grands."

Inspector Gavigan stepped forward and probed the body's interior. His operative technique might have been open to professional criticism, but it got results. Merlini held a pillowcase, and Gavigan filled it with banknotes. Finally he produced two account ledgers, and his face beamed as he leafed through them.

"The Weissman evidence," he said. "More motive. To certain people these books are worth twice that cash. It means curtains for some of Maxie's racketeer pals whom we haven't been able to pin anything on. Especially Jerry O'Bryen, the Brooklyn real-estate operator—the two-faced crook who throws a smoke screen over his underworld connections by his donations to charity. The D.A.'s been hoping to get him with his pants down for a long time—and this does it. Maxie didn't trust O'Bryen, and he's put enough evidence in these books to send Jerry up the river until about the year 4000."

"Motive enough for half a dozen murders," Merlini commented. "O'Bryen would pay plenty to get his hands on those books." He paused a moment, and then continued, "Since you know who the murderer is, it's obvious why the technique of the crimes was so expert, why so few clues that one could really get one's teeth into were left."

"I don't see them," I said. "If, at this late date, you are going to turn into one of those psychic detectives who solve their cases by character analysis or plain and fancy hunches, you can find yourself a new Boswell, starting now."

"Do you think the Inspector would have let me pull anything as dramatic, anything that smelled as much of the footlights, as that ventriloquism stunt, if I had only hunches? There were just three really decent clues, but they were whoppers. It's a practical possibility, even in this day and age of scientific detection and F.B.I. trained detectives with their spectroscopes, their moulage methods, and their vacuum cleaners, to commit one murder, perhaps even two, without a slip. It happens every day, somewhere. But if you try it with the investigators sitting right in your lap, and are forced to attempt a third and then a fourth murder, even a Napoleon of crime can be excused for making a misstep. It's pretty nearly impossible, unless the investigators are complete dunderheads. The law of averages gets you eventually."

"Oh, so! Dunderhead, is it? Some day I'm going to cross you up and report one of your cases with you on the short end. It may be my last assignment, but I'll have fun writing it."

Merlini looked down his nose at me, said, "Sour grapes," and then continued on his explanatory way. If asked to explain one of his own tricks, the man is as close-mouthed as a clam, but when he begins describing the inner workings of a murderer's hocus-pocus, he lectures *in extenso,* complete with prefaces, marginal notations, footnotes, and appendices.

"The law of averages," he repeated, "gets you in the end. Complications creep in, unforseen hitches occur, snap decisions must be made. I doubt if even a lightning calculator could run that gamut. Our murderer, though an experienced criminal tight-wire walker, took three bad falls. Even then Lady Luck still smiled, because the evidence, though it completely exposed the criminal's identity, was still not quite the sort that a good trial lawyer couldn't fog with a lot of reasonable doubt. That was why I set the trap I did. That and the desire to avoid a messy court trial which would have put the fact of Pauline's illegitimacy on all the front pages."

Impatiently Inspector Gavigan said, "Merlini, skip the long-winded introduction. I've heard you do them before. Your reputation as an impromptu lecturer is safe enough. Get down to cases. You told me earlier who the killer was and supplied some evidence. But I want to know how you arrived at those conclusions. Why—"

"What's your hurry, Inspector? The conflagration is over. You're not going any place."

"But *you* may be," Gavigan came back. "There's still a blotter full of law violations hanging over your head, in case you don't remember. Get on with it!"

"Sour grapes from Ross. Ingratitude from you. I don't know why I bother." Merlini grinned, apparently little disturbed by Gavigan's threat. Then he got to the point. "The missing head—I said more than once that it was the crux of the matter, that if we could find it—"

"But we haven't found it," Schafer said. "Or did you?"

"No," Merlini replied. "If I had, there would have been no need to set the trap we did. How many good reasons are there for the removal by the murderer of his victim's head?"

"We discussed two," I offered. "It might have been done to conceal the victim's identity; in this case, to hide the fact that the body was the missing and wanted Paula. But that's out, because, if it were the motive, the clothing labels would have been removed as well.

"Secondly, as I said before, it might have been done for the exact opposite reason—to hide the fact that the body was *not* Paula—but someone else. You eliminated that on the score that no attempt had been made to remove Paula's fingerprints from her trailer, or the hands from the body. The only other motive I can suggest is insanity."

"Which," Merlini answered, "is improbable on more than one count. Separating head from body is a fairly unusual form for psychopathic body mutilation to take. Furthermore, everything else about the crimes indicated a cleverly operating, sane mind—always supposing that your definition of sanity includes the possibility of murder. There's one other possible motive."

Captain Schafer said, "I get it now. The bullet was in the head, and the murderer knew that ballistics tests could link it to his gun."

"Exactly. The head was removed for the simple reason that it contained evidence that would have brought the murderer's whole house of cards down about his ears. The bullet itself couldn't be extracted because the murderer hadn't the time or any decent probing instruments."

Gavigan nodded. "Yes. I'll agree there. I've seen cases where the bullet ricocheted inside the skull, and the medical examiner had to do a complete cranial dissection in order to locate the slug. But how did that indicate identity? Several suspects were in possession of firearms."

"That wasn't too difficult," Merlini replied. "I merely asked myself why it was the murderer hadn't gotten rid of the gun instead of troubling to saw off the head. You see?"

"Well, yes. This hick town doesn't offer any firearms stores where a similar gun could be purchased and substituted. You'd have noticed its absence. And the other boners?"

"Were worse. The business about the gun couldn't be helped. Fate played that card. But the other clues were out-and-out boners. The rubber gloves should never have been planted in the Headless Lady's trailer to make us think that she had committed the crimes and lammed. The nitrate test is getting commoner year by year. Four or five years ago few people outside the Crime Detection Bureau at Northwestern had ever heard of it. Now every dick who's had the F.B.I. training can do it with his eyes shut."

"Stop editorializing," I objected. "The test showed that the gloves had been worn when a shot was fired. So what?"

"So," Merlini said, "if you hadn't poked your nose down so close to that paraffin mold you'd have noticed that *the nitrate stains appeared on the left hand!* There was one person among our suspects who was obviously left-handed."

"There were two," Schafer corrected. "I'm not quite so blind that I missed the paraffin-mold clue. It was obvious as hell that the murderer was a southpaw. Burns saw it, too. But we didn't mention it to you. We were saving that for your court trial. I thought that if you saw the molds, it might throw a scare into you."

Merlini said, "You thought *I* was left-handed?"

"Sure, aren't you? I saw you vanishing that half-dollar of yours with your left hand."

"Teach you not to make generalizations about queer people like magicians. Look."

Merlini took out his half-dollar, dropped it onto his open left hand, closed the hand, said "Abracadabra" three times, and slowly opened his fist. The half-dollar was gone. Merlini bent forward and took it from Schafer's coat pocket. Then he dropped it on his right palm, repeated the whole process and spread both hands wide, fingers open, palms empty. "The coin is in your pocket again, Captain."

Schafer reached in sheepishly and removed it himself.

"Oh," he said, "both hands, huh?"

Merlini nodded. "Ambidextrous. One result of the practice of conjuring. While the spectators watch the right hand doing some ordinary, above-board action, the left hand is often busy getting in the dirty work. Magicians' left hands consequently are well trained.

"The third and final boner was the bit of information that, when it showed up in O'Halloran's story, clinched the case. I told you the other night, Ross, that *everyone* had an alibi for the monkey business with the lights—except for Joy. She, Mac, and Keith were apparently the only ones on the lot who knew that Pauline was about to give the Sheriff some headline news. Then tonight Joy was with us when the sword was stolen, and she had an alibi at last.

"But when O'Halloran, busily spinning a yarn aimed at making the Duke the fall-guy, got so engrossed in his careful pussy-footing between truth and falsehood that he stumbled and *admitted that he had eavesdropped outside the trailer window,* he elected himself as the murderer!

"O'Halloran was the man who owned a gun distinctive enough so that he couldn't, in a tank town like this, obtain a duplicate.[1] He was the man whose first-hand acquaintance with crime supplied him with an expert murder technique; whose first-hand acquaintance with violent death had hardened him to the point that he didn't boggle at sawing off a corpse's head to save himself; whose first-hand acquaintance with detection made him realize the danger that lay in that bullet if ballistics tests were ever performed. O'Halloran was the southpaw. You'll remember that when I gave my demonstration of the gentle art of pocket-picking, I found his gun in his *left* coat pocket and his billfold in his *left* trouser pocket. It was possible that he might carry his purse there to foil pickpockets, but he would only carry his gun in a left-hand pocket if he was left-handed. O'Halloran

---

[1] O'Halloran was probably aware of the fact that his Metzger .32 not only had an individual ivory grip, but also, as I discovered later, could be easily matched with any bullet fired from it, since it is the only left leed (rifling twist) pistol made that has but five lands (raised surfaces between the spiral grooves). All other pistols known so far to have left leed have six lands.

also manipulated his cigarette with his left hand." [2]

"Your solution," I criticized, "still has as many loose ends as a Spanish shawl. I still don't see why he had to kill the Major. And why, once he did get his hands on the cash, didn't he lam instead of hanging around waiting for us to catch wise?"

"Because, Ross, when the locomotive initial event in this case pulled out of the station, all the others hitched on in logical order and rattled along behind. Briefly, O'Halloran's thought processes must have gone something like this. Having run Paula to ground here on the circus, he tumbled to the fact almost immediately that the Duke was on the show. Casing Paula's trailer as he was, he could hardly have missed the visits the Duke paid her—like that one we ourselves saw. He didn't nab the Duke at once because it wasn't the reward he was after, but the Weissman money. Since the Duke was living in the clown car, and since he noticed that both Paula and the Major always kept their trailers locked, he deduced that the money was hidden in one or the other—probably Paula's. But she stuck to it too closely. Simple burglary, he realized, might not do the trick—he might have to get the money at the point of a gun. So, to eliminate it as much as anything else, he investigated the Major's trailer first.

"Using the glass cutter, he got in at the window. But, while he was searching the place, the Major and Pauline returned unexpectedly, trapping him there. He picked up the bull-hook and ducked into the wardrobe. When Pauline left, the Major opened the wardrobe to get his slicker. O'Halloran knocked him out with the elephant hook to prevent recognition. He finished his search and found that the reason the Major had always locked his trailer was because he had a bank roll there—the remainder of the Duke's initial payment after Saturday's salary payoff. But far worse, he found that

[2] See page 167. O'Halloran, signaling Merlini with his right hand, is therefore holding his cigarette in his left. I accused Merlini later of having taken a terrific chance when he let O'Halloran fire at the mummy. The man might have taken pot-shots at the rest of us. Merlini's answer was that, on the ride back from the jail when he had been in possession of O'Halloran's gun, he had removed all but one bullet.

the Major's heart, which he hadn't known was bad, had stopped.

"He was in a jam. He didn't want to lam without the money he had committed murder to get. An investigation would endanger his impersonation of Towne and probably scare off Paula and the Duke before he could hijack them. That left only one course. He had to make the murder look like an accident and no questions asked. He refrained from touching the Major's money so it's absence wouldn't contradict the accident setup. We didn't find it there later because Pauline had removed it the next morning, and Schafer didn't find it when he searched Pauline's trailer because she had it, with the will, in bed with her.

"Then, when he thought his staged auto-smash had gotten by nicely, Harte and myself arrived; and he began to worry. Not knowing why Pauline had visited my shop or what was behind her apparent vanish from it, he couldn't understand where we fitted into the case and decided we needed some investigation. Then, ironically, although he himself was familiar with pickpocket argot, he wasn't aware that the real Towne knew any; and he made the mistake of denying such knowledge.[8] He didn't know this was an error then, but later he got a jolt when, listening at the trailer window, he not only heard us shoot holes in his phony accident but also heard Pauline announce that what she had to say would make headlines. He knew that meant that she suspected Paula and the Duke, and was intending to stool on them. This, in itself, later proved to be a clue to the murderer's identity since it meant that only someone knowing the Headless Lady's identity could have translated Pauline's cryptic statement.

"O'Halloran still hadn't gotten his dukes on the money, and he saw that unless he could quiet Pauline he never would. His flair for the impromptu showed itself here when he quickly concocted one of the year's better pieces of dirty work. With Pauline engaged in her perilous and dizzy feats

[8] O'Halloran, once on the force, had been a member of the pickpocket squad. Most dicks or cops however, are not familiar with the argot since criminals seldom choose them to confide in. You can test the truth of this by trying Farmer's argot anecdote on page 141 on your official friends.

aloft, he unplugged the light cable—a murder attempt that left no clues at all, that was simple and direct to the point of genius. The only reason he didn't plug the cable in again, making the light failure not only clueless but downright mysterious, was that he wanted to prolong the confusion the lack of light caused. Harte incidentally mentioned the point that a circus person wouldn't have counted on Pauline's being killed in such a fall. That was the reason I began to suspect that the murderer might not be a circus person—a deduction which made me give O'Halloran some serious consideration.

"You will also notice that he made no serious attempt to dish up any alibis, but instead promptly did something of even more importance. He hotfooted it back to the Major's trailer. Finding us gone, as he hoped he would, he destroyed or made off with all the evidence in the matter of the auto accident. He wiped away the rubber glove prints and took the hat, the broken lens pieces, and the photo. This effectively staved off any immediate official investigation.

"The important thing after that was speed. I think, like ourselves, he saw the Duke enter Pauline's trailer and decided against a holdup on the circus lot as being too risky. The Duke was the sort of person who would start shooting, and the battle would bring the whole show down around their ears. So he lay low, thought hard, and during the night his criminally fertile mind hatched the plan of the chalked arrow which early the next morning sidetracked Paula down a little-frequented road. He held her up, handkerchief over his face probably, and knocked her out. This next, I'll admit, is guesswork based on the finding of a gun among Paula's effects. Mindful of the fact that the night before he had struck the Major too hard, he now pulled his punch too much; and, while he was in the trailer finding the money, Paula came to and put her head in at the door, gun in hand. O'Halloran managed to fire first—but got her in the head.

"Dilemma. He now had the money, but also another body, a body whose head held a bullet from his gun. He knew only too well that the rifling marks on the slug could be matched with the gun. He couldn't discard the gun without arousing suspicion, and he couldn't get a substitute. He had neither time nor instruments to probe for the bullet. Someone might drive down that road at any moment and catch him red-handed. But if he conceals the body and removes Paula's luggage so that she appears to have decamped, he again conceals the fact of murder. Then he got too fancy.

"He *had* been the eavesdropper at our hotel-room door and had heard me deduce the use of the rubber gloves. He saw that if he planted the gloves and the torn envelope in the trailer, so that they looked hidden but would be sure to be found, suspicion might be switched to Paula, Harte, and myself; and the official investigators, when they arrived eventually, could be expected to ride off in all directions after a vanished and impossible to find Paula. In addition, since he now had the money, he could dispense with the false whiskers of the Stuart Towne impersonation, disclose himself as a detective, and join the hunt—with the quarry everyone is chasing, reposing secure, but dead, in the trunk compartment of his own car!"

"And," Gavigan added, "once that happened he'd have all the time he wanted to remove the incriminating bullet and dispose of the body miles away. He could even arrest the Duke to make his intentions look good and collect the reward! I hope I never meet any more murderers like him."

"No, Inspector," Merlini contradicted. "He's the kind you want to hope for. He did make those boners, you know."

Schafer said, "That sounds like a watertight schedule. Why didn't he go through with it?"

Merlini said, "He couldn't start that train of action until someone had found the empty trailer; and he'd rather not do it himself—though if he had, he might have pulled it off. He came back to the hotel and put on his shaving-in-the-bathroom act for my benefit. That was the nearest he came to attempting an alibi, and it was an error.

"Then Fate did him dirt. Because I happen to collect circus posters, I had to be the one to find the arrow on the pole and discover the trailer. I realized that the arrow pointed directly to foul play. If Tex, as Harte wanted to have it, had driven Pauline down that road to her death and a substitution of identities with Paula, there'd have been no necessity for the arrow. The arrow indicated foul play, and the absence of the rug suggested blood, and thus—murder.

"Later when we arrived on the lot O'Halloran was all set to announce his identity and carry on, but I perversely refrained from making any general announcement of having found an empty trailer, and he couldn't, without arousing suspicion, quizz me on the subject. Then, while he was impatiently champing at the bit, Captain Schafer and his minions arrived with a boy who had heard the shot; I announced that the Headless Lady had not vanished, but was murdered—and the fat is in the fire, sizzling like anything!

"Paula's body hidden in his car was more dangerous than the sword that threatened Damocles. O'Halloran couldn't do a thing but hope like hell that darkness would fall before the troopers started a search. His luck held that far, and when nearly everyone was in the cookhouse he got his chance to swipe the Swede's sword. In the darkness behind the sideshow top he hacked off Paula's head and transferred the body and other things to my car. You'll remember that his car was parked right next to mine." [4]

"And," I added, "he placed the money in the mummy because it wasn't likely that a search would include the interior of a corpse on exhibition."

"But he didn't put the head there," Schafer said. "And my men are out there now trying to find it. They haven't uncovered it yet, or I'd have heard about it. I wish you'd look into your crystal, Merlini, and give me the answer to that one."

Merlini replied, "I rather think that tomorrow, after the show moves, if you'll do a little excavating you may find it. I don't think he put the head in the mummy because it was just possible that someone might stumble on that hiding place accidentally. O'Halloran would rather take a chance on losing the money than have Paula's head found and lose his own. He cut off the head because he didn't have the time nor tools to bury the whole body, and even so he couldn't have done it without leaving too many traces. The head was less of a problem; he could manage to bury—wait, that's bad too. Burial is better than the mummy, though there'd

[4] See pages 156 and 187.

still be some danger of accidental discovery. It's not perfect enough, and O'Halloran was a perfectionist. I don't think he'd have let the head leave his possession until he'd removed that bullet. It must still be in his car."

"But we searched it," Schafer said. "Besides, if there were a hiding place in the car for the head, he'd have put the money there too."

"You may have something there, Captain," Merlini said. "The first time you searched the car you didn't know what you were looking for. Look again. Look for a place where he could have put the head, but one in which it would be inadvisable to put the paper money."

"I'll be damned," Schafer said. He strode to the door and put his head out. "Stevens!" he called. "Beat it in to town. O'Halloran's car is parked in front of the jail. Give it a good going over— and look under the hood!" [5]

"O'Halloran," Gavigan commented, "was certainly efficient enough. He got rid of the body and got you jailed all at one and the same time. Then, since he couldn't follow his plan of chasing after Paula, he dealt another hand and tried to work the same stunt using the Duke. O'Halloran probably intended to warn the Duke to lam so he could appear to go chasing after him as soon as he'd lifted the money from the mummy again. But the Duke, who had already got the wind up and taken a powder, gets himself caught and leaves O'Halloran high and dry."

Merlini nodded. "Yes, and even then he still thought he was pretty safe because he only knew about one of the boners he had made—the gloves. Harte and I barged in on him in the Sheriff's office when we were escaping and found him

---

[5] Schafer's suspicion proved correct. The head, containing a bullet that matched O'Halloran's gun, was found beneath the hood. Gavigan's guess that the bullet might possibly have ricocheted inside the skull also proved good. The bullet, entering the right temple at an oblique angle, had made a nearly complete semi-circle inside the skull over the vertex, producing a gutter on the surface of the cerebral hemispheres, tearing the dura, and perforating the longitudinal sinus. The bullet was found in the petrous portion of the left temporal bone with its base upward.

examining those paraffin molds. I suspect he was wondering if he could fake some blue specks on the right-hand mold and scrape them off the other. That was our tough luck. If he'd had time to attempt that we'd have had him."

Keith said, "And at the finish he swiped a leaf from your book, Merlini, and desperately tried misdirection to make us think someone else had crowned him. He told us someone had taken his gun and fired, because once again there was a telltale bullet in the victim's head."

"Yes, and the blood on his face was from a self-inflicted cut. The case of the Headless Lady had two headless women and a headless man. But the murderer had a head and used it nearly every minute."

"If guillotining," Gavigan added, "was used hereabouts rather than electrocution, the case *would* end with a headless murderer after all."

"And that," Merlini said, "reminds me of a story Earl Chapin May tells. The Mabie Bros. show was playing through Texas, season of 1857. A booted, spurred, large-hatted sheriff came to the ticket wagon one afternoon and said, 'See heah, sah. I've got a triple hangin' on today. They's a heap of folks driv into town from as much as fohty miles aroun'. They's fond of hangin's like they is of circuses. 'Less you give tickets to me and my prisoners, I'll have my hangin' when you open yoh dawes and I'll get the crowd. I know my people!'

"The ticket agent was a practical psychologist too. The sheriff and his prisoners saw the performance, but the management wasn't passing out paper for nothing. Near the end of the show when the concert was announced, 'tickets for which will be sold by the gentlemanly agents who will pass among you,' the announcer added: "Ladeez and gen-tul-men, immediately following our after-show the hanging will take place at the first big tree to the right as you pass out of our tent'!

"They all stayed for the concert and the hanging was held as advertised!"

"Getting back to a more cheerful subject and speaking again of heads," Keith said, "*I'm* reminded of the fact that two are better than one—or, for that matter, none—and does anyone know where I can find a Justice of the Peace at this time of night?"

"Captain," Merlini smiled, "can you produce one from thin air? It's a conjuring trick you troopers always seem to able to do whenever you make an arrest for speeding. It's amazed me more than once."

"I guess," Schafer admitted, "that it can be arranged."

A half-hour later in the only tent that still remained standing, the menagerie top, the personnel of the Mighty Hannum Combined Shows attended a wedding. Lohengrin was supplied by a band whose repertoire no longer included Suppé's "Cavalry March," and incidental sound effects were furnished by the "strange and wonderful congress of curious jungle beasts and zoological wonders" who paced their cages nervously, still apprehensive of the now-diminishing storm outside.

Once, when it was the bride's cue to say "I do," Rubber, the smallest elephant, lifted her trunk and answered for Joy. On circus lots they still ask Keith if he's quite sure which of them he married.

"All out and all over!"